# The Irishman's Deception

A
Conor McDermott
Novel

The Irishman's Deception


Published by Anthony J. Harrison


Copyright© 2017 Anthony J. Harrison



ISBN: 978-1-3707781-2-6 (eBook version)
ISBN: 978-1-7324081-0-4 (print version)

**Cover design by:**
Robert Gray of Channel Islands Design
http://www.channelislandsdesign.com


**Editing service provided by:**
Lawrence Editing
http://www.lawrenceediting.com

## This book is dedicated to:

My cousin Brian McBride, for showing me the courage it takes to trail-blaze your own path and chase after that "pot of gold" as only we Irishmen can!

# TABLE OF CONTENTS

# PROLOGUE

The docks of Southampton were especially busy this week. The arrival of three freighters from the continent and two car carriers from the Far East crowded the moorings. Six large gantry cranes, resembling metallic praying mantis, moved back and forth along the length of each of the freighters, extracting cargo containers from the ships. The dock was alive. Workers with flags or lighted wands directed the flow of traffic below each crane. There was a continuous exchange of tractor-trailers loaded with containers in a steady and orchestrated flow of traffic.

Due to the busy schedule loading and unloading the ships, many of the laborers on the dock in the past few weeks were temporary hires from the local union hall. Supervisors could use them, allowing regular workers to keep their normal hours, and not have to work until fatigued.

In the shadows of the French freighter *M/V Joan of Arc*, Trevor Ogden, a temporary dockworker, and a member from the freighter were completing a clandestine transaction. Trevor had been given a chance to work as part of his probation agreement for assaulting a local constable and chose the night shift on the busy docks. Trevor was acting as the local drug dealer amongst some of the other temporary workers. Tonight, he was handling the package of hashish from Guillermo Ochoa, the second engineer from the *Joan of Arc*.

Taking a small fisherman's scale from his satchel, the young dockworker took the opportunity to weigh the package, insuring it met the agreed upon quantity. Placing the package in the small sling and then on the hook, the package swayed slightly as the spring-loaded needle bobbed up and down until it settled on two kilos. As each of them saw the number register on the scale, Trevor reached into his satchel, pulled a brown envelope out, and passed it to the Frenchman.

"I promise you it's better than what you get from those in the Caribbean," the engineer said, handing over a sample of the hashish to Trevor, alluding to the fact he thought his supply was better than the drugs from the Caribbean.

"It better be, Ochoa, for the money we've given you," he said, "because it'll be my ass if I can't deliver the goods as promised."

Taking the offered envelope, the engineer said, "Goodbye, my friend," and made his way back towards his ship tied along the dock.

Trevor took the sample, placed it into his makeshift pipe, and lit the pungent drug. He drew on the mouthpiece, inhaling deeply, which caused him to cough unexpectedly. Looking about the container, he made sure his wheezing didn't draw attention. The intensity of the hashish and cannabis resin cocktail slowly began to take effect as Trevor entered a zombie-like state, the drug causing his sense of awareness to slow down to that of a crawl.

After what seemed like hours but was just minutes, Trevor began making his way from behind the container. In Trevor's mind, he was in complete control. However, the drugs were causing him to act in a much different way.

"Trevor; get yourself back to the loading area!" the shift supervisor yelled, noticing the young man walk out into the vicinity of the off-loading cranes. As the supervisor returned his attention to the current ship offload, he heard men yelling from behind him.

The shouts of the other dockworkers and the shrill blast of the gantry cranes' horn jarred the dockworker back to his senses momentarily enough to cause Trevor to stagger across the path of a moving gantry crane that was proceeding to the next vessel to begin off-loading cargo.

Because of the noise and movement of all the vehicles, the alarm sounded by his co-workers came too late. Trevor stepped into the path of a moving gantry crane and was crushed by the large machine as it moved into position. As the accident unfolded, safety horns and sirens sounded across the harbor. As the sound faded, an eerie silence fell over the dock. Trevor's body lay motionless and bloody for all to see under the glare of the dockside floodlights.

***

The tone of the meeting was becoming tense as the six subordinate directors of Scotland Yard's Drug Enforcement Task Force listened to their superior. It was this office's responsibility to investigate and, when possible, apprehend all parties involved in drug trafficking throughout Great Britain and its sovereign states.

"This is the third such incident in the last month and a half," Commander Lewis said to his staff gathered in the conference room. Referring to the forensics report, the senior officer said, "Each individual had the same blend of high-end hashish and cannabis resin in their system at the time of death."

Pointing to the display screen, the commander identified the proximity of the incidents to his staff. "This deadly combination of drugs was not only linked to the recent dockworker's death here in Southampton, but also causing of death of a young Royal Navy seaman from Portsmouth, who drove his motorbike into an oncoming lorry on the motorway, here south of the Naval installation.

"And we've also linked to the death of a female student, an Edna Gallagher from Aberdeen, who was attending a party near the local university and fell to her death from the roof of a third story flat, here in the center of the city.

"Gentlemen," Commander Lewis said, pausing to drink some water, changing the tone of his dialogue. "The only lead we seem to have is a French freighter leaving port within hours of each death. That and our American friends at the Drug Enforcement Agency advising us of a growing contingent coming from off-shore, possibly Northern Africa, becoming more involved in the drug movement into the British Isles.

"Now, I've reached out to our French counterparts, and they're pledging their assistance when we have the evidence to support their involvement. Until then, it's our problem to get a hold of."

Looking at the assembled group of chief inspectors before him, his gaze stopped at one. "Mister Collingsworth, there were documents found amongst the drugs on the recent victim that described a meeting in Aberdeen. Dispatch several of your men to consider a possible connection, but limit the number of people in the circle," he added to his instructions for the chief superintendent on what was expected of him and his investigators.

"Gentlemen, the commissioner himself was called upon by the prime minister, wanting us to gain a handle on this, so you can see it is a national priority," Commander Lewis said, ending the meeting.

# Chapter One

The squawking of seagulls filled the air as they glided high above the quay on the afternoon breeze. The horizon was dotted with silhouettes and exhaust trails of the workboats servicing the oilrigs that sat out of sight and of oil tankers transiting the North Sea, as it was nearly every day off the eastern coast of Scotland.

As the workboats drew closer to shore and the harbor, one could make out the bright-colored hulls and funnels. This might make a casual observer to wonder why one color was chosen over another. However, to the seasoned sailor or maritime aficionado, the bright colors meant the difference in another boat seeing them during a winter's gale or remembered as part of a eulogy.

The breeze blowing in from the North Sea this afternoon had the familiar smell of fuel oil, seaweed, and sea life. *The stench never gets any worse than this.* Chief Inspector Conor McDermott reminisced about his childhood, watching the various workboats, barges, and tankers ply the River Dee with their cargo of men and machinery. Regaining his focus, he continued walking along the quay towards the stack of shipping containers.

Leaning against one, McDermott inhaled deeply, relishing in the heavy scent of the sea cascading in from the east. The chill in the air always brought a sense of life to him, reminding him of growing up in this part of Scotland and living in a part of the seaside town known as 'Old Aberdeen' south of the university.

As part of the domestic Drug Enforcement Task Force at Scotland Yard, he and his partner, Inspector Andrew Fletcher, were working an investigation into the drug trafficking, which included a lead from the local office of Police Scotland. They'd been advised that a group of longshoremen had taken to selling drugs to crew members of the working boats that supplied the numerous oil rigs dotting the North Sea. The constant work on the oilrigs insured that the nation's economy would keep receiving a much-needed influx of cash.

It was McDermott's good fortune that his superior at Scotland Yard in London allowed him to take this assignment with Fletcher. He was working this investigation with a sense of trepidation, having a personal reason to find the group behind the drug movement. Reviewing the case files in London, he learned that one of the fatalities from the drugs included the death of his cousin, Edna, the only child of his uncle, Duncan Gallagher.

Teeth chattered as the sea breeze assaulted the young inspector from London. "Bloody hell, Conor, but it's cold!" Fletcher said, walking out of the shelter of the stacked containers, shoving his hands deeper into his jacket pockets.

"Aye, Andrew. It is inviting, isn't it?" McDermott said jokingly. *How in the hell did he ever survive it as a Royal Marine?* McDermott loved the sea, spending time in the Royal Navy as a lieutenant in the Signal Corps. The shrill blast of a workboat's horn as it entered the harbor at the quay's edge caught the chief inspector off-guard, jumping in surprise.

"You're a bit on edge, I see," Fletcher said.

"I'll cuff your ear if you keep that up," McDermott said, a foolish grin on his face for displaying his nervousness. Walking slowly along the supply pier, he and Andrew skirted numerous motorized lifts moving cargo when he noticed several men gathering near one of the warehouses lining the quay. "So, do you recall the bloke's descriptions the police report had, Andrew?"

"Of course; why in bloody hell don't you write things down?" the young inspector replied.

"Because I've got a young lad like you tae keep things in order."

Resigned that he would lose the argument, Fletcher pulled out his notepad and glanced at the writing. "Let's see. One chap is just over six feet tall and about one hundred seventy-five pounds, with brown hair and a handlebar moustache, another one, rather thin, shorter, about one hundred sixty pounds with blond hair."

McDermott could see in the distance what appeared to be the second man Fletcher described as part of the group. Two of them had the obvious look and mannerisms of stevedores working the docks, while one was dressed as if he had just come off an oilrig stint. The last two, one being the blond described by his partner and his 'companion' looked too well-dressed for the type of workers who toiled over the boats, oil rigs or containers.

This last person, with dark complexion, stood nearly six feet tall. His dark hair that was barely visible appeared to be closely cropped.

Wearing a slicker that hadn't seen much weather with a woolen sweater under it, it appeared he paid good money to try and fit in at the waterfront.

"What country do you think that one fella comes from, heh?" McDermott asked his partner, nodding his head in the direction of the group at the dock.

"He looks like he's from the Middle East," Fletcher replied, "but I've never been good with nationalities, mind you."

"I recall some of the 'hired help' on the boats as being from southeast Asia, but that bloke is a tad too tall for someone from the south of Asia," McDermott responded, keeping a keen eye on the odd man in the group. "And the rest of the crew could easily be from the Continent, like Norway or Denmark," he added.

***

Having provided local crime syndicates with the drugs entering Aberdeen, 'Louis Remesy' didn't usually supervise transactions in person, but was making an exception this time. Leaning against a pallet of supplies destined for the oilrigs, he watched with a nervous and wary eye as several dockworkers made their way towards him and his contact.

Trafficking drugs was the second step of his expanding criminal empire, with the help of a German contingent posing as work crews on the oilrigs making it difficult for the local authorities to track the drugs. It was the personal request by the financier of the drugs to increase the quantity of hashish for distribution that brought 'Remesy' to the Aberdeen docks today. He was uneasy because the buyer was an English-speaking man he only knew as 'Mr. Higgins'. Meeting briefly in Algiers several months ago, the message he received was simply to assist in the transaction between his distributor and the buyers.

Remesy was put in touch with Ewan Sutherland, an individual known locally to police for a few minor crimes. Now he was stepping into the larger circle of underworld crime syndicates that dealt in the drug trade. After an awkward introduction at the Edinburg airport, Remesy and the young Scot made their way to Aberdeen, and their appointment with the vessel crewmembers and dockworkers.

"Ewan, do you know of any police activity on the docks today?" Remesy asked. His gaze caught the movement of two men passing the local union office just off the frontage road along the quay.

"Aye. My source said we'd be clear for about ninety minutes from three till about, mmm, say four-thirty or so," the blond Scotsman said.

Remesy looked at his watch. *Nearing half past three, well within the time identified by Ewan's source.* Still, he couldn't shake the feeling that something was amiss with the two strangers. *It seems all too familiar.* Looking about the docks, his nervousness gnawed at his better judgement. "I believe we need to complete this transaction later, gentlemen," Remesy said.

The two dockworkers handling the drug and money transfers for Sutherland and the deckhand from the workboat looked rather bewildered. "Eh? What are you saying?" a chorus of uncertainty being spoken by several of the group.

"As an American would say *'we've been made'*, gentlemen," *Louis* said, losing sight of the two suspicious men from earlier.

***

Leery of the group they were observing, McDermott and Fletcher had gained access to an office that allowed them to observe without being seen. Standing to one side of a dirty window, Fletcher steadied the small digital camera on the dusty window ledge of the empty second floor office in the vacant building.

"Get a clear picture of the bloke with the tan," McDermott said.

"You'll get the best I can get. I'm not able to pose them, you know. Unless he turns and starts to wave, all you'll get is a profile shot," Fletcher said, clicking away at the group. "I've two or three clean shots of everyone else, just not him."

"Don't forget to take a group photo as well."

As his partner tried to zoom in on the faces, McDermott noticed that the group began to disband in several directions. "It appears they've either concluded their business, or they're keen to us being in the vicinity."

"Should we try and follow them?" Fletcher asked.

"*Nae*, it's no good unless we catch them doing something illegal, now, is it? We need to go back to the office and give the chief superintendent a call. Let him know we have a new player on the pitch to defend against," McDermott said.

Heading back to their car parked at a nearby pub along the waterfront, McDermott couldn't help but replay the image of the Middle Eastern suspect. *He wasn't local, even though he wore a heavy woolen sweater and foul weather slicker like most boat crews do. Something just doesn't fit.* Conor focused on the little details that caused him to feel the way he did, climbing into the driver's seat of the unmarked police car.

It was fifteen minutes of slow, silent, and circuitous driving back to the police station, which did nothing to relieve the uneasy feeling about the men he saw at the docks. McDermott pulled the police car into the parking space at the building on Victoria Road and climbed out. "I'm famished, lad, come on, a pint and portion on me," he said to Fletcher, starting his walk down the road.

Working with the Scottish inspector for the last year, Fletcher was catching on when Conor wasn't in the mood for discussions with their supervisor. Most likely, his partner wanted to ask for an opinion on today's events. Fletcher also knew he'd do this at the nearby fish and chips shop located a few hundred meters from the police station.

In the three weeks since they arrived in Aberdeen, they'd been to the small eatery on at least seven different occasions, always discussing things away from the office and the other constables.

The original interior of the shop was once white, though with the air heavy with the scent of cooking oil and fish, caught fresh that day, it looked more like jaundiced yellow. Customers eating their meals occupied a handful of the small tables located inside. Stepping up to the counter, Conor nodded to his childhood friend Malcolm standing next to the fryer, keeping a keen eye on the recent order he was cooking.

"Good day to ya, Conor. Will ya be having the usual?" Sadie, the young lass working behind the counter, asked.

"Aye, but make it two this time, love," Conor responded. "And two pints of Tennent's as well," before moving off to settle at the last table situated in the corner of the shop.

"So, what's on your mind, Conor?" Andrew asked, taking the opposite seat, placing his back against the wall.

"Thinking back to the Middle Eastern chap, he seemed a wee bit outta place, didn't he?" Conor asked.

Andrew paused before responding, giving Sadie a chance to place their drinks on the table. He slid one of the pints towards his partner before answering. "He's certainly not a local player, if that's what you're asking," Andrew said before taking a sip of his lager.

Conor's expression was thoughtful. "He didn't seem exactly comfortable in his surroundings tae me. It was almost as if he expected us tae show up."

"The desk sergeant, ah, McCord, is it? He didn't say anything about a foreigner being involved." Andrew leaned his head back, hitting the wall. "Damn!" he cursed rubbing his hand on the back of his scalp. "So, you think he was aware we were watching him?"

"I'm not sure it was *'us'*, but more that he knew police might show up if he stayed longer than a few minutes. I think we might need to be more mindful whom we discuss our business with. These blokes just might have a set of ears in the station," Conor said.

A robust and muscular figure loomed over the two inspectors. "You visit so often, I might have to hire you, Conor," Malcolm Smythe, the shop owner, said, bringing them their plates.

"I'd make a lousy dishwasher, Malcolm," Conor replied, reaching for the half-empty bottle of malt vinegar to douse his fish and chips in.

"He's not very hygienic either," Andrew quipped, breaking off a piece of the freshly cooked fish. Malcolm snorted at the jab to his good friend and went back to the fryers and his cooking.

"Since getting briefed about the drug trafficking back in London, and in the last two and a half weeks that we've been here watching the docks, we've never caught a glimpse of any Arab type. Have we?" Conor asked.

"I've not really been keen on keeping details on the nationalities we encounter," Andrew said, wondering what Conor was alluding to with the question. Just two years after serving as a Royal Marine, he had difficulty keeping details from the reports he read and who he was observing in the field.

"Our only lead on this case has been a brief reference to an Irishman working with the Glasgow syndicate, attempting to move drugs through the Aberdeen waterfront," Conor said, looking off at a point on the wall, wishing that more information would come to him.

"True and the fella we saw is no Irishman or Scot by any stretch of the imagination," Andrew said, wiping his hands of the salt and oil from his lunch.

***

Sitting in the front room of a drab rented flat off the A90 in Portlethen, Remesy was listening to the young Scotsman Sutherland discussing the appearance of unscheduled detectives and their activity with his police contact.

"Yes, we're sure that we were being watched," Sutherland said to his informant on the other end of the phone. "What do you mean there are two chaps from London working out of the Victoria Station?" he asked, exasperated at hearing this detail. "Don't you think that would've been something I needed tae know 'bout before I arranged for a meeting? Aye, when did they arrive? Just over two weeks ago, you say," Sutherland said, a terse tone in his voice.

Remesy took a sip of his tea, his mind beginning to race at the multitude of possibilities and pitfalls if he remained in Scotland. He became more concerned listening to Sutherland, without the benefit of hearing the informant's answers. *See if your contact can obtain their names,* he wrote on a piece of the local newspaper and slid it so Sutherland could read it.

The Scot read the note and nodded his head in understanding. "It'd be good of you to provide me with their names by tomorrow evening. I'll contact you at 6 p.m. Goodbye."

Finishing his tea, Remesy stood and walked to the kitchen sink, placing the empty cup on the counter. His mind was racing, getting an uneasy feeling about the transaction and the presence of the police inspectors. "Two individuals from London, possibly from Scotland Yard?" he asked.

"Aye, that's what I was told," Sutherland said, folding his arms across his chest, tilting his head back.

"The next question that needs asking is simple. What do they know and from whom did they learn it from?" Remesy said, alluding to how someone might've known about the meeting. *Did it come from one of my people, or is it the Scots?*

Running his hand through his close-cropped blond hair, Sutherland looked at Remesy, a sense of apprehension beginning to dwell in his mind as to what would come next. He did not expect the meeting to end like this, certainly not one that involved members of Scotland Yard.

"I need to return to my office and begin looking at what might have happened from that end," Remesy said, looking at his watch. *It would be too late to try and catch a flight from Edinburgh tonight.* "Can you muster a ride back to Aberdeen, Ewan?"

"Aye. I've a few friends I could call."

"Good. You call your friends for a ride. I'll take the rental back to Edinburgh and arrange for my flight," Remesy stated in a dismissal tone to the young Scotsman. Leaving Ewan in the rented flat earlier and driving the ninety minutes back to Edinburgh, Remesy found himself sitting in a hotel room, making plans for a morning flight back to Marseille.

"Yes, ma'am, a connection through Paris would do fine," he spoke into the phone.

"Half past nine will be fine as well."

Twenty minutes later, Louis Remesy had completed his travel plans back to his home in the south of France. Thinking back on the activities leading up to what happened, he took stock on what could have caused him to cancel the meeting. So much could be attributed to what happened, he soon began to have a headache with the myriad of thoughts, from being double-crossed by the young Scot to finally being identified by the French National police agency.

Next, he dialed a number on his cell phone from memory to inform his partner that he would be returning. "Hello," he said, hearing his friend answer.

"I wasn't expecting a call from you until Friday," the partner said.

"I'll explain everything when I arrive tomorrow. I'm coming in on the Ryanair flight from Edinburgh via Paris," Remesy said.

"I'll be waiting for you."

Remesy hung up, a constant suspicion and paranoia of exposure to eavesdropping devices used by the police gnawing at his psyche. Over the years, he'd learned hard lessons when it came to insuring his safety.

Several years earlier while handling a transaction in Tangier, Remesy escaped being apprehended by the local police based on his instinct and a faulty phone connection. During a discussion with a local drug dealer, he heard a slight click in his ear, and then an echo of his breathing before his conversation ended. He later found out from an old friend that the police were using radio transponders to track the local drug dealer's movement when using certain cell phones. He'd never forgotten that lesson.

***

Finishing their supper, McDermott and Fletcher returned to their office at the Victoria Station where Conor struggled typing his thoughts on the computer, filling in the report on the afternoon's observation. *Having a pint does nae help the fingers does it*, hunting, and pecking with two fingers. Fletcher, in the meantime, strolled down to the forensics lab where he found Sergeant Sheila Gordon, the young Scottish lass with chestnut-colored hair, hazel eyes, and a very inviting, curvaceous figure standing at one of the analysis machines, her back turned to the door.

"Evening, Sergeant Gordon," Fletcher said, entering the lab with the camera and data card from earlier. The young woman had caught his eye early into the posting at Aberdeen, and he always looked forward to seeing her at every chance. Though he was not the shy type, he wasn't sure if his time in Aberdeen would last long enough to start seeing someone.

"Evening, Inspector, and what might I do for you?" Sergeant Gordon asked with her soft lilting Scottish accent.

"I'm returning the camera that was signed out, and I need the images from this data card printed, please," Fletcher said, leaning onto the counter, drawing closer to her, catching the light scent of her Chanel No. 5 perfume. *I'd think it would be quite enjoyable waking up to her wearing nothing but that perfume,* he thought, recalling the vintage commercial with the Hollywood actress declaring it was the only thing she wore to bed.

"What will it be inspector; black and white or color?" Sergeant Gordon asked, filling out the custody form for the film. Even though they had not documented a crime, it was still protocol to make sure it was logged properly. As the senior lab technician, she was a stickler for having everything filled out properly and this time was no exception.

"Color, 8x10 glossy with a shiny gold frame," Fletcher quipped, attempting to lighten the moment with the attractive lab technician.

"Color will take a wee bit longer, and I don't do framing services," she said with a slight giggle. "It'll be ready by morning, just after tea." She walked towards her lab area, leaving him to his thoughts. Stepping away, Sheila considered the newly arrived young inspector quite the catch, not the type of one to be had for a fleeting one-night pass or weekend fling. *I wonder if he'd like a lunch date?* She completed the form to process the film he had dropped off.

An hour later, having finally finished his report, McDermott was discussing the afternoon's events with his chief superintendent and colleague. "I'm sayin' he'd a Middle Eastern look about him, William," Conor emphasizing his observations to his superior in London.

With sunset reflecting off buildings surrounding Scotland Yard, Chief Superintendent William Collingsworth looked out his window at the serene grounds of Christchurch Gardens, listening to McDermott over five hundred miles away.

"He came across like he knew what he was doing or involved in," the inspector said. "But out of place at the same time," continuing his monologue. Conor wasn't known to have many *'gut instincts'*, but this time he had an uneasy feeling with the events from this afternoon.

"Let him know we'll have the photos sent to him as soon as the lab finishes developing them," Fletcher said, interrupting McDermott's conversation.

"Put everything in your report then Conor," Collingsworth said.

"Aye, I'll do that. And we'll have the photos to you by the morn' as well," Conor said.

***

At nearly half past ten, Conor realized he wasn't going to function normally in the morning if he stayed any longer in the office. Getting up from the desk and taking the reports he'd been working on, he placed them in the folder and slid them into the drawer, locking it for safekeeping. Fletcher had already left since he was staying in the spare room the chief superintendent assigned to the station. Conor, on the other hand, had reacquainted himself with his lady friend from his Royal Navy days.

"You're a wee bit late." The soft and sleepy voice came from the prone figure curled up on the sofa situated in the front room of the small flat.

"Aye, I told you not to stay up," Conor admonished his roommate and lover.

Ailene O'Leary and Conor had met ten years earlier, with her working as a clerk for the maritime magistrates' office. During his Royal Navy days, his ship made a port call to Aberdeen, where Conor had the good fortune to meet the raven-haired beauty working in the communications office.

"Hush now and take me to bed, you scoundrel," she whispered, drifting in and out of sleep.

Looking down on her, he remembered fondly the first time they had spent time together. He was a young ensign delivering communiqués to the maritime magistrates' office for destruction when he saw her. *Soft curls of black hair cascaded over her shoulders, her blouse fitted snugly around her breasts, her pencil skirt accenting her slim figure as she stood at the counter asking the obviously very nervous Royal Navy*

*Ensign McDermott what his business was.* The thought of that first meeting brought a sheepish grin to his face. *Now that was a time ago.*

Succumbing to her request, Conor leaned down, pulled the limp figure from the sofa, and made his way into the bedroom where he laid her gently onto her side and covered her with the blanket. With the glow of the streetlights cascading into the room, Conor stripped out of his clothes and slid gently next to Ailene, who was in restful slumber based on the soft breathes she was taking.

Sleep came hard for Conor that night as his mind continued to ask questions about the stranger on the quay he saw earlier in the day. An odd sense told him he would see him again. *And it might not be a pleasant encounter if I have my way.* With that last thought cascading through his head, he drifted off to sleep.

***

The music from the local radio station grew louder as it reverberated off the walls of the small bedroom, bringing Conor out of sleep. Rolling over onto his back, he realized he was alone in bed. Rolling back onto his side, he silenced the radio, as the music had grown louder at each passing moment.

Slowly, Conor swung his legs over the side of the bed and stood, all six feet and four inches of taut muscles stretching from one side to the other. With one noticeable tattoo on his right arm and a scar along the right side of his stomach, he didn't exhibit an overly muscular build. Nevertheless, it was obvious to most that he did well to keep himself in shape. Pulling on his trousers and a clean shirt, he walked into the small kitchen where Ailene was fixing him a cup of tea.

Standing in the small kitchen with a loose pair of men's boxers and a thin tank top on, Ailene was a welcome sight for a poor soul's eyes. "Good morning, *'Mr. Stormy Seas'*," she quipped, handing him the steaming mug of tea.

"What do you mean hen?" Conor asked, taking a careful sip so as not to burn his mouth.

"You tossed and turned like the North Sea during a gale storm last night," she said, sitting at the table with her own cup. "You also mumbled a lot too."

"Sorry about that," Conor replied. "I've got a *Times* crossword puzzle dancing around inside me head that I can't seem to solve, and that's a bugger."

"Well, while you try and find the answers to solve your puzzle, I'm going to shower and get ready for work," Ailene said.

"I'll just fix me some toast and ponder the meaning of life," Conor said, pouting like a child.

"You do remember it's a small shower?" She walked past his outstretched hands, knowing he was planning to join her.

"Aye, but I've lost a few pounds since the last time," he chirped, rising to follow her.

***

Sitting quiet amongst the officers of the Victoria Station, the inspector from Scotland Yard took in his surroundings, contemplating how it be having a permanent assignment in Aberdeen. "Morning, Chief Inspector," Fletcher said, noticing his senior partner enter the office. "Running a tad bit late this morn', are we?"

"I dinnae sleep well, thank you very much," McDermott responded, removing his field coat.

"So, you have a roommate that snores, do you?" Fletcher asked, knowing full well Conor was staying with Ailene.

"That'll be enough out of you," McDermott growled at his young partner. "Did you get the photos from yesterday?"

"I was just about to go and see if they are ready," Fletcher responded, rising from behind the desk.

"Well, be quick about it then," McDermott directed, beginning to fix his second cup of tea for the morning.

Fletcher hurried to the forensics lab, ready to see Sergeant Gordon upon entering, but instead found himself greeted by one of the other uniformed technicians assigned to the lab. The dejected look was probably quite evident on his face stepping to the counter in the lab.

"Can I help you?" the technician asked, stepping to the counter where Andrew was waiting.

"Yes. I was hoping the photos on this order were ready for pick-up," Andrew said, handing the technician his copy of the custody sheet.

"One moment, sir," the technician responded, turning to the files stacked on the desk behind the counter. Thumbing through the stack of papers, the technician came across the order, second from the bottom. "Yes, it's ready. Won't be a moment," the technician said, walking to the back of the lab towards a counter with what appeared to be a large Xerox machine on it. Pulling a large manila envelope from the stack, the technician walked back to Andrew and handed the custody document to him. "Please sign in box twenty if you would," he said.

Andrew signed and was handed the envelope containing the photos as well as the data cards. "Thanks," he said, turning and exiting the lab, photos in hand.

Returning to the office, Andrew saw his partner entering the last few notes from their observations onto the report being sent to London, a comical scene, as McDermott typed with his two index fingers. "Here you go," Andrew said, placing the large envelope over a copy of the local newspaper on the desk.

Taking the envelope from the desk, McDermott asked, "Did you look at them yet?"

"No, I was going to give you that honor," the young inspector replied, going to the bookcase that held a small electric hotplate with a tea kettle perched on its element.

Pulling the photos from the envelope, he saw the profile of their Middle Eastern suspect. "Well, you were right, Andrew," McDermott pointed out to his partner. "You took an exceptional profile picture of this bloke's face. No distinguishing facial features unless he had turned to look at us." He thumbed through the near dozen photos in his hands.

***

Sitting alone in the rental flat, Ewan Sutherland felt nervous pulling the slip of paper from his wallet with his contact's mobile number. Yesterday evening, he'd contacted his informant at the Divisional Headquarters building and received information he knew wasn't pleasant. He not only learned the names of the two Scotland Yard inspectors, but also that they worked within the agency's Drug Interdiction Unit.

The information he received was rather dour, learning that they were working on a tip about a connection of the drug trafficking between Glasgow and Aberdeen. Ewan knew that not only would he need to speak with the Frenchman, who he only knew as 'Louis Remesy' about this, but also his boss in Glasgow. Dialing the number, he wondered how *Louis* would respond to the news regarding the inspectors from London.

Sitting in the café of the hotel, Remesy felt the vibration of his phone and pulled it from his pocket. Looking at the number, he answered, "Hello?"

"Good morning, 'Mister Remesy'," Sutherland started, not wanting to exchange too many pleasantries, "your two acquaintances in question are from London and they're interested in the same line of work you are, it seems."

Remesy took a moment to let the news sink in before responding to the young Scotsman. "Thank you for this news. I'll be in contact with you later this week," he responded before hanging up.

Sutherland was a bit taken aback at this sudden exchange because Remesy failed to ask for the two inspectors' names. "I'll just keep that to myself," he muttered, going back to his cup of tea. Next, he scrolled through his phone, listing, and coming across a number for a hotel. He selected the call button.

"Hello?" the voice of a middle-aged man answered on the first ring.

"Good morning," Sutherland answered nervously, "I need a room with a king-size bed for one night."

"When do you need this?" the voice asked.

"Tomorrow."

"That can be arranged, we'll see you tomorrow."

***

Back in Aberdeen, McDermott and Fletcher were back at the docks. This time they were discussing foreign visitors with several of the workboat captains. This was not always an easy task as some of the captains employed crewmembers who had *'questionable'* work documents.

With the help of the harbormaster, the inspectors were given the opportunity to meet with four captains who called the Aberdeen harbor home. As they gathered on the dock beside one of the large workboats, Fletcher passed out the best photo they had of the Arab they were looking to gain information on.

"I've seen a few coming out to work the derricks, mostly engineer-types, but none of them fit your bloke's description," one of the burly captains said, returning the photo the young inspector had handed him.

"He might give you the idea he knows his way about a boat, but not the type to get his hands dirty," McDermott said, gazing at each of the four captains.

"Aye, an engineer then, they never get their hands dirty," one captain chuckled.

Each one had a stern, business-like look about them, but they also appeared to have a slight disdain for law enforcement types as well. The weathered and tanned faces were hard to fathom for Conor trying to read their expressions.

"This fella might also give you the impression he was working for someone on the Continent," he said. In doing so, Conor was hoping to paint a picture the Arab might be someone to be wary of without disclosing the drug trafficking connection.

Glancing at each other, none of the captains could recall in recent memory of coming across the stranger from the Middle East.

"If you come across something or someone of interest, you can contact us at Victoria Station, using this number," Fletcher said, handing out generic police business cards with their desk number written on the back.

"We appreciate your help regarding this matter, gentlemen," McDermott said, shaking hands with each of them. "Safe sailing." He turned away from the boat captains and headed back to the car, walking away from the captains, who had now closed ranks to discuss the inspectors' presence on the docks.

"Why didn't you mention the possible drug connection?" Fletcher asked as they got into the car parked at the end of the quay.

"If we did mention something about drugs and their boats, then we'd *nae* find any evidence," McDermott said, adding, "because accidents happen at sea."

Fletcher looked at him with a quizzical expression on his face, then it hit him, and he knew exactly what McDermott meant. A captain at sea had the right to apply the justice he saw fit for the crime, just as it had been for centuries. The thought of a vessel's captain acting as judge, jury, and at times the executioner sent a chill down his back.

# Chapter Two

Gazing out his office window, the mysterious 'Mr. Higgins' was not happy with the turn of events in Aberdeen yesterday. He received a call earlier in the day from a source in the Aberdeen police office, who described the situation that led to cancelling the scheduled meeting of the Frenchman and the young Scot from Glasgow. Sitting in his comfortable office in Belfast, he motioned to his counselor. "Contact our man in Glasgow," he directed. "Ask him if he has the means to discern who those gentlemen are."

"Yes, sir," the counselor responded, leaving the room.

As the barrister stood and left the office to make the call, the mysterious Irishman was left to his own thoughts. *Business was becoming promising, and I don't need the Yard stepping in and ruining what I've started.* Having built a legitimate business with his partner, he used it to create a shadow company for its illegal activities, which could all come crumbling down if the wrong people caught wind of it.

***

Pacing about his office, Chief Superintendent William Collingsworth reviewed the report of the observations made by his two agents in Scotland, including the photos they'd forwarded to him. *Conor was correct. The Arab certainly appears too comfortable in this meeting.* Stabbing the intercom button on his phone set, the inspector called, "Officer Jones, please come to my office."

In a moment, a rosy-cheeked officer from Wales stepped into the office. "Yes, sir?"

"Jones, please get me the last three months' dispatches from INTERPOL regarding potential drug trafficking operations between the UK and the Middle East."

"Right away, sir."

"Oh, include all activity across the Mediterranean coast of Africa as well if you would," the chief superintendent added.

"Bloody hell," Officer Jones mumbled to himself, returning to his cubicle outside the inspector's office, turning on his computer. Located deep in the bowels of Scotland Yard and protected with multiple security protocols, the database of activity recorded within the United Kingdom was nearly astronomical.

"Good morning, my dearie," Officer Jones said to no one in particular, entering his security code to begin the search for the INTERPOL files. As the screen image shifted to the department's database page, Officer Jones began entering the information based on Collingsworth's request. He started with setting the dates of the search, then the activity, and finally, the locations. "There we are. Let the music begin," he said whimsically, pressing the *'enter'* key.

As the electrons raced back and forth across the miles of cables, bits and bytes of information began to gather, the program looking for the key components that Officer Jones had entered. Seeing the program icon twirl endlessly on his screen, Jones went to the nearby beverage station and prepared himself a cup of tea.

"Slow day, Jonesy?" Officer Ethan Taylor asked his fellow constable.

"Somewhat. Chief Superintendent Collingsworth asked if I could gather up some information. I'm just waiting for it to finish."

"Doesn't the *'high and mighty'* inspector work the drug side of the wall?" Taylor scoffed.

"He does; but I'm not keen to question why he wants the information," Jones said, walking carefully back to his desk, trying not to spill the cup of tea.

Officer Ethan Taylor was not only a lowly constable working in Scotland Yard, but he also acted as an informant for a South London crime syndicate, who paid well when the information was fruitful.

What he didn't know was the syndicate he occasionally supplied information to was also in contact with his uncle, Alistair Hunt. Ethan knew his uncle did *'questionable'* things from time to time, but he never questioned or knew the depth of his involvement, nor did he push to find the answers about it. Things were about to change today, since he would soon gain a glimpse into what his uncle was involved in and how deep that involvement went.

***

An hour later, Chief Superintendent Collingsworth was poring over the documents Officer Jones had extracted from the Yard's extensive database. *Nothing 'jumped out' as it were from the pages of dispatches he reviewed*, he noted with a sense of irony, looking at the stack of paper he'd sorted by country, hoping to establish a link between the Continent activities and the UK.

"Will there be anything else, sir?" Officer Jones asked, looking in the doorway at Chief Superintendent Collingsworth's office.

"No. Not for the moment at least, thank you, Jones," he said, turning his attention back to the reports.

"If you don't mind, then I'm off to lunch," Jones said. Looking up at the clock, the senior inspector noticed he'd spent the better part of two and a half hours reading the dispatches.

Meanwhile, as Jones was leaving the office the desk phone rang. "Don't worry, I'll handle it," Officer Taylor said, picking up the phone in his cubicle, answering a few questions from the caller.

"Yes, sir, we are interested in information that would lead to the apprehension of criminals, especially those who deal in narcotics," Officer Taylor said. "I'll see that your information is passed to the inspectors and handled accordingly," he responded. "Thank you and good day to you as well," he said, placing the receiver down. A cold sweat began building on his brow after hearing the caller ask his questions. This was the first time speaking directly with his uncle regarding a matter such as this.

Alistair Hunt didn't like contacting his nephew in London, but he'd no choice this time. Receiving the call from the counselor for 'Mr. Higgins' sent a mild shiver down Hunt's back, especially when the question was asked.

"Identify the two inspectors from Scotland Yard that are in Aberdeen," the counselor said to Hunt.

His first action was contacting Ewan Sutherland and asking if his contact at Police Scotland's district headquarters in Aberdeen knew the names. Sutherland helped Hunt with his decision to call his nephew when Sutherland traveled to Glasgow from Aberdeen to speak directly to him.

Sitting in the railcar away from the other passengers, Sutherland said, "Yes. I was asked by the Frenchman, 'Mister Remesy' to find out right after he sacked the meet at the docks," he told his boss when the question was asked. "I asked our contact at the district office in Aberdeen, and he confirmed the two names."

"Very well," Hunt said. "After you get into town, plan to stay for a day or two, then return to Aberdeen and wait for my call." He hung up the phone.

Hearing this disturbing news from Sutherland, Hunt's next move was to make the cryptic call to his nephew. Without getting into details, but asking a specific question, he conveyed to his nephew what information he needed. All he had to do now was wait for his nephew to contact him outside the office to insure no prying eyes or ears could place who he was talking to. After what seemed like an eternity but was just ten minutes, his private phone began to ring.

"Hello?" Hunt said, answering the call to his private phone on his desk, being wary of who might be on the other end of the conversation.

"A Scot named Conor McDermott and an Englishman named Andrew Fletcher," the voice on the other end said.

"Thank you," Hunt said, before the line went dead.

His nephew had just confirmed the names of two members of Scotland Yard who were involved in the investigating drug trafficking activities in Aberdeen. With this knowledge, Alistair Hunt knew he needed to begin searching for a mole in his organization, but he wasn't sure where to start. His first call was to the counselor for 'Mr. Higgins' to advise him of what his nephew had just told him.

Sitting in the cubicle, his hands were shaking as he put the phone receiver down, Ethan Taylor felt uneasy having made the call to his uncle, providing the names of two fellow officers he knew nothing about. Getting up from his desk, he told a fellow clerk he was going out to grab a bite and would return shortly. Walking across the street from the office, he entered the coffee shop and ordered a large iced coffee and a scone. Taking a seat outside, watching the patrons of the shop as well as pedestrians walking the streets, he wondered how he could ever escape the grip of the syndicate.

***

"We've confirmed the names of the individuals in Aberdeen, sir," the counselor said to 'Mr. Higgins' entering the luxurious office suite. 'Mr. Higgins' had chosen his office with care, situated in a high-rise building that was tall enough to see both the harbor as well as the airport, and overlooking the River Lagan, in the heart of Belfast.

"Well done Mister Gilmore; see that the information is sent off to 'Mister Remesy'," he said, turning in his chair to look out upon the city landscape. The counselor left the office quietly and returned to his desk where he sat down and pulled an old-fashioned Rolodex cardholder from the side drawer. Pulling out the cell phone he used to make the call to associates such as this, he slowly punched in the number, beginning with the country prefix for France.

The cell phone Remesy purchased for this trip chimed as it sat in the middle of the table. Both he and his partner looked suspiciously at the device as it rang for the second time. Picking up the phone, he thumbed the 'on' button. "Mister Remesy, please?" the voice asked as 'Louis' brought it to his ear.

"Yes, this is 'Monsieur Remesy'."

"There are two new employees in Aberdeen, a Mister McDermott, and Mister Fletcher," the counselor said, passing on the information obtained by Hunt's nephew.

"I understand, two additional employees," Remesy responded, a chill filling his body.

"Please be sure you make proper arrangements for their indoctrination on the working platforms," the counselor said, which to Remesy meant that no harm was to come to them unless it was at sea. Accidents at sea are easily forgotten and, in most cases, don't involve the authorities who are adept at thorough investigations.

"Yes, I'll see the word is passed along. And thank you for the update," Remesy said as the conversation ended. Closing his phone, he looked across the table. "We have names and a place," he said, turning to his partner.

***

With the sun beginning to set behind the city landscape, McDermott and Fletcher walked back to the car. The inspectors were quiet, having spent the better part of five hours scouring the docks for their mysterious Arab. With eighteen registered workboats using Aberdeen as a base of operations, they observed activity on nine of them. This made sense as each boat would rotate between platforms with another, ensuring a constant flow of men and material working the offshore platforms.

"It's like he just up and vanished," Fletcher said, sliding into the passenger seat, rolling down his window just a touch.

"Aye, sudden and complete," McDermott replied, rubbing his hand over his face. "It would seem like he was here for a purpose, but not for a holiday."

Rubbing his hands together to warm them, Fletcher said, "Funny how we saw the stevedore and one of the crew members from the other day, but not the blond either," pointing out the absence of Ewan Sutherland.

"Aye, you're right about that too. So, we've three of five missing, with one that was apparently a 'visitor' to the area," McDermott said. *Why weren't they here today?* He thought about the significant fact his partner had just pointed out.

Driving back to the station, Conor mentally worked at placing the puzzle pieces into the voids, recalling the events of the last few days. *An Arab, the Scot who's a known criminal, two boat workers, and a stevedore from the docks working together. If the handling of drugs was the connection, was the Arab the supplier and the Scot playing the intermediary? Moreover, where does the transaction take place?* He was ready to ask his partner a question.

"Andrew, if you've a stevedore on the wharf and a worker on the boat, how would you pass something between the two?" he asked, arriving back at the police station car park.

"Well, the stevedore would know what was being passed," Andrew said. "And if he saw the right worker on the boat, who to pass it to."

"Or vice versa," Conor said, the method of transferring the drugs becoming clearer to him. "We just need to identify which party is involved," maneuvering the police car through the evening traffic.

***

Sitting back at his desk with the phone to his ear, Conor once again conversed with their superior in London. "Chief Superintendent, can we get our hands on the movement records of the work boats out of Aberdeen?"

"I suppose it's possible, but the Aberdeen officials could get it quicker and easier, don't you think?" Collingsworth said as both a question and a statement to his subordinate.

"Aye, we can do that, but I think we might be asking those types of questions to the wrong person if we do," Conor said, alluding to the fledgling alliance between the Police Scotland officers and Scotland Yard inspectors.

"I see. Let me make a call or two and I'll be in touch tomorrow," the senior officer said, not wanting to think that his two inspectors might be at risk of harm by one of their own. With that, Collingsworth made a call to a friend, colleague, and senior insurance investigator working with Lloyd's of London on all matters involving shipping.

"Thomas, this is William Collingsworth, how are you today?"

"I'm fine. What can I do for you, William?"

"I'm wondering if we can sit down for a chat on a rather interesting subject, say at 4 p.m. today?"

Thomas looked at his calendar and then at the clock. "Tomorrow's fine. How about the Bulldog Arms, I'll give them a call to set a table aside for us."

William smiled at the answer from his colleague. "That will be fine. Thank you, Thomas." Looking at the report from McDermott and Fletcher, Collingsworth quickly made a few notes based on what had transpired so far in the investigation. *Transit of vessels from the Mediterranean to the English Channel and beyond would be the key*, he wrote down. Looking at his calendar, he jotted down a few dates as a reference based on his earlier review of INTERPOL communiqués and folded the papers together and placed them in his jacket pocket.

At a quarter to five, Collingsworth went about the routine of closing his office up for the evening. There was a brief knock on his office door, "Come in," he replied to the knock.

"Excuse me, Chief Superintendent; a moment, sir?" It was Officer Jones.

"Yes, what is it? I have an appointment at four that I need to be at," Collingsworth said, glancing at the wall clock.

"The desk sergeant was wondering if you've seen Officer Taylor about the office this afternoon."

"No, I haven't seen him at all. Why do you ask?"

"Well, sir, just after I provided you with your documents earlier this morning, he answered a call as I left for a wee break and hasn't been seen since," Jones said, a touch of concern in his voice.

"Has the desk sergeant notified the foot patrols about the area?" the senior officer asked.

"Yes, sir, but we're asking all on the floor as well, just in case Officer Taylor said something to someone in passing."

"Well, I haven't seen him nor have I talked with him today, but I'll keep my eye open for him as I head out."

"Thank you. Good evening, sir," Jones said, leaving the office.

*****

The pub was just beginning to receive the after-work crowd, young boisterous office workers, some dressed for the office, while others were more casually attired, as Collingsworth was shown to the table where his colleague was already seated.

"So, to what do I owe this impromptu visit to William?" Thomas queried his friend.

"I've a couple of chaps working in Aberdeen, and they're trying to fit a few odd pieces of information together," William said as the server came to the table.

"What will it be, gents?" she asked, pad and pencil at the ready for their order.

"I'll have a Boddington and an order of fish and chips," William answered.

"And I'll have a Newcastle with the chicken and mushroom pie," Thomas added.

With the food ordering out of the way and drinks on the horizon, William began the discussion with his friend regarding the Yard's involvement in international shipping. "My two chaps need to know if we can link shipping from the Mediterranean to the North Sea?" he asked.

"Intriguing to say the least," Thomas replied, pulling his hand across a long and stylish handlebar moustache. "We're looking at several incidents in the channel between flagged carriers too," he said just as their drinks arrived.

"To your health," William said, raising his glass to his friend.

"And to you as well," Thomas said. "So, in the last six months, we've noticed a trend in smaller container and bulk cargo vessels making their way out of the Mediterranean. This would normally be quite innocent, mind you. But, we've seen at least half of them making a stop in Tangiers before making their way up the coast and entering the channel."

"Are you saying there are no stops by these freighters along Portugal, Spain, or France then?" Collingsworth asked, drinking his beer.

"Not with the ones we have tracked, based on the information provided by INTERPOL," Thomas added. "Why is this matter of concern for you, William? I was under the impression you were handling domestic issues?" Thomas asked.

"It seems there is a new angle to supplies and or supplier that my inspectors have come across while in Scotland," William said. Before his colleague could ask another question, the server came to their table carrying their supper and a fresh round of drinks.

"We didn't order these," William said, pointing at the second set of beers.

"No, sir, but the gentleman at the bar asked that I bring you both a fresh one anyway," she said, pointing to the African-American sitting at the bar.

Looking over at his counterpart at the bar, William waved him over and asked that the server bring another chair to the table. "Well I'll be. Charles. What a surprise to see you in London!" William exclaimed, rising to greet the American.

"Good to see you as well, William," the American said, shaking hands with his friend.

"Thomas, I'd like you to meet Charles Baldwin, senior detective with the American FBI," William said, making the introductions.

"It's a pleasure," Thomas replied surprised at the size of the agents' hand.

Taking a seat at the table, Baldwin leaned towards Collingsworth. "I'm no longer with the FBI, my friend. I'm working with the DEA these days," Charles said.

"Then what brings you to this side of the pond?" William asked him, finishing his first drink.

"What else? Drugs," Charles said, drinking his rum and cola.

# Chapter Three

The pleasantry of having a meal cooked for him instead of reheating a box of leftovers was beginning to take hold of the chief inspector. "That was a delightful meal," Conor exclaimed, pushing his chair back from the table.

"I'm pleased that you found it so wonderful," Ailene said, as she stood and gathered the dishes from the table. "So, you've been here for four weeks, but I'm still waiting to know for how much longer?"

"I'm not sure, maybe a week or two more," he said. "It all depends on how things go with the investigations."

"Did you ever stop to see your mum and dad?"

"Aye. I stopped by and paid a wee visit the day after arriving," Conor said. "Cleaned up the space and had a wee drink with Dad and placed a few flowers out for Mum."

Walking into the small kitchen, Conor wrapped his arms around the waist of his lover. "I wish I could make a commitment to you, but working for the Yard makes things rather unpredictable," he said, gently squeezing his arms together.

"Well, if you stay longer, I'll be charging you a thousand euros rent a week," Ailene said jokingly.

"Aye, and if I had a thousand euros a week to give, I'd buy this flat me self and you'd rent from me," Conor said, leaning down and placing a brief kiss on the nape of her neck.

"That activity will not get you any privileges as a renter," she said in a low and sultry tone. "If you plan to interrupt me, you can dry," she squealed, handing Conor a dishtowel.

After helping Ailene clean the dishes and straighten the kitchen, Conor cleaned up and retired to the bedroom for the evening. Lying in the darkened room, he continually tossed the thoughts about his head, trying to put the puzzle back together, until he fell asleep.

What felt like two hours of laying in the dark bedroom next to Ailene, was actually six. As the music from the radio grew louder as Conor propped himself on his elbow to see what time it was. *Half past five*, he thought to himself, turning the radio off, and laying his head back down on the pillow.

Rolling to his opposite side, he could see the soft silhouette of Ailene lying next to him, the outline of her breasts hidden under the bed sheet, lifting, and falling gently with each breath. *I'm nae sure of this.* He slid gently from beneath the sheets and walked to the bathroom, hoping not to wake her. Over the last several weeks, he'd grown accustomed to coming to her flat after working at the office, meeting her at the door as she returned from work or being greeted coming in late.

Standing at the stove, the kettle was coming to a boil. He felt her presence walking up from behind. Turning around, he saw she'd a sheepish grin on her face, the ever-present tank top slung lazily over her shoulders. "Good morning," he said, pulling her close.

"Good morn', *Left-tenant*," she replied in a mockingly military tone.

"I'd say you're out of uniform, Seaman O'Leary," he said, noting all she had on was the tank top, barely falling past her waistline. Bending down to place a kiss on her pouting lips and just as she was reaching across to slip her arm out of the tank top, the phone rang.

Begrudgingly, she stepped into the living room and answered the phone, leaving Conor to stand and contemplate what might have been, seeing her ass cheeks sway as she walked.

"Hello?" she said, answering the intruder to their moment. "Yes, he's here, just a moment." She held up the phone for him. "It's for you."

"Hello, this is McDermott."

"Conor, it's Andrew," his young partner said on the other end of the call. "I think I found a mole at the district office."

"And this couldn't wait until I came in, lad?" he said, gazing at the half-naked figure of Ailene walk into the bathroom. With the moment between him and Ailene interrupted, Conor queried his partner for more information. "So how did you come to this conclusion now?"

"Well, last night I was discussing things with Chief Superintendent MacCallum after supper about the investigation," Andrew said. Moreover, he mentioned that one of his desk sergeants took a call from one of the workboat captains we talked with the other day at the docks. He clearly overheard the sergeant providing the caller with a description of you and me as well."

Closing his eyes, his mind reeled at the news. *This doesn't seem likely that someone in the Aberdeen district office would be able to have firsthand knowledge of our purpose.* "I'll be in the office in thirty minutes," Conor said.

"Are you having trouble with the young inspector?" Ailene asked, exiting the bathroom, her only clothing being a lace bra and matching bottoms.

"It seems I might need to have a talk with the chief superintendent," Conor replied, tracing his hands across the round cheek of her exposed flesh.

"You'll be late if you start that," she said. "Plus, it'll ruin my makeup."

Knowing she was right, Conor sighed in defeat, pushing his way into the bathroom for a quick shower and shave. "You did leave me some hot water now, lass?" he called out, turning the spigot in the shower.

"Right now, you need a cold shower to relax, laddie," she called out from the bedroom, slipping into her skirt.

***

Meeting his partner in the office, McDermott listened to Fletcher retell his version of the conversation with the chief superintendent regarding a possible mole among the constable ranks.

"Write up a wee report and lock it away," McDermott said.

"Why?"

"Consider it a 'get out of jail' card. While you're doing that, I'm going tae look for a clue at the docks," leaving the young inspector in the office.

Sitting in the unmarked police car, Conor peered through the marine-grade binoculars at the various workboats tied up at the docks along Regent and Albert quay. *Do you see me?* Scanning the upper deck of the boats, he attempted to catch a glimpse of the captains he and Andrew had talked to the other day.

Suddenly one of the bridge wing doors opened and a figure appeared. Although this bloke was sporting a weathered, Greek fisherman's hat of grey tweed, Conor recognized him as one of the captains from the other day. Having identified the captain, Conor quickly glanced at the forward hull to see the name of the vessel, *PSV Nordic Supplier. Now all I need to do is find out who owns her, and I know just the lassie to ask.* A sheepish grin came across his face.

***

While Chief Inspector McDermott was observing the crews of the vessels in Aberdeen, a young drug runner was getting ready for breakfast. In the restaurant of a Glasgow hotel, Sutherland was looking over the breakfast menu. "I'll have the eggs and toast and a ration of bacon," he said to the waitress.

Sitting in the hotel room for the last two days had given Sutherland time to think about the past few days' events. *How did Mr. Hunt know this Frenchman named 'Messier Remesy'? Moreover, how was it that I need to be involved in Aberdeen and not here in Glasgow?*

"Here you go, sir," the waitress said, setting the plate of food in front of him. "More tea as well?"

"Yes, that will be fine, thank you," he replied. The more he thought of his involvement and the various angles; he was left with more questions than answers.

The shrill ring of the cell phone interrupted his attempt to take the last bite of his toast. "Hello?" he answered, clearing his throat.

"Good morning, Ewan. When you're done with your breakfast, please meet Mr. Hunt at St. George's Tron in one hour," the voice of the mysterious caller said.

"Aye, I'll be there," Sutherland replied, looking at the clock above the checkout kiosk. A cold shiver ran down his back, suddenly realizing that someone in Mr. Hunt's employment had been nearby to keep an eye on him. With that thought, he quickly swallowed the last of his tea and went to pay for his meal.

Stepping outside, Sutherland felt the sting of an early summer rain, walking to the car park. The nice part of returning to Glasgow the other day was the luxury of driving his own car, which was a vintage BMW 2002 coupe. It was one of the last possessions that he still had after selling everything he owned to settle his gambling debts.

Alistair Hunt was no stranger to the locals that lived around St George's. He was known to attend the odd Sunday service when it wasn't interfering with a business meeting or a football match, having grown up a staunch Celtic supporter. With the passing of the early morning shower and sitting on a bench outside the church feigning to read the morning addition of *The Herald*, he began to think through the current situation.

*What to do with Ewan?* With the interest of 'Mr. Higgins' concerning the events from the other day in Aberdeen, Alistair Hunt knew he was being closely watched for any sign of weakness. *Could Ewan make the hard decision if it came down to it?*

"Mr. Hunt," Ewan said, greeting the older Scotsman.

"Good morning, lad, have a seat," Hunt responded, motioning to the bench. "It seems I've placed you in a wee spot of bother."

"Aye. I've noticed that myself," Sutherland said in a nervous tone, unsure of what was to come next.

"You realize that with your meeting the other day I need you to step up to the challenge?" Hunt said in a fatherly manner. "But with all challenges comes a level of uncertainty and risk."

"I'll be more than ready, Mr. Hunt," Sutherland said, a slight queasy feeling beginning to creep into his stomach.

"I'm sure you will, lad," Hunt said, glancing up at the church steeple, wondering how long the young man would survive in the coming months.

After his early morning meeting with Ewan, Alistair Hunt was back in his office on Argyle Street, needing to discuss the matter of protecting the young man in Aberdeen. With the possibility of some 'wet work' as it were, he called his associate, Stuart Ross, who was best suited for this task to join him.

Thirty minutes later, Ross was shown into Hunt's office, listening to the elder crime boss' concerns. "Stuart, what can you do to help look after the lad?" he asked his associate.

Stuart sat across from his boss, looking at him sitting behind the mahogany desk, but also past him, envisioning Sutherland standing at the docks in Aberdeen. "I could spare a man or two to mind the young lad," he said, contemplating the potential trouble that his men could encounter.

"I want them to be discreet, but close enough to take care of things if need be," Hunt replied.

"Aye, I have a few I can trust to blend in," Ross said.

"Good then, see to it that they are ready. I'll be sending Ewan back to Aberdeen tomorrow and I'll want them close by."

As Ross left the office, the phone rang on Hunt's desk. Picking the handset up, he answered, "Hello, can I help you?"

"Mr. Hunt, please hold for 'Mr. Higgins'," the voice on the line said. A cold chill fell upon Alistair when he realized his private line had been compromised. After a moment of silence, a distinct voice of an Irish gentleman came on the line.

"Good morning, Mr. Hunt," the gentleman said.

"Good morning, sir," Hunt replied. "What can I do for you today?"

"Mr. Hunt, I need to know if you can prepare a group of individuals to provide some protection during a transaction?" the mysterious 'Mr. Higgins' asked the Scottish crime boss.

"Aye, I'm quite capable of gathering over twenty loyalists when the need arises," was Hunt's reply, wondering what might be in store for him and his colleagues.

"Good then. My counselor will be in touch later this week with details. Good day, sir," 'Mr. Higgins' said before hanging up on the Scotsman.

*What the bloody hell was that all about?* Hunt stared at the handset.

Reaching forward, he selected the intercom. "Janice, please contact Gordon Wallace and ask him to come see me as soon as possible."

"Yes, sir."

Standing up from behind his desk, Alistair walked over to hutch below the windows that allowed him to look down Brown Street to the River Clyde. Opening the hutch, Alistair reached in and pulled a crystal tumbler and the open bottle of single malt scotch from the shelf, pouring himself a drink. *Nae time for the weak, is it, Ali boy?* He finished the dram in one gulp.

***

Sitting at his desk in the Victoria Station police station, Inspector Fletcher was busy reviewing the passage logs from the Maritime and Coast Guard Agency office that had been filed for the past six months. *What in bloody hell does Conor expect me to find in all this rubbish?* He turned what seemed to be the hundredth page of listings.

Suddenly, something caught his eye on the page he'd noticed at least two other pages earlier. Pulling back the last ten pages, he looked closer at the listings, mindful to keep his hand on the last page he was looking at. "There you are, silly bugger!" he exclaimed.

"Who's the 'silly bugger'?" a female voice asked, startling Fletcher nearly out of his chair.

The voice belonged to Sergeant Gordon, the technician from the forensics lab providing him with more reports from the printing station.

"Damn you women and your quiet shoes. You scared the hell outta me," Fletcher exclaimed at the intrusion.

"Sorry, Inspector, but I wanted to bring you these other prints before I went to lunch."

"I'm sorry for the outburst, and thank you," he said, rather embarrassed to be caught off-guard. Gathering his wits, he boldly prepared himself for what was to come. "For being such a help, can I buy you lunch?"

"Aye, I'd like that. I'll meet you at the front desk, in say 'bout an hour then," she said, walking out of the office.

"I'd like that," he said softly to himself, repeating her acceptance to the lunch date. With that, Fletcher went back to reviewing the last ten pages. Taking a pencil, he circled the information he found on each of them. *This just might give Conor and me a leg up on the blokes and their activities,* the young English inspector thought to himself proudly.

***

Standing at the front desk, Fletcher feigned reading a notice on the bulletin board, hoping he didn't appear overly anxious about taking the young forensic technician to lunch. Preparing to look at his watch for the third time, he spied Sergeant Sheila Gordon walking out of the stairwell. *Quite the sight,* he noted as the young woman walked his way.

"Hope I didn't keep you long, Inspector?" Sheila asked.

"Not at all," Andrew replied, Gooding her through the front doors of the station, "and please, do call me Andrew. Inspector seems too formal. Now, do you have any preference for lunch?" he asked as they stepped out onto the sidewalk.

"I fancy the wee bistro around the corner," Sheila said.

"The bistro it is then."

"So, what's brought you and your partner up from London, Andrew?"

"Well, my associate and I are looking at a possible connection to some activity that originated near Portsmouth several months back."

"Oh, so that's why you need to look at the ship docking records?" she replied, quick to put a piece of the puzzle together.

"Well, yes. That's part of it, but we are also looking for a group of gentlemen who might have transited aboard certain vessels as well," he replied, a sense of panic beginning to rise in his thoughts.

"Well, if you need a second set of eyes, I'll be free later today," the young woman said.

Coming to the storefront of the bistro, Andrew opened the door as a true gentleman would, making sure he followed closely behind, less someone rudely step between them. *It might just do me well to have a second person look over those files.* They reached the entrance to the bistro. "I must admit. I'm surprised that you prefer wearing Chanel No. 5 over the more modern scents."

"I'm surprised you even noticed?" Sheila asked.

"It's a very distinct fragrance. Why, my aunt in South Africa and her sister in America would wear nothing but. I always knew when they were visiting on holiday."

"I'm not keen of the current trends. They seem overly fruity or heavy," she said.

"What would you like to order, miss?" the young lad behind the counter asked.

"I'll have a ham and Swiss cheese sandwich, and a bottle of Perrier," Sheila answered.

"And I'll have a ham and cheddar sandwich with a bottle of Perrier as well," Andrew added, stepping next to Sheila, pulling his billfold out to pay.

***

Conor parked in an empty space outside the Maritime and Coast Guard Agency on Blaike's Quay. Grabbing a ratty looking moleskin notebook from the passenger seat, he stepped out of the car and walked through the front entrance.

"Can I help you, sir?" the young woman at the reception desk asked.

"Yes. I'm here to see Miss Ailene O'Leary," he replied, showing his Scotland Yard credentials.

"Just a moment, Chief Inspector," she said, picking up the phone and dialing a number. "A Chief Inspector McDermott from Scotland Yard to see you, Ailene," she announced. For a moment, there was no discussion, and then the receptionist hung up. "You can go down the first corridor on your left. It will be the fourth door on your right," she directed Conor.

"Aye, thank you, cheerio," he replied, moving toward the corridor in question. Looking at the nameplates on each door, he finally came across the fourth door and read, *Services and Payments, Ms. O'Leary. She's done well.* He knocked on the door and entered the office.

"And to what do I owe the pleasure of this visit, Inspector?" Ailene said, seeing Conor enter her office.

"Well, I could think of several things, but your desk seems a wee bit cluttered."

"Seriously, Conor, what is it that you need?" she asked. "I'm quite busy."

Knowing that this was not the place to exhibit his wanton desires, he came to the point of his visit. "I need your help in finding out who owns a vessel."

The look of shock that came across her face was probably quite evident upon hearing his question. Ailene recovered by asking him, "What's the name of the vessel?"

"It goes by the moniker *PSV Nordic Supplier* today," he said, looking at his notebook.

"Very well," she said, "it'll cost you a 'nice' dinner and twenty-four hours. Now, off with you, I've a meeting in ten minutes," she demanded.

With that dismissal, Conor stood up from the desk before stepping out the door as he felt Ailene pulling on his arm, placing a kiss quickly on his cheek.

***

Walking through the streets like most common and law-abiding citizens, one wouldn't know that Gordon Wallace was a senior member to one of Glasgow's notorious crime syndicates. Beginning his life of criminal activities at an early age, he helped incite fights and discord during football matches at Ibrox Stadium for his hometown Rangers club.

It was during one of these early, youthful melees that he crossed paths with Alistair Hunt. Standing opposite each other, Gordon and Alistair went to blows, each one standing fast to show support for their respective football clubs. After their arrests and a night in jail, they each came to understand the other's level of commitment, and a newfound respect was developing between the two. Today, Gordon Wallace was known as a hired enforcer for the top bidder, which always seemed to be Alistair Hunt.

Entering the outer office, he introduced himself to the receptionist, Janice.

"Good morning, miss. Mr. Wallace to see Mr. Hunt," he said in a polite manner.

"Just a moment, sir," Janice said, picking up the phone. "There's a Mr. Wallace here to see you, sir."

"Show him in," Alistair said.

Getting up from her seat, Janice said, "Please follow me," leading the guest to her boss' doorway.

"Gordon, what a pleasure to see you again," Alistair said, seeing his friend come through the door behind his receptionist.

"Alistair, it's always good to see you too my friend." He took the offered hand and shook it firmly.

"Please, have a seat," Alistair said, pointing to the sofa on the side of the room. "A wee dram?" he offered, holding up the bottle of Scotch from the hutch.

"Aye, but a wee one now," Gordon said, knowing he was here to discuss business and not cricket or football with his rival.

Having poured two glasses of the golden liquor in the crystal tumblers, Alistair offered the first to his associate.

"To your health." He raised his glass, sitting in the easy chair opposite his guest.

"Aye, and to you as well," Gordon replied and took a sip.

Alistair looked at his guest and began to discuss the reason behind his request for the visit. "I asked for you to meet me because I'm in need of some additional help for a transaction that's being planned in the coming weeks," he said, pausing to take a sip of his own drink.

"How much 'additional' help is it that you need?" Gordon asked.

"Oh, say, no more than ten men maybe," Alistair said. "I've a dozen of my own available, but the party in question stated at least twenty would be needed."

Gordon leaned back in the chair, slowly raising the glass to his mustachioed lips, all the while contemplating his next response. "I'll need at least three days' notice to insure I don't have other commitments," he answered. With his response, he was looking to determine the level of Alistair's involvement and how committed he would be in the transaction.

"Fair enough," Alistair answered, "but they need to be ready to travel at the time of notice," he added. *This 'Mr. Higgins' seemed keen on having something done in Aberdeen.* He knew he needed to share this with his associate seated across from him.

"Will this task be taking place offshore?" Gordon asked, as this would increase the price and limit whom he could call upon.

"No, not that I'm aware of," Alistair said.

"Well then, let's say three hundred quid a day per man." Gordon started the bidding.

"Done," was Alistair's response, without a moment's hesitation. *I'll just let 'Mr. Higgins' foot that bill.*

"And will we be the only ones in contact during this effort?" Gordon asked.

"No, you'll be contacted by my counselor, Robert Burns," Alistair said, leaning over to hand a business card to him.

"All right then, I'll need to make a few calls," Gordon said, tilting the crystal glass back and emptying the contents in one swallow.

Standing up, Alistair offered his hand. "Good to see you again, my friend."

"Good seeing you as well, Ali," Gordon replied, shaking hands, knowing their discussion was now over.

Upon showing Gordon to the door, Alistair returned to his desk and picked up the phone, dialing a number from memory. Contacting his counselor, he provided the following instructions, "Robert, you're to find out as much on Gordon Wallace as possible," he said.

"Understood, sir," was the response and the line went dead.

***

Returning from a pleasant lunch with Sergeant Gordon, Inspector Fletcher turned his attention to the reports on his desk. *PSV Standard-Hercules* is shown making three trips to the 'Erskine' gas fields as well as making several unscheduled rendezvous with *PSV Standard-Apollo*, and what business does one boat need to do with another away from the docks? Andrew mulled, sitting back in his chair.

Suddenly the door opened and Conor entered, catching his young partner unaware.

"Try being a bit more civil, Chief Inspector," Andrew said, catching himself before he fell out of the chair and hitting the floor.

"Taking a wee nap, are we now?" Conor asked.

"Hardly," was his response, pulling the reports up for Conor to look at.

"So, what is it you've toiled over all day?"

"I believe I've come across a connection between two boats," Fletcher said. He then proceeded to tell Conor what he had come across in the way of inconsistencies in the passage logs. "So, I asked myself,

'Why do two boats meet in the middle of the North Sea when they can just meet at the docks', right?"

"Well, first thing is they might need assistance," McDermott said, providing his thoughts to his colleague's hypothesis. "Secondly, they might have had a medical emergency or the captains might have had a wager that was being paid off."

"Come on now Conor, the same two vessels, on at least three occasions?"

"Aye, I'd admit it seems queer to have it happen to the same two vessels," McDermott said, starting to formulate his own ideas on the possibilities. Placing his field coat on the door hook, he pulled his chair back and sat at his desk, hands folded in front of him like a pupil, waiting for his grades from an exam. "So now let me in on your lunch date, lad."

"How the hell did you find out?" Fletcher asked.

"It's all the gab of the front desk now," McDermott said. "You and the young lass from the forensics lab."

"For the record, it was quite pleasant," Fletcher said, "and quite innocent," he added, seeing the look on Conor's face, whose lewd thoughts betrayed him. With that exchange done, Fletcher returned to work, reviewing the ship dock records.

* * *

Sitting in her office at the Maritime and Coast Guard Agency, Ailene O'Leary had the good sense to leave well enough alone, but Conor had asked for help that she knew she could provide without breaking the law. Opening the third drawer of the immense file cabinet, she leafed through the tabs listing each vessel's name, finally coming across the one Conor asked about, *PSV Nordic Supplier.* Pulling the folder out and replacing it with a placard noting its removal, she pulled the lone desk chair from the table and sat down.

*Who christened you?* She reviewed each document carefully. Seeing the listing of the initial owner, she quickly jotted down the name and turned the page to see the launch date and current operator. The next page was not the information she expected as it turned out to be a bill of sale. *Why was this placed there, and why didn't the new owner change the name of the vessel?* Continuing to look the document over, she noted the new owners were a holding company in Belfast, '*Callaghan, and Higgins Limited'.*

She continued with her review but found nothing more that she could provide Conor without violating the confidentiality laws of the Magistrates' office and the vessel's owner. *Now, where do I want to go for dinner?* She mused, replacing the file, knowing Conor was now indebted to her for an evening out.

Returning to her desk, Ailene picked up the phone and dialed the number for the police station on Victoria Road. "Yes, CI McDermott, please?" she asked as the constable was answering her call.

"Just a moment, I'll forward your call, ma'am."

"Chief Inspector McDermott, can I help you?"

"You most certainly can, Inspector," Ailene said with a giggle.

"And what might that be, miss?" Conor replied, not wanting to alert Fletcher as to his lady friend's call.

"You owe me a dinner, and I was thinking of the Japanese-Korean shop off Summer Street, say 6 p.m. or so."

"Certainly, miss. I can see that it's taken care of by 6 p.m."

"Cheers," Ailene said, hanging up.

"Good day to you as well, miss," Conor said to the static on the phone.

"What was that all about?" Fletcher asked.

"I have a few outstanding bills to pay on," Conor said, standing to leave, pulling the keys from his pocket, and tossing them to his partner. "You keep the car. I'll just take the bus to run my errands for the rest of the day. We'll go over the findings you have tomorrow," he said, walking out the door. Leaving the police station, Conor quickly pulled out his cell phone and called the restaurant Ailene mentioned, securing a table for two at 6 p.m.

***

Stepping off the bus at the corner from Ailene's flat, Conor saw she had arrived ahead of him from the office. Walking up the street, he saw her silhouette through the drapery as she walked from the front room.

"It's *nae* fair, mind you," Conor exclaimed, walking through the door of the flat.

"What's not fair?" Ailene responded from the bedroom in the back.

"You did *nae* have a partner to tell a fib to before you left work," he said, removing his field jacket. "And you also have your own car." He pointed out the fact her Ford Focus was parked on the curb.

"Oh, aren't you such a poor lad," she said, reaching out to him, walking down the hall towards the bedroom. "Should I give you a head start the next time?" she said, with a feigned pout on her lips.

"Aye, that and a wee bit more," he said with a sheepish grin on his face.

"You owe me a dinner, and if you start something we can't finish, it'll be cold mince and tatties for you the rest of the week," Ailene said, placing a gentle kiss to his lips.

"Aye, lass, I know," he said, sulking, squeezing her ass cheek, moving down the hall.

"Damn you, Conor. I'll have a bruise for a week if you keep that up," she squealed, rubbing the spot where his thumb and forefinger came together on her ass.

Thirty minutes later, they were walking from the car park towards the restaurant.

Entering, a young Asian woman met them at the door. "Can I help you?" the host asked, greeting Conor and Ailene.

"Yes, we've reservations, under 'McDermott' for six o'clock," Conor said.

"Ah, yes, please follow me," the host replied, picking up two menus and two sets of silverware.

"After you," Conor directed toward Ailene. As she stepped around him, Conor could finally enjoy the shapely figure of Ailene, which was hidden under the red silk of her dinner dress. *Nary a panty or bra line to show. She's feeling frisky tonight.*

Sitting down at the offered table, Ailene and Conor were handed their dinner menus as the hostess asked, "Would you like a drink?"

"I'll have a vodka tonic with a lime twist," Ailene said.

"And I'll have a bottle of Asahi with a glass, please," Conor said.

As the hostess nodded and left, Ailene looked at Conor and asked him, "Did you enjoy the view?"

"Was I that obvious?"

"Not quite, but I'm sure you weren't the only gent getting his eyeful," she said with a sense of pride. Ailene could still turn a head or two of most men while walking the streets, especially when she dressed for the occasion. In this case, she dressed for the evening after dinner, selecting something she could shed quickly, with nothing but her 'Obsession' perfume to act as defence.

The arrival of the server, dressed in a traditional kimono, with their drinks spoiled her from completing her thoughts of the festivities she was beginning to conjure together. The last few weeks sharing the same bed with Conor had rekindled her feelings for the man. *At least I'm sure he doesn't have any more women in a far-away port like most sailors,* she thought as the drinks were placed on the table.

"What can I have our chef prepare for the two of you?" the server asked, pulling her pad and pen from under the *'obi-age'* or sash of her kimono.

"We'll have the *'yorokobi'* set with the soup, scallop tempura, volcano roll and the bull-back beef," Ailene said in a matter-of-fact manner.

"I'll have the same," Conor said jokingly, knowing too well that his lover had just ordered dinner for them both to share.

"Cheers," Conor said, lifting his glass of beer, and saluting his dinner companion.

"Cheers," Ailene replied, lifting her glass in return.

"Now, hen, what did you find out that's costing me a hundred quid for dinner?"

"What I found at the office can wait until breakfast."

"Oh, it can wait?" Conor asked in bewilderment.

"Aye, you didn't think this was all about dinner and no entertainment, did you?"

"Well, I suppose I could behave myself and not spoil the evening then," he said, looking at his beer, now half-empty.

"Your soup," the server said, interrupting both of their thoughts of what was to come later in the evening.

# Chapter Four

The sun was already beginning to cast its glow upon the eastern sky when the alarm on the radio came to life in the bedroom Conor and Ailene shared. Reaching across the bedside table, he deftly turned the radio off before shifting his position back. Rolling onto his side, he spied the gentle contour of her breasts under the bed sheet, just like the morning before, rising and falling with each breath.

With a sense of being watched, Ailene slowly opened her eyes to see Conor gazing down upon her. "I hope you are not expecting a repeat of last night?"

"Aye, I'd fancy another go, but I suspect we'd both pay the piper for our transgressions if we did."

"I agree." She slid slowly away from him and out of bed, heading to the bathroom.

Conor rolled in the bed to keep the image of his lover's naked form in view, as she walked through the flat. "Do you nay catch a draft walking about like that?"

"Normally no, but if you keep flapping your gob, I just might."

Shaking his head, Conor walked past the bathroom and into the kitchen to put on the tea kettle for the morning. "Don't spend a lifetime in there. I need to go me self," he said, returning to just outside the bathroom door.

"You may enter," she said with a grin as she attempted to walk past him and back to the bedroom.

Conor reached out, pulling her close. "If you don't mind." He leaned against her, his stiffening member rubbing against her flesh. He kissed her lips. "Fix me a cup a tea now, lass."

"Is that all you want?"

"Aye, for the moment."

***

Ewan Sutherland sat melancholy in the front seat of his car. For the second time in as many weeks, he had to leave it in the parking garage near his flat in Glasgow so he could travel to Aberdeen. Resigned to the fact he would miss his train if he stayed any longer, he opened the door and stepped out into the cool morning air.

"There he is," Reggie Brown, one of the two henchmen in Stuart Ross' employment, pointed out. They were sitting in a non-descript motorcar, having just followed Ewan Sutherland from the hotel he had been staying in instead of his nearby flat.

"You gather he'll be catching the train to Aberdeen?" Clyde Smith, the other member in the car, asked.

"Aye. I would, and then he could pick up a rental and *nae* worry about his own car," was Brown's reply.

Ewan walked to the boot of the BMW and unlocked it, grabbing an old tattered duffle bag with his clothes that he had packed the evening before. Closing the back end, Ewan turned and began the walk towards the stairwell and the street below.

"Hurry now, before we lose sight of him," Brown said to his partner as they exited the car and headed to the stairwell Ewan had just entered.

Ewan entered the Glasgow Central Station, looking at the large display panel above the ticket kiosks. Every thirty seconds the display changed for each train's information on the route to Aberdeen. *Twelve-fifteen on track seven.* Ewan saw on the screen. Walking up to an empty kiosk, he put in his destination and waited for the screen to refresh. Next, he fed three twenty-pound notes into the machine to cover the cost of the ticket. Seeing the information displayed before him, he selected the destination and the departure time and waited again for the system to process his request. *Finally, ya silly twit,* admonishing the kiosk as it spat out his ticket and his transfer pass.

"Look, he's at the kiosk," Brown said to his partner as they too entered the train station. "Go see what train he selected," he said to his companion.

Clyde Smith approached the kiosk that Ewan was standing at just close enough to see the train selection. "He's taking the twelve-fifteen to Aberdeen," Smith said, returning to his companion's side.

"Then I say we get our tickets and move smartly to the platform," Brown said, walking towards an empty kiosk, away from Ewan.

***

Sitting at the kitchen table and taking a sip of his second cup of tea, Conor asked Ailene about the information she learned the day before. "So, what did you learn about my 'mysterious' vessel?"

"Well, the only significant information on your vessel is that it has a new owner from the original one who filed for port access."

"Is that common?"

"No, most new owners will change the name of the vessel and then file for port access under the vessel's new name and registration number, but in this case the new owners didn't do that," she replied, finishing her tea.

"So, you're saying the new owners kept the old name and left the access under the original owners," Conor said.

"Why, yes," she said, realizing her notes were still in her handbag. Getting up, she pulled the lined notepaper from the side pocket. "And it's now owned by *'Callaghan and Higgins Limited'* from Belfast." She sat back down at the table.

"Interesting," Conor said, beginning to try to piece together yet another cog to his ever-growing puzzle. "I believe I need to make a call or two." He rose from the table and placed his tea cup in the sink. "Fancy a quick shower?"

"Quick and cold," she said, looking down at the bulge in his briefs as it began to stir.

***

Once again, Inspector Fletcher found himself in the office first this morning. Setting his coat across his chair, he spied a call listing stuck on the desk lamp sitting on McDermott's desk. *'Call me immediately'* it read as he pulled it from the lamp, and it was from Chief Superintendent Collingsworth in London.

"Keeping close tabs on me, I see," McDermott said, entering the room to find his young co-worker pulling the call slip from the lamp.

"No, I just noticed the slip."

"Very well then, what does it say?"

"Call me immediately," Fletcher said, "and it has Chief Superintendent Collingsworth's phone number at the bottom as well."

"Well, let's give him a call then, shall we," McDermott said, picking up the phone and dialing.

***

Sitting in the coach section of the railcar, Ewan Sutherland watched the green rolling countryside of eastern Scotland pass by. *I didn't even get a chance to contact Caroline.* He reflected on the last few days spent in Glasgow. A sudden jolt of the train as it approached a switching section of the track brought Ewan back to the present. Looking out the

49

car window, he could tell they were entering the outskirts of Aberdeen, near Cove Bay.

Less than an hour later, Ewan was stepping off the train, not knowing that two of Stuart Ross's men were also stepping off, carefully watching his every move.

Looking for the exit, Ewan pulled his cell phone from his jacket and dialed a local number. "Hello, Ian?" Ewan said, hearing the voice on the other end. "Aye, I'm back. Can you come to the station and give me a lift?"

"*Nae* worry, I'll be there in five or so," the friend said.

"Cheerio."

Looking over his shoulder, he spied the men's room and turned to join the line of other gentlemen entering to relieve themselves before his ride showed up to the station.

"Good idea," Brown said to his partner as they watched Sutherland walk through the men's room doorway. As both men entered, they saw Sutherland standing along the wall, waiting for an open stall, not looking particularly concerned.

"Seems that he's not too concerned being here?" Smith said to Brown as they too stood and waited for an opening at one of the stalls to relieve themselves.

Finally, Ewan could step up and relieved himself after the three-hour train ride. Walking away from the stall, he innocently bumped into one of the spotters from Stuart Ross. "Excuse me," he said, brushing by the other gentleman.

"No worries, lad," Brown said.

Finishing their own business, the two members stepped outside and suddenly realized they had lost contact with their target. Trying to calmly gain the upper hand, they agreed to split up, each walking toward an exit, to see which direction Ewan had gone.

*Aye, I've got you two.* Standing in the back of the small food stand, Ewan watched the two men Stuart Ross sent to keep an eye on him. As the gap between the two men grew larger, Ewan stepped away from the stand and strolled to the exit immediately in front of the men's room, and spotting his friend Ian, he waved him down. Opening the car door and sliding in, he said, "Let's go, Ian, I'm being followed."

"Did they follow you from Glasgow?" Ian McLeod asked, placing the Nissan in gear and pulling away from the station.

"Aye, I saw them follow me from the kiosk onto the car," Ewan replied, wondering if he should contact Alistair and let him know of this development.

"Well, in a few minutes we'll be safe and on our way to the flat," Ian said.

Ewan looked out the window as his friend drove through town, wondering why he suddenly felt all alone in the world.

***

Sitting at his desk, Chief Superintendent Collingsworth was a picture of serious and mindful concentration. Each morning upon his arrival to his office at Scotland Yard, he would spend the first fifteen minutes looking over the '*The Times*' crossword puzzle, trying his best to solve the most questions. However, this morning he would not be given the chance to complete his review as the phone began to ring.

"Hello, Chief Superintendent Collingsworth."

"Good morning, William. It's CI McDermott in Aberdeen."

"Good morning, McDermott, you're in early for a work day."

"Fletcher and I are returning your call from last night," the chief inspector said, giving his young partner a comical thumbs-up addressing his superior.

"So, I see," Collingsworth said. "I've some interesting news from my friend regarding the vessel movements."

"Do tell then, we're listening," McDermott said, placing the call on speaker, allowing Fletcher to listen in.

"It seems there are more vessel movements coming out of the Med that skip all ports until they enter the Channel," Collingsworth said, retelling the story his friend Thomas Sinclair provided to him from the other evening.

"Interesting situation that creates," McDermott added. "And I found out several of the workboats here in Aberdeen have new owners, but the port access documents are still listed with the original buyers of the boats. Can your friend also check on the firm of '*Callaghan and Higgins Limited*', William?" he asked his superior.

"I'll ask him, but what's the connection?" Collingsworth asked.

"They're listed as the new owners of a workboat that's in question," he said. "Also, Fletcher is working on a connection of the workboats, making '*at-sea transfers*' before entering the harbor."

"Very well, you've ruined my routine with '*The Times*', so I guess it's back to work then," Collingsworth said with a chuckle.

"Fair enough," McDermott replied. "We'll go about earning our own few schillings then, cheerio."

As the day wore on, he and Fletcher conducted another review of the shipping logs, attempting to develop a solid connection between the workboats and their routines.

"I'm quite knackered looking at all these numbers," McDermott said, attempting to stifle one of the numerous yawns from sitting at his desk for so long.

"Fancy another cup o'tea then?" Fletcher quipped, knowing that neither of them could stomach another cup.

"No, thanks. I'm saving me self for dinner," he jokingly replied, standing, and stretching for what seemed like the tenth time in the day.

"Well, it's nearly supper time and I have an appointment to keep," Fletcher said, beginning to place the shipping logs in his desk drawer for the night.

"Oh. Are you and Sheila doing dinner and a show now?" Conor asked with a smile, thankful that his young partner had found someone to spend his off time with instead of work.

"Yes, we are actually. She's taking me out to a small club by the university," Andrew said with a smile.

"Well, dinnae be late tomorrow morning," McDermott said with a laugh as they walked out of the office.

"Look who's calling the kettle black; you are a cheeky bugger," Fletcher replied, spying his lady friend at the station entrance.

***

Walking up the street from the car park near the university, the two off-duty police officers approached the nightclub entrance. Squeezing past a couple leaving, they made their way towards an empty table. "This place has quite a buzz," Andrew quipped to Sheila as they squeezed into their seats.

"I would come here every Friday after class, and come to think of it, I've had every item on their menu," Sheila replied with a friendly smile.

"Evening, Sheila," the server said, stepping to their table amongst the crowded aisle.

"Hello, Geoff," she replied. "I'd like you to meet Andrew."

"Pleasure, Andrew." He shook hands with the inspector from London.

"What can I start you out with?" he asked, pen and paper at the ready.

"I'll have a Sierra Pale," Sheila answered, looking at Andrew.

"And I'll try a bottle of the Dogfish Ale," Andrew said with a quizzical look on his face putting the drink menu down.

"No worries, you'll like it," Geoff said, seeing Andrew's apprehensive expression.

"You seem quite popular here," Andrew said as the server went to the bar to place their orders.

"As I said; I was here almost every Friday evening. Also, Geoff and I dated for a wee bit while I was in school, but it didn't work out," Sheila said, trying to reassure her friend that she was committed to their evening together.

"My good fortune then," Andrews said, gently placing his hand on hers, giving it a squeeze.

"Yes, it is," she replied, reciprocating the gesture.

After having their share of drinks and the meal, Sheila took the opportunity to display her years of dance practice to her date, as one of the local bands provided the evening's musical entertainment. After an hour or so, and with a glistening sheen of sweat on their brows, Andrew and Sheila finally decided to call it an evening, each knowing that they had work to attend to in the morning.

"I must say, that was quite the evening's meal, not to mention the entertainment," Andrew said, escorting Sheila to her car.

"I'm glad you enjoyed it," she replied, leaning into his arm as they walked to the car park. "And I'll make sure they never find out you're a 'Sassenach' either," she chided him, noticing the confused look on his face.

"I'm a what?" Andrew asked sharply.

"It's an old Scottish term for an 'Englishman' or 'outlander' used mostly by the clans in the highlands," Sheila said, trying to calm her friend down. "Don't think for a minute I consider you a 'Sassenach', Inspector Fletcher," Sheila said in a soft and gentle tone, pulling him close and kissing him.

After what seemed like an eternity, their lips parted. "Thank God for that," he replied, returning her kiss with his own, this time with more passion.

"I take it you'll be staying at my flat for the night?" she said, catching her breath as they reached the car.

"Umm, I'd like that," Andrew said, stumbling over the response.

"Then let's not waste the night, shall we." She took the keys from Andrew and slid behind the steering wheel.

"No, I guess we shouldn't," was Andrew's reply, opening the passenger door and sitting down next to Sheila.

***

Settling down in Ian's flat, Ewan went over the events of the day. *The first time I saw the two 'police' were in the car park.* He closed his eyes to concentrate. *Then just after the ticket kiosk and then the railcar.* He continued to recall the moments that had presented themselves. *After the train arrived, it was in the loo.* He chuckled to himself at the humor in thinking that they would be spying as he relieved himself. "But what if they were police from Glasgow, why follow me?" he muttered to himself, sitting in the empty room.

"Is it you, or is it you helping them get to someone else?" Ian asked, entering the room, knowing that his friend was trying to align the thoughts into a cohesive sequence.

"I *dinnae* know who they are, Ian," Ewan said.

Suddenly, Ewan began to put together a twisted thought. "Mr. Hunt," he said.

"What does he have to do with it?" Ian asked, taking a sip of his beer.

"I was sitting with him at St. Georges, talking about the Frenchman," Ewan exclaimed. Over the next few minutes, he related to Ian what had transpired in Glasgow and how the two men from the train must be police trying to connect him to their boss.

"You're *nae* thinking they're after the *'Big Yin'*, are you?" Ian questioned Ewan, not wanting to think of the consequences for being his friend if the police were to come knocking at his flat.

"The best way to make this right is to call him," Ewan said in a shaky and uncertain tone, pulling out his cell phone.

"Good evening, Mr. Hunt," Ewan said as his boss answered the phone.

"Good evening, Ewan, I take it you made it back to Aberdeen without cause?"

"Not exactly, sir, that's why I'm calling," the young Scot replied.

Hearing this comment come from the young Scot on the other end of the call caused Hunt to place his scotch and cigar down and lean forward in his chair. "Tell me, what seems to be the problem, lad?"

"Well, I might have been followed from Glasgow by the police," he said, continuing for the next several minutes, relating what he saw in the form of the two men sent by Stuart Ross.

"They didn't try and apprehend you, though?" Hunt repeated back to the younger Scotsman.

"No, sir, but I got the feeling they were close to pinching me at the Aberdeen station," Ewan replied. "After my mate, Ian picked me up and we made it to his flat, I thought everything through and concluded that if they were after me, it was because you and I talked at St. George's earlier this week," he added to his tale, "so I thought it best to call you."

"You did the right thing, Ewan," Hunt said, working hard to control both his anger and his pride thinking that the young man was willing to warn his boss of possible danger. "I want you to keep inside for a day or two until I can contact someone here in Glasgow."

"Yes, sir," Ewan replied with a sense of relief.

"I'll contact you when it is clear for you to be out in town, and you can continue with your original task working with Captain Duncan," Hunt finished just before hanging up the phone.

Picking up the phone receiver again, he pushed the intercom button. "Janice, please contact Stuart Ross for me and ask him to join me for lunch tomorrow."

"Certainly, sir," she replied. "Where will you be dining at?"

"The Chinese restaurant on York Street will do. Please make the arrangements," he added, hanging up the phone.

Opening her desk drawer, Janice pulled out a folder with several menus from the local eateries that Mr. Hunt would frequent. She selected the one for the Chinese restaurant and called the number to reserve a private table for two for a working lunch.

Next, she pulled out an old rotary-style Rolodex from her drawer, selected a well-worn card from the "R" section, and dialed the number listed on the back. "Mr. Ross?" she asked of the person who answered the phone.

"Yes, this is Mr. Ross," Stuart replied, knowing who was calling by the number listed on his cell phone screen.

"Mr. Hunt would like you to join him for lunch at the Asian restaurant on York street, twelve-thirty sharp, if you please," Janice stated.

"Certainly, I will be there promptly at twelve-thirty," he responded as the hair on the back of his neck began to rise.

"Thank you, sir." Janice hung up, leaving Mr. Ross to his thoughts. *It's not like Alistair to call so quickly after he has assigned me a task.* He returned to his desk. When the phone rang, he had expected the call to be from one of his two henchmen that he assigned to tail young Ewan Sutherland back to Aberdeen.

***

On a non-descript workboat tied to the quay in Aberdeen, the vessel's captain picked up his shore-based phone and dialed a distant number and waited for the connection.

"Good evening. *'Callaghan and Higgins Limited'*. May I help you?" the voice of a female receptionist said on the other end of the call.

"Good evening, ma'am," Captain Duncan spoke. "May I speak with Mr. Gilmore, please?"

"Just a moment and I'll see if he is in," the receptionist said, placing the captain's call on hold. Several moments went by before she returned to the caller. "He's currently in a meeting, but I'll be happy to pass your name and number to him."

"Please tell him that Captain Duncan of the *Nordic Supplier* called to discuss a missed transaction. He already has my number," the captain said in return to her query.

"Certainly, sir," the receptionist replied. "Will that be all?"

"Yes, that's all, thank you very much," Captain Duncan said, hoping to hide his displeasure at not being able to talk with his contact regarding the young lad from Glasgow's sudden disappearance. Walking across the bridge wing of his boat, the captain stepped outside and leaned against the rails, looking down at the River Dee and out towards the breakwater at the harbor entrance.

*What information do the local police have on the Frenchman?* He drew out an old briar pipe from his shirt pocket and stuffed it with a pinch of tobacco. Pulling out his lighter, he turned his back to the breeze and lit the pipe. Looking about, he caught his own reflection in the bridge window, and with it, a plume of blue-grey smoke curling upwards from the pipe. *Aye, the life at sea is the simplest to have, because ya only have one mistress to please, don't you, Clive?* He took in the grizzled image staring back at him in the window's reflection.

57

# Chapter Five

Returning to Sheila's flat after dinner, Andrew walked confidently to her door in a veiled attempt to hide his nervousness from her.

"Do you fancy a cup of tea?" Sheila asked, unlocking the front door.

"I'm really not up for tea, but thank you," Andrew responded, not wanting to waste an opportunity with the young woman over a cup, following her through the door.

"Be a dear and lock the door," she asked, tossing her coat and purse onto the small sofa in the front room.

"Certainly," Andrew said, turning his back to her for the moment. Having locked the door as requested, Andrew turned back towards his date, only to find her standing in front of him wearing nothing but a smile and her camisole. "Comfortable, are we?" he stammered, off-guard by the sudden and bold appearance of his co-worker before him.

"Yes, quite comfortable," Sheila answered reaching out and drawing him closer against herself, placing her lips to his in a slow and passionate kiss, her tongue teasing his lips. After what seemed to be an eternity to Andrew, Sheila broke off the kiss, allowing him to catch his breath.

"I think we should retire to your room before we find ourselves on an uncomfortable piece of furniture," he said.

"So true, Inspector," Sheila replied, walking him down the hall and into her bedroom. Within minutes the couple were engaged in an intimate embrace, each one struggling to remove the others clothes. For the next hour, they became lost in each other's hold, inter-twining grasp.

Lying next to Sheila in the darkened bedroom, Andrew found himself looking up at the ceiling and contemplating what his next step should be. *Can I have a relationship with Sheila after just a brief visit?* He listened to the soft rhythmic breath of the young woman beside him. The last few weeks working in Aberdeen had led to this point, and he knew he had no one he was seriously seeing back in London to interrupt anything further with Sheila. *The real question is if she feels the same way I do?* Slowly turning onto his side, he looked at the slumbering lass lying next to him.

Just as Andrew had shifted his position in bed, Sheila lifted her head from the pillow, asking, "What time is it?" in a groggy voice.

"Half past five," he said looking at his watch

"Oh, bloody hell Andrew! We've got to get going," the woman exclaimed.

Watching the nude form of the young woman stride around bed, Andrew asked, "What's the rush?"

"I've got the early shift in the lab, and we can't both fit in the bath at once."

*What a shame.* He recalled the soft touch of her hands and the smoothness of her alabaster skin from earlier in the evening. Hearing the water run in the bathroom, Andrew tossed the covers back and got himself out of the bed, put his trousers on and went to the kitchen to put the kettle on for tea.

*Shame we couldn't squeeze in here,* she thought as the warm water cascaded across her back. *The evening went quite well.* He recalled the event from earlier in the evening. *Andrew was the perfect gentleman and a more than adequate lover in bed,* Sheila mused, rinsing the shampoo from her hair.

Her thoughts from the past evening were quickly interrupted as Andrew called out "don't forget to leave me some hot water, now, will you," walking past the bathroom door, returning to the bedroom with a cup of tea.

"Aye, you'll have plenty in a wee bit," she said, turning the shower off and grabbing a towel.

Andrew placed the cup he fixed for Sheila down on the dresser and collected the rest of his clothes from the floor where she had discarded them.

Opening the door of the bathroom, Sheila stood in the doorway, the towel loosely wrapped around her breasts and barely covering the remainder of her wet figure. "You're up."

"I fixed you a cup of tea. It's on the dresser."

"Thanks." She gave him a brief kiss on the lips.

Closing the door behind him, Andrew realized it wasn't a hot shower he needed, having felt her hand brush across his crotch as he entered the bathroom.

***

Across town in Ailene's flat, Conor was going about the same routine Andrew was, showering and preparing for another day of chasing down his elusive quarry. *Why haven't we seen the Arab?* he thought as the water beat down on his chest, washing away the soap. *Andrew found out that the Aberdeen Police might have a mole in their midst.* He recalled their discussion over the phone from the other day that had rudely interrupted a potential repeat of sex with his lover. *In addition, that our names are now being floated out there to someone we don't know.* He considered the potential for retribution against the two Scotland Yard inspectors.

"Fancy some eggs and toast?" Ailene said through the bathroom door.

"Aye, that'll be fine, hen," Conor said, turning the spigot off and stepping out of the shower. Soon afterwards, Conor was sitting at the small kitchen table, finishing his meal that Ailene had fixed for him.

"Busy day ahead?" she asked, looking at his facial expression change for the umpteenth time this morning.

"Aye, the puzzle still has missing pieces." he said, picking up his plate and cup and placing them in the sink. "I'm hoping Andrew had a pleasant evening and is ready to work," Conor said with a sheepish grin, turning to Ailene.

"Oh, why is that?" she asked.

"He's gotten friendly with the young lass working in the lab," Conor said, explaining the relationship he believed his partner had begun.

"Good for him," Ailene said, getting up from the table. "He deserves the company just as much as you do." She placed a kiss on his cheek.

"Aye, I suppose you're right."

They each picked up their coats and walked to the door to begin their day.

# Chapter Six

Entering the office at the police station, Conor noticed he had arrived first, ahead of his partner, Andrew. *Well, things must be looking up for the wee lad.* He took the kettle off the burner and filled it from the sink in the men's room.

As Conor was tending to the kettle in the detective's office, Andrew did his best to look relaxed with Sheila as they walked into the station from the car park.

"Good morning!" the desk sergeant boomed with his heavy highlander accent. This came more as an announcement rather than greeting since most of the police members in the station knew of the blossoming relationship between the inspector from London and their senior lab technician.

"*Gae an boil yer heed, John,*" Sheila snapped back at the burly sergeant, keeping her sheepish school girl grin on her face, strolling down the hallway towards the lab.

"Have a pleasant day," Andrew said to the sergeant, Sheila striding past him toward the forensics lab, he too with a humorous grin on his face, walking towards his office.

*Thank God,* thinking that he had gotten in before his partner McDermott. Pulling his chair out from behind the desk, he hung his coat across the back and turned to grab the tea kettle when he realized it was gone.

"I see you finally arrived," the voice said as the door swung open to reveal McDermott carrying the now full kettle of water.

"Why, yes, I'm just a few minutes behind you," Fletcher replied, looking a little forlorn at the prospect that he had been caught entering late behind his superior.

"*Nae* worries, laddie, you had good cause for it," McDermott said in a joyful tone. "But, I highly recommend that you keep a few extra duds at her place so you ne'er need to wear the same shirt twice." He nodded to the wrinkled dress shirt Andrew was wearing from the previous day.

"Point taken," Fletcher replied to his partner with a Cheshire cat grin on his face.

"Now, shall we go about the business of catching a few bad guys?" he asked his partner, pulling the shipping reports across the desk. "Let's do our best to get through these before lunch, shall we?"

***

The drudgery of the morning work finally gave way to the lunch hour for people working in downtown Glasgow. Patrons hustled to their favorite eateries for a quick meal before returning to their desks.

The interior of the Chinese restaurant was adorned with the typical rice paper dividers and paper lamp shades of red and yellow, fierce dragons painted on the outside of them. Sitting at the private table, Alistair Hunt was waiting for his subordinate to arrive.

Walking in, Stuart Ross spied the crime boss sitting at a private table in the back, with his back to the entrance for the kitchen. "Good afternoon, Mr. Hunt," Ross said, pulling the chair away from the table and taking his place across from his boss.

"I'm glad you came on time, Stuart," Hunt said in a rather neutral tone. "Before we get to talking business, I suggest we order before it becomes too busy." He waved the waitress towards the table.

"Yes, sir," the diminutive Asian woman responded, reaching their table.

"Kim, I'll have my usual, with a Perrier and glass," he said, having been a patron to this specific eatery for some time.

"And you, sir?" she asked, turning to Ross, who was still looking over the menu, trying to determine what he should order.

"I'll have a number twelve, with egg drop soup and a vegetable egg roll," he said, pointing out the beef and green peppers with steamed rice, "and a Perrier as well."

"An excellent choice," was her answer, gathering the menus and walking back to the order window that led to the kitchen.

"So, have you heard from your two men following Ewan?" Hunt asked.

"Not yet, but I suspect it'll be soon," Ross said, knowing a bit of what this meeting was about.

"Well, you'll be happy to know I've heard from Ewan and he made it safely to Aberdeen," he said with a slight touch of sarcasm.

"Is that so?" Ross said, looking at his boss for a hint of what was to come next.

"He also told me that two blokes followed him and he considered them to be police trailing him because of me," Hunt replied, relating part of his conversation from Ewan to Stuart.

"You're telling me the young lad made my men that quickly?" Ross asked with a sense of disbelief.

"It seems so, which means you might think about dispatching a couple more of your lads if the first two were that easily spotted," Hunt directed. "And be ready to compliment the young man for his intuition."

Ross sat there across from his boss, trying to think through how two of his most 'seasoned' men could have let the young Scot get the best of them. Getting ready to explain his plan to the crime boss, the waitress brought their meals to the table, which placed any continuation of their conversation to the side.

***

Just nearing the lunch hour, McDermott and Fletcher were still looking over the shipping logs, trying to find a key to the workboat habits. Each vessel was 'logged out' as departing the harbor and, was 'logged in' when reaching its intended platform. There were also notations when a vessel radioed in a position change or when they were at station, keeping away from a platform for more than an hour's time.

"Conor, remember I said two of the boats showed that they rendezvoused at least twice during the last three months out at sea?" Andrew said.

"Aye, and you were *nae* sure of why."

"Well, maybe we need to look at another vessel or vessels that were in the same vicinity?"

Leaning back in his chair, the chief inspector flicked his pen against his chin in thought. "Aye makes sense to look for that third point to reckon on when you put it in those terms," Conor said.

As the two inspectors discussed the possibility of a third vessel, the desk phone began to ring. Looking up from the printed reports, each one glanced at the other, wondering who would be the one to answer it.

Reaching across the papers, Conor grabbed the handset before his younger partner could pick it up. "Hello?" he asked in his Scottish lilted tone.

"Good morning, Chief Inspector McDermott," Sergeant Gordon said. "May I speak with Inspector Fletcher, please?"

"Aye, hen, just a minute," Conor said, holding out the handset. "It's the *'missus'* for you."

With a scowled look on his face, Andrew reached for the handset from the Scotsman. *I'll never hear the end of this,* he thought to himself, taking hold of it and speaking, "Inspector Fletcher."

"I'll be ready in about ten minutes or so for lunch," Sheila spoke, reminding him about their noontime date.

Looking up at the clock, Andrew realized they'd worked uninterrupted for four hours. "I'll be there in a few minutes," he said, trying not to give Conor any more fuel to chide him regarding his relationship with the forensics technician.

Conor was feigning that he was back to work, turning his attention to the list of shipping movements, allowing Andrew to finish his call with Sheila when he noticed something odd on the page he was currently looking at. "What was the name of the two workboats, lad?" he asked Andrew.

Pushing aside several stacks of reports and his tea, Andrew pulled a notepad from below the third stack of papers, handing it to Conor. *PSV Standard-Hercules* and *PSV Standard-Apollo* were written across the notepad, and Conor was looking at a transcription of a point in the North Sea where they both were at the same location and with a third vessel.

"I'll see you then," Andrew finally said, hanging up the phone.

"We just might have a connection with our boats and a freighter," he exclaimed as Andrew looked back at him. "The *M/V Joan of Arc* is shown making an emergency stop at these coordinates," Conor pointed out to the younger inspector. "And your two PSVs are also shown as 'providing aid' in the same vicinity, but not identifying who they are providing the assistance to."

"So, we've a potential link, but where does it show the *M/V Joan of Arc* making port at after the encounter?" Andrew asked his senior inspector with the obvious question.

"Per this report, after six hours of station keeping, she made port in Hamburg the following evening," was Conor's answer.

Looking at his watch nervously, Andrew said, "Let's take a fresh look at this after lunch, shall we?" He got up to grab his coat.

"Aye, don't want you being late with the young lass, now, do we," Conor replied with a grin, sending his young partner off to his lunch date.

While Andrew was having lunch with Sergeant Gordon, Conor decided to continue digging for clues regarding the shipping anomalies they had come across in the last few days. Due to this, he decided the best place to look was with Ailene at the Maritime and Coast Guard Agency office.

Picking up the phone, he dialed the number for Ailene's office. After the third ring, the call engaged *'Hello, you have reached the office of...'* Conor heard Ailene's voice as the answering function was recording. "Bugger," he said aloud to the empty office, hearing the message that she was unavailable. *I could let William in on this and have him contact his chap at Lloyd's,* he mused, not wanting to wait for the investigation to begin after someone's meeting or lunch date. Not wanting to waste any more time, Conor picked the phone back up and dialed his supervisor's number in London.

"Scotland Yard Narcotics Division, Officer Jones speaking," he heard from the unfamiliar voice.

"Officer Jones, this is Chief Inspector McDermott calling for Chief Superintendent Collingsworth, if you please."

"I'm sorry, Inspector, but Mister Collingsworth is currently in counsel with the assistant chief constable," Officer Jones said.

"Well, could you please have him call me when he returns? He has my number," Conor directed the officer in London.

"Why of course inspector. Is there anything else you'd like me to pass along?" the desk clerk asked.

"No, that will be all. Good day," Conor added, hanging up the phone.

Looking up at the wall clock, he noted it was nearly a quarter past twelve. *No sense going hungry.* Grabbing his field coat, he headed out of the office for lunch.

Walking out from the police station, Conor headed down the street to his Malcolm's shop. *So, we've at least one freighter to consider, but where did the freighter originate?* It was the next logical question that came to his mind. *And who might the owner be?* He knew that one vessel had a questionable ownership. *We already know the where, that's Hamburg,* he mused, thinking of the vessel's destination. Entering the local eatery, Conor was greeted by Sadie, the young server from Bermuda, who seemed to work as many hours in the shop as his friend Malcolm did.

"Afternoon, Sadie," Conor said, returning the afternoon greeting from the young lass.

"The usual?" she asked, pencil at the ready.

"Aye, but *nae* ale, just a cola," Conor replied, placing a twenty-euro note on the counter as payment and tip.

With a smile and brief wink, Sadie rang up his order and placed the change dutifully in the jar for all to share, as was the standing rule set by the owner Malcolm.

Walking over to an empty spot at the counter, he pulled the chair away and sat down, watching one of Malcolm's two young cooks fixing the batter for the next round of fish to be fried. *Can Ailene help me with finding the 'Joan of Arc' owners? And, what connection does the captain of the 'Nordic Supplier' have with the two other PSVs for Chevron?* referring to the *Standard-Apollo* and *Standard-Hercules* that Andrew had initially found during their search of the docking records. No sooner had he finished his second thought, Sadie came over to where he was sitting and placed his lunch order in front of him.

***

Sitting across from her lunch date, Sheila contemplated the response she would get for the next question she was about to ask. "So, I was wondering if the chief inspector would mind letting you go for a few days," she asked, finishing a bite of her grilled chicken salad.

"What do you have in mind?" Andrew replied, wondering where this peculiar question was leading to. *Well, that certainly came unexpectedly.* He looked over his lunch at her.

"Well, I've got a few days of holiday time to take and thought it might be nice to spend it in the highlands," she cooed at her lunch date.

Thinking of the ramifications if something were to happen, Andrew considered the fact that the young woman across from him was becoming accustomed to his being with her.

"I don't think Conor has any say in the matter since I need to clear it through Chief Superintendent Collingsworth in London," he replied, wondering what a full weekend with Sheila would result in. Taking a quick drink of his Perrier, his next question didn't surprise her. "Where exactly in the *'Highlands'* were you thinking of going?" Andrew asked, not knowing much of the landscape.

"I was thinking we could go to a resort near Colyumbridge. It's supposed to be very posh and relaxing," Sheila said, not wanting to give in that she had already begun making some of the arrangements. She had in fact already considered how she would ask to have the room arranged with beverages and snacks.

Taking the last bite of his sandwich and taking another swallow of his sparkling water, Andrew contemplated his response. He was getting used to having Sheila as his female acquaintance, enjoying their off time as they continued their budding relationship.

"Let me contact the chief superintendent and see if he could do without me for a few days," Andrew replied, deciding he needed to show some resolve of his own to Sheila.

"Good, I'll call the resort to see what days are available, and you can pass that along to your inspector," Sheila said with her hazel eyes aglow.

***

Having learned that his two best men had been compromised in Aberdeen during his lunch with Alistair Hunt, Stuart Ross left the restaurant and headed straight for his own '*office*' to make a few phone calls of his own. In this case, Stuart's office was a room in his apartment on Renfrew Street where he made all his calls to his subordinates.

Picking up the phone on the small roll-top desk, he carefully dialed the number written on the back of the worn business card. The slip was passed to Ross allowing him to contact one of the 'independent' operators in Glasgow's criminal underground.

"Angus, it's Stu," he said as the phone was answered after the fourth ring.

Angus Dunbar was well respected among the Glasgow crime syndicates, for his ruthless enthusiasm and known more for his ability to completing a task without being observed, but at a price.

"Aye, Mister Ross, what can I do for you today?"

"I need you to help with a situation in Aberdeen."

"And what might this be?"

"I need you to shadow a lad working for Mr. Hunt; you know, keep him safe, and keep yourself out of sight," Ross said, hoping the use of his boss would persuade him to accept the request.

"Okay, when do I need to be there?"

"Leave as soon as you can. I'll give you the name of one of my men already there to help set you up," Ross said in the hopes he wouldn't embarrass himself or his two members already in Aberdeen.

The syndicate's hired man knew that the transaction was not complete until a price had been agreed to, and he had a number in mind. "It'll be three hundred fifty quid and an additional one hundred fifty if I have to make myself known," Dunbar replied, always wanting to keep his anonymity in every situation.

"Done," Ross answered without hesitation, knowing Dunbar was a man of his word when it came to this type of deal. "Send a text to this number with the usual information for payment."

Angus wrote down the number, saying, "You'll see it in a few minutes."

Ross also provided the mobile numbers for his two men in Aberdeen as well so Dunbar could contact them. "*Good* day then," he said, hanging up. *Now to let Clyde and Reggie know they're getting company.* He dialed the mobile number to his men in Aberdeen.

***

Having finished his fish and chips at Malcolm's shop, Conor took his time walking back to the police station, still puzzled about the development of the service vessels and now, a freighter. Strolling back into the office, Conor saw the message ticket left by the constable at the front desk on the shade of his desk lamp, *'Available for call at 14:30'*, it read, and it was from Chief Superintendent Collingsworth. *Well, at least I'll know when he will be in and I can call.* Looking at the clock on the wall, he made note that Andrew had yet to return from his lunch with Sheila. Sitting down at his desk, Conor heard the door open and saw Andrew walking in, a puzzled look on his face.

"You look a wee bit perplexed, lad."

"Why, yes, yes, I am," Andrew replied. "It seems Sheila…, I mean Sergeant Gordon, wants me to join her for a weekend getaway to the highlands."

"So, after we talk with the chief superintendent at two-thirty, you can ask for a few days' holiday to spend with her."

"But, Conor, this is getting a bit serious between us."

"Aye, it is, but are you fond of the lass?"

"Why, yes, of course," Andrew replied, feeling his face grow warm, blushing at the thought.

"And she's kin on you as well?" Conor asked.

"I believe so. She's not given me any reason to think otherwise."

"Then all's well. Let's get back to work before our call with the chief superintendent then," Conor said, ending the conversation about his young partner's romance.

Pulling the report open on his desk to the pencil he left as a marker, he read the transcript to himself before he spoke. "So before lunch we had two support boats meeting a freighter in the Channel," Conor said, getting their focus back on subject.

"Yes, and the coordinates place all three vessels approximately one hundred fifty kilometers south of the *'Erskine'* gas fields where the support boats were last reported to be at," Andrew said.

"And we know they were possibly alongside for six hours per the freighter's position report," Conor said, completing three quarters of the circle of the *'who, when, and where'* just not adding the *'why'* to the puzzle.

"So, we need to find out about the freighter and who owns her?" the young inspector stated. Conor had asked this same question himself walking to lunch an hour before.

"Aye, and that will be our question for the chief superintendent," Conor said, putting his feet onto the edge of his desk, leaning back on the chair.

***

Returning to her lab at the police station after lunch, Sergeant Sheila Gordon was all smiles. *Now, to get a room at the resort for Andrew and me-self.* She put her purse in the desk drawer and grabbed her lab coat from the chair. Looking through the brochures she had picked up from the railway station, she found the one she had previously circled. *Large suite with views of the River Spey, complete with separate sitting area and soaking tub,* the literature read.

Reading the information, she became moist with excitement at the thought of having Andrew to herself for three days. Turning back to the front of the brochure, she pulled her cell phone out and dialed the number for the front desk.

"Ardmore Resort, may I help you?" the young woman's voice asked as Sheila's call went through.

"Yes, I was wondering if you had any rooms available for the weekend on the eleventh." Sheila said to the desk clerk.

"Just a moment, I'll check," the clerk responded.

In the background, Sheila could hear the faint tapping of fingers on the keyboard as the desk clerk searched the availability for the time in question. "Yes, I have a non-smoking suite with a king-size bed and two rooms with a pair of queen-size beds available during that time," the desk clerk stated.

"I'd like to book the suite then," Sheila said, not wanting to miss the opportunity to have her time with Andrew in anything but a comfortable and private setting.

"Very well, the name for the reservation, please," the clerk asked.

"Fletcher," Sheila replied with the sensation of a warm glow spreading through her body.

# Chapter Seven

Looking up from the dwindling stack of reports piled on his desk, Conor noticed it was nearly two-thirty, the time his boss was to be available. "*Gae a heid* and give the inspector a jingle," Conor said to his young co-worker from across the desk.

Putting a pen in the spot he was looking at in the reports so he could return to it later, Andrew set them aside. Picking up the phone, he dialed the number for the chief superintendents' office at Scotland Yard in London. "One ring a ding, two ring a ding," the young Londoner muttered, hearing the chime of the phone on the other end.

"This is Chief Superintendent Collingsworth. May I help you?"

"Good afternoon, sir, this is Inspector Fletcher calling from Aberdeen."

"Ah, yes, Fletcher, how are you and McDermott faring there in Scotland?"

Reaching over the desk, Conor punched the *'speaker'* button on the phone set so he could hear what was being said to his young partner.

"Fine, sir, we believe we might have a link with the service vessels here in Aberdeen and freighters that come up the Channel," he said with a sense of accomplishment.

"Is that so?" Collingsworth said with a somewhat surprised tone to his voice. "Do tell then." Sitting in his office, he preferred that his subordinates speak their minds while thoughts were fresh.

"Aye, sir." This time it was McDermott's turn to provide his shillings' worth of information. "Fletcher actually came across the first bit of information when he found the two service vessels meeting away from shore and from their original destination."

"Go on," the senior officer in London said, knowing the importance of not interrupting the conversation.

"Then as we looked at other vessels after your talk with your man Thomas, we stumbled across a *M/V Joan of Arc* that was listed as being in the same vicinity as the other two," McDermott said, completing his statement of what they had found so far to their superior.

"So, what's your next step?" Collingsworth asked his two inspectors sitting in their office over five hundred kilometers from London. Not only did he expect his inspectors to talk openly of what they thought, but he also wanted them to consider options as well.

"Well, we're hoping your friend at Lloyd's would do a wee bit of research and find out who might be the registered owner of the freighter," McDermott replied to the question his inspector had asked.

"Very well. I'll contact Thomas and see if he can give us an assist on this," the chief superintendent said.

"Chief Superintendent, one other thing?" This time it was Fletcher asking the question.

"What's that?" Collingsworth queried the young inspector.

"I was hoping to take a few days' holiday, if there's no problem?" he said in a matter-of-fact tone. Sitting there, Andrew unknowingly closed his eyes as if he were a child asking for permission to buy some sweets from his mum.

"McDermott, do you have any objections?" the chief superintendent asked his senior inspector, wanting to hear from the Scotsman on this issue as well.

"I've *nae* problem, sir," was his reply, knowing that this time off would be spent with Sergeant Gordon of the forensics lab.

"Very well, just submit the proper chit to the Administrative office, Fletcher," the superintendent said before hanging up.

"Thank you, sir," was the only thing Andrew could muster before the line went dead from the other end.

Sitting back in his chair, McDermott gave his young partner a stern look of concern. "So I guess you'll need to go and let the wee woman know you have permission to run away with her."

"Yes, you're right, I should."

***

Back in London, sitting outside the assistant chief constable's chambers at Scotland Yard, Constable Ethan Taylor looked paler than usual to his co-worker Constable Jones.

"Don't fret, Ethan, you were only gone a day without notice. You'll probably get a written letter in your packet," Jones said in a veiled attempt to ease his fellow officer's worries.

The thought of a written letter of discipline was hardly the item that had Ethan so concerned. During his absence, he had heard from his uncle Alistair Hunt's counsel. The barrister from Glasgow had informed Ethan they needed to obtain information on a Mister Gordon Wallace of Glasgow. This request, as well as the earlier one asking for the names of the two inspectors in Aberdeen shook the young officer's resolve to continue his dual role as a constable and an informant for the London crime syndicate, and now his uncle.

Recalling the other day, Ethan replayed the actions he took after calling his uncle. Once he paid for his coffee and scone at the coffee shop, he sat alone, trying to make sense of his situation. Having been away from his desk for several hours, Ethan realized he had no excuse for his prolonged absence, so he returned to his apartment.

Here, the young constable found himself contemplating the possibility of ending his troubles at the working end of the 40-caliber pistol he kept. *I'm stronger than this,* he mused, holding the weapon in his trembling hands. Turning the pistol around, Ethan ejected the magazine from the grip end of the gun and pulled the slide to the rear to eject the bullet that sat ready in the chamber. With a renewed sense of being, the young constable stood and placed the weapon back in its place, a lock-box bolted to the bottom of the dresser.

"Come on," it was Constable Jones' voice ringing in his ears that brought Ethan back to his present surroundings.

"Constable Taylor, front and center," the senior constable sergeant said, stepping out of the assistant chief constable's chambers.

Standing up from the hardwood bench just outside the chambers, Ethan adjusted his dress uniform and marched into the chamber room so he could face his superior and receive the disciplinary action that was to be dispensed. "Constable Taylor, reporting as ordered, sir," he sounded off, saluting the assistant chief constable in the process.

"Stand fast, Constable Taylor," the booming voice of the senior constable sergeant roared in the chamber. Ethan removed his traditional *'custodian helmet'* but stood still at attention, waiting to hear his fate.

The assistant chief constable stood at the podium directly in front of Ethan, reviewing the documents that held his fate, and more importantly, his future within Scotland Yard. "Constable Taylor," the assistant chief constable spoke with a level, but firm tone, "you are being disciplined for being absent from your post without purpose," he said. "Do you understand this charge?" he asked, concluding the brief statement.

"Yes, sir," Ethan responded with a positive tone, resigned to his fate.

"For that you will be reassigned to the security force at Heathrow Airport for a period of one hundred eighty days," the assistant chief constable said, "at which time you will be given a second hearing to determine your future assignment at Scotland Yard," adding the duration of Ethan's 'sentence' as it were.

"Understood, sir," Ethan responded, knowing he had no opportunity to say anything in his own defense.

"Constable Taylor; dismissed." The senior constable sergeants booming voice once again echoed off the walls of the chamber.

Coming to attention, Ethan donned his helmet, offered a crisp salute, that the assistant chief constable returned in kind, then he spun on his heels and marched out through the same entrance he had just come through less than five minutes earlier. Exiting into the hallway, Ethan allowed himself a chance to relax for a moment.

Seeing his co-worker exit the chambers, Constable Jones walked up and asked him, "Well, good news?"

"Reassigned to Heathrow Security for six months and then another hearing," Ethan responded to his coworker.

Before Constable Jones could ask another question, the senior constable sergeant came up to Ethan and spoke.

"Constable Taylor, you're to report to Room 201 for reassignment, sharply now, lad," the sergeant said in a softer, almost fatherly tone.

"Yes, sir," Ethan replied, turning away from his friend, heading to the office as directed.

Leaving Room 201 after signing his reassignment papers, Constable Ethan Taylor knew he had one last thing to do before he reported to the Security Office at Heathrow to assume his new assignment. Recalling that his uncle needed information on Gordon Wallace, he needed to inform him he wouldn't have the access to the records to give them anything on the Scotsman. Walking out of Scotland Yard, he took out his cell phone and dialed his uncle's office number where Janice picked up his call, all the while walking to the parking garage to his car.

"Hello?" she asked, not knowing the caller's number that was displayed.

"Good evening," he said. "Is Mister Hunt available?"

"Why yes, he is. May I ask who's calling?" the secretary asked, unsure of the caller's identity.

"Please let him know it's Mister Taylor of London and it's very important that he take my call," Ethan said, stopping outside the parking garage, knowing he would lose the reception on his phone if he entered.

"One moment, please," Janice said, placing the call on hold. Selecting an alternate line, she rang Alistair's office phone.

"Yes, Janice?" he asked, answering the call.

"There's a Mister Taylor of London calling. Says it's important for you to take his call," she said, repeating the message from Ethan.

"It's okay, Janice. Put him through," Alistair said, trying to hide his surprised tone hearing that his nephew was calling him directly.

"Mister Taylor," Alistair said, not sure if his nephew was under any duress.

"Yes, Mister Hunt," Ethan started. "Thank you for taking my call this evening." He tried to keep his voice even and professional.

"What can I do for you?" the uncle asked, wishing to keep the call short in the event it was being recorded somehow.

"I am sorry to inform you that the GW transaction will be placed on hold for six months because of a clerical error," Ethan spoke, hoping his uncle would understand his meaning.

"That's rather unfortunate to hear," Alistair said, trying to fathom the reason for the delay.

"I can assure you, sir, I will be doing everything I can to provide you details within a fortnight, if not sooner."

"I understand the situation. I look forward to hearing more news when it comes available," Alistair said. "Have a pleasant evening."

"The same to you, sir, good evening," Ethan said, ending the call.

Still holding the phone, Alistair pushed the intercom and asked Janice to come into his office.

"Yes, sir?" she spoke.

"Janice, contact Mister Burns and ask him to join me tomorrow for breakfast at Celtic Park," Alistair requested, referring to his counselor and confidante.

"Yes, sir, eight o'clock as usual?" she queried her boss for the time.

"Yes, that will do just fine," he said, turning his chair to look at the lights of the passing vessels along the River Clyde at the end of Brown Street. *What have ye gotten yer self into now, lad?* He replayed the phone call he just finished with his nephew through his mind.

***

Entering the forensics lab, Andrew noticed Sheila had her back turned, giving one of the other technicians' instructions on a bag of evidence. Taking in the view of the young woman in white from behind was quite a treat, as the lab coat did little to hide her sumptuous curved bottom and shapely legs. *A full weekend to explore those curves will be quite the adventure. If the other evening is any indication, I might want to start working out again to bring up my stamina.* "Excuse me, Sergeant Gordon, may I have a word with you?" he asked from the opposite side of the counter at the front of room.

Turning around at the sound of Andrew's voice, she answered, "What can I do for you, Inspector?" An obvious smile of happiness graced her face.

"I need to discuss the request from earlier regarding the shipping reports," he said, trying his best to hide his enthusiasm in knowing he had permission to spend a few days with her.

"We'll discuss the rest later," Sheila said to her colleague, half-turning away from Andrew, who was standing at the counter. Stepping up to the counter, she asked her beau, "What seems to be the issue, Inspector?"

Seeing the other lab technician had stepped to the back of the room, Andrew whispered, "It appears that I've permission for a few days' holiday time."

With a schoolgirl giggle, Sheila replied, "Then we best get our plans in order, tonight, after dinner."

"I'll see you at your car then," he replied with a wink and a quick squeeze of her hand.

***

As the morning sun crept above the horizon of the Irish Sea, 'Mr. Higgins' was just finishing his jog along the shore road near Ulster University. Taking in a deep breath, the cold marine air stung his lungs, slowly bringing his pulse rate down and calming his breathing in the process.

Shortly after his run, 'Mr. Higgins' entered the study of his spacious home on the barren shore of the sound that entered Belfast harbor.

Sitting in the leather winged back chair, he read each series of dispatches his counselor, Sean Gilmore, had left the previous evening. Each of the dispatches addressed a certain aspect of *'Callaghan and Higgins Limited'* business ventures. From shipping, pharmaceuticals to livestock, he had a hand in a portion of an operation or had ownership of the entire operation.

One dispatch caught his eye thumbing through the sheaf of papers. *'Gazelle Transport'* was the title of the dispatch, and reading the text, a faint smile came across his face. *'Five hundred units are prepared for distribution at three thousand one hundred rand each for a total of one million five hundred fifty thousand rand upon receipt'*, it read, which equaled one hundred thousand euros at today's rate of exchange. *'Shipment to be arranged overland to departure dock in Tangier'*, the dispatch continued announcing where the items would be shipped from. *'Estimate date for shipment is September 10'*. It was a date that 'Mr. Higgins' needed to know since he would be arranging for shipment via freighter.

Having finished this part of his morning routine, 'Mr. Higgins' walked to his bedroom and adjoining bathroom, where he showered. Exiting the shower, he wiped the condensation from the mirror where he could see his reflection. It wasn't the normal physique of a fifty-five-year-old business man, but that of an individual who had spent time in the jungles of French Guinea, Indonesia, and the deserts of the African Sahara and American Southwest during his time in the French Foreign Legion. The only visible reminder of that time other than his physique was the slightly faded tattoo, an outline of a stallion's head with a drawn sword resting on the crown of his right shoulder.

Having finished bathing and getting dressed to begin his day, 'Mr. Higgins' called for his driver to take him to his office in Belfast. Within minutes, a stately, 1986 Jaguar XJ6 Series III sedan, in *'British Racing Green'* pulled up the gravel driveway. Stepping out of the driver's door, the young robust Ulsterman walked around and held the rear passenger's door open for 'Mr. Higgins'.

"Good morning, Geoff," the Northern Irishman said, greeting the driver.

"Good morning to you as well, sir," he said in return, closing the door behind his employer, who took a seat in the rear of the sedan.

Geoff Brennan had come to 'Mr. Higgins' employment as a favor to his uncle, who worked for Mister Callaghan. Growing up in Belfast's west side, the young man learned early in his youthful years that survival depended on strength and guile. Once he and several of his friends were confronted by a gang of youths that had a disagreement with their way of life and a raucous fight broke out. In the end, one of his friends had been stabbed and soon died in his arms.

***

"As you can all see, the shipment of the approved narcotics has been successful from our pharmaceutical plant in Limerick," 'Mr. Higgins' said to the three men and two women who were part of a board he chaired. "Are there any questions?" he asked, ending the meeting.

After the members left the boardroom, he picked up the phone and asked his secretary, "Erin, please arrange for a table at *'Mathew's Bar'* and contact Mr. Gilmore and have him meet me, say at one o'clock."

"I'll see it's taken care of sir," the young woman responded, hanging up the phone before selecting the counselor's business card from the listing on her computer file. Before contacting 'Mr. Higgins' counselor, she called and secured a private table at the establishment that had been requested. She then dialed the counselor's number, which was finally answered on the third ring.

"Hello, this is Mister Gilmore," the counselor said, slightly out of breath.

"Mr. Gilmore, 'Mr. Higgins' would like your company for lunch today at one o'clock at *'Mathew's Bar',"* she said.

"Certainly, Erin," the counselor said, making a note of the time and location of the requested meeting.

Morning soon became afternoon as two men gathered in the local eatery. Sitting in the secluded area of the bar, 'Mr. Higgins' was just finishing his discussion with his counselor, Sean, on how best to handle the shipment of weapons from the dealer, Kurt VanHoorst.

"In past instances, sir, we've used our facility near Dublin to accept the cargo because of the distance from your office here," the counselor replied to 'Mr. Higgins' questioning.

"That's true, but we were also dealing with a smaller item," 'Mr. Higgins' pointed out to the counselor that the facility in Dublin was ideal for moving narcotics, but not weapons. "Also, I was planning to have Mr. Hunt and his people provide the *'expendable'* security while it was being off-loaded and transported to the warehouses." He concluded his statement.

Pausing for a moment to finish his lunch and collect his thoughts, 'Mr. Higgins' contemplated a very bold action. "Do you believe that our current 'shipper' could handle an 'at-sea transfer' like the ones we do out of Aberdeen?" he asked of his counselor.

The counselor closed his eyes briefly, picturing the movement of a shipping container from a freighter to the deck of a service vessel and vice versa. "Captain Duncan would be more qualified to answer that question," he said, pointing out his limited knowledge of activity at sea to his boss.

"Umm, seems you're correct, let's plan to entertain Captain Duncan in Edinburgh in, say, three days' time," the syndicate leader said before picking up his glass of mineral water.

"Very well, sir, where in Edinburgh would you like to meet the captain?" Mr. Gilmore asked.

"At the Asian tiger exhibit at the Edinburgh Zoo," he replied with a whimsical smile on his face. "Should be rather easy to talk without eavesdroppers about. Oh, and then contact Mr. Hunt. Let him know I'll call him tomorrow at nine so that we can discuss the next step of the security plan and inform him of the tentative timetable for his services," 'Mr. Higgins' said, confident in the knowledge that he had the upper hand in the transaction.

"As you wish, sir," Mr. Gilmore replied.

"And one last thing. Let's contact our principal working with *'Papillion Transport'* and put into motion the plan we discussed, changing the way the container is handled from our usual methods," the Irishman spoke, contemplating the need to tighten control of how the narcotics would be brought onshore.

***

Returning to his small office in Belfast, Sean Gilmore, counselor and barrister, went about the business of making the two phone calls he was instructed to make. The first call he made was quite easy, since the recipient of the call was not fighting the wind or tide in the North Sea as Captain Duncan could very well be doing. Picking up the phone, he dialed the number for Alistair Hunt in Glasgow. The line connected and he began to hear the tone of the phone ringing.

"Hello?" the familiar voice of Janice Gordon, Mr. Hunt's receptionist, said.

"Good evening, is Mister Hunt available?" Mr. Gilmore asked, hoping the syndicate figure had not left for the evening.

"May I ask who's calling?"

"Mr. Gilmore, ma'am," he replied.

"If you'll hold for just a moment, I'll see if he's free, Mr. Gilmore," she said, placing the caller in electronic limbo.

Getting up from her desk, Janice walked the few paces across the room to the closed door that led into Alistair's private office. "Excuse me, sir," she said, "a Mister Gilmore is calling for you. Should I put him through?"

Looking at the clock on the wall, he saw it was a quarter past five in the evening, and he had plenty of time to make his dinner engagement at seven. "Yes, please put him through," Alistair replied, waiting for the call to be transferred. Answering the call on the first ring, he spoke, "Good evening, Mr. Gilmore."

"Good evening, Mister Hunt, I apologize for the late call, but 'Mr. Higgins' would appreciate your availability for a conference tomorrow morning at 9 a.m.," the counselor said, relaying the instructions from his boss.

"If you'll excuse me, I need to check my calendar for the day. Can you hold for a moment?" he asked.

"Of course," came the reply from the counselor.

Placing the call on hold, Alistair opened the calendar program on his computer that was meticulously kept up to date by Janice. Seeing that he had no meetings scheduled at the requested time, he punched the hold button again, opening the line.

"Mr. Gilmore, please inform 'Mr. Higgins' that I'll be available to take his call," he replied.

"Thank you for confirming the time. I do hope you have a pleasant evening," the counselor answered as the line went dead.

Meanwhile back in Glasgow, Hunt placed the phone back in its cradle, then stood, and walked to the outer office where his receptionist was in the process of leaving for the evening. "Janice, please make a note that I have a conference call at nine o'clock tomorrow morning and that I shouldn't be disturbed during it," he instructed her.

"You already have an appointment with Mr. Burns at eight, should I move it?" his receptionist questioned back to him.

"Yes, please contact him and have him meet me at seven o'clock instead," Hunt said, hoping he could catch the train from Celtic Park to downtown in time tomorrow morning for the call.

"Certainly, sir," she replied, making a note on her legal pad sitting next to the phone.

Returning to his office, he closed the door, went to the maple hutch, and slid the door back revealing the half-empty bottle of liquor on the shelf. Taking the scotch and the small crystal tumbler, he poured himself a drink and sat on the couch that was situated against the wall opposite his desk. *What's next wee, Higgie?* he mused, having received yet another call to discuss things with the mysterious 'Mr. Higgins'.

***

Having placed the first call, Sean Gilmore now went about contacting Captain Duncan of the *Nordic Supplier* in Aberdeen. Pulling up the captain's information on his computer, Mr. Gilmore located the marine frequency call number that he would use to contact him with. Dialing the operator's number for the Maritime Magistrates office in Aberdeen, his call was finally answered on the fifth ring.

"Maritime Magistrate Office, which vessel do you need connected to?" the voice of the operator asked of the caller.

"*PSV Nordic Supplier*, Captain Duncan," Gilmore said, answering the operator's question as briefly as possible. After a series of clicks and chirps, Gilmore was finally connected with the vessel at sea.

"*Nordic Supplier*, First Officer Spiers," was the response.

"Captain Duncan, please?" the counselor asked.

"Stand by for the Cap'n."

"Cap'n Duncan here," was the next voice Gilmore heard from the vessel.

"Evening Captain. Mr. Gilmore, counselor for 'Mr. Higgins' calling," he said. "'Mr. Higgins' wishes to meet you in Edinburgh in three days' time. Can you meet with him?" the counselor queried the vessel skipper.

"Aye, I'll be in port tomorrow evening. I'll call from my regular number, out," was the answer Gilmore heard before the line went dead.

*As you wish, Cap'n Duncan,* the counselor thought to himself, hanging up.

***

Sitting in the front room of his friend's flat, Ewan Sutherland stared blankly at the meal on the table. It was the third take-out dinner he was eating since returning to Aberdeen at Mr. Hunt's direction.

"Not fancy enough?" his friend joked, pushing a forkful of mashed potatoes into his mouth.

"I'm *nae* craving Chinese tonight," Ewan said, thinking on how he just wanted to get out and away from his current surroundings.

"If you're not keen on being caged, give the old bloke a call then," Ian suggested.

"I plan on doing that tomorrow," the young Scot said, picking at the deep-fried prawns in the white container. *Aye, I'll do that tomorrow, or just go for a walk regardless.* He wondered about the chances of crossing paths with the two *'policemen'* from Glasgow he saw the other day at the train station.

# Chapter Eight

Having finished his breakfast early, Alistair Hunt strode quickly along Argyle Street towards his office in anticipation of the call from the mysterious Irishman. The morning had started out grey and damp, making his way from the local coffee shop near the central rail station. Looking at his watch, he saw he had thirty minutes to walk from the station to his office and still receive the expected call.

Nearing the office, he spied Janice exchanging a kiss with a gentleman before exiting a car just outside the building. It was the first time in nearly a year that he had seen her out with anyone. He remembered with a heavy heart how Janice's husband had succumbed to pancreatic cancer the previous spring and how devastated she was.

With a fatherly sense, he provided for her and the funeral, then made sure she was always occupied to help ease the pain of her loss. The only thing he couldn't fathom was the absence of her estranged daughter at the funeral. However, seeing her out with someone made him smile, reaching for the door at the building entrance. Entering the office, he exclaimed "*Good* morn', Janice."

Somewhat startled at the volume of the greeting, she took a step back away from the coat tree where she was hanging her sweater up. "Mister Hunt, you gave me a fright there," she said with a more cheerful tone than usual.

"I'm sorry, but I noticed you had a gentleman drop you off this morning, and it made me somewhat happy to see you're getting out," Alistair said.

"Well, yes, I am," Janice replied, now embarrassed at the fact her boss knew she was seeing someone.

"*Nae* worry, lass," Alistair said, "I'm pleased if you are." He walked over and gave her a brief hug.

"Thank you, Alistair," she said in a soft tone, tears forming in the corner of her eyes.

"Now, shall we get to work," he said, walking into his office, "and don't forget my coffee," finishing the declaration that life was back to normal in the office.

"Yes, sir," Janice said with a smile on her face, dabbing away her tears.

***

Across the Irish Sea, a similar event was taking place. Entering his office thirty minutes earlier than usual, Sean Gilmore took to collecting his notes from last night's discussion with his employer about the handling of the container of narcotics. Looking through his listing of contacts, he selected the one for *'Papillion Transport'* and dialed the international operator's exchange to initiate the call.

"Hello, *'Papillion Transport'*, how can I help you?" the voice of a Frenchwoman asked the caller.

"Hello, Monsieur Adrien Richelieu, please," Sean asked the young woman politely.

"Yes, one moment, please. I'll see if he's in," she said to the request for the head of the shipping firm.

Unknown to Sean Gilmore, the supposed owner of *'Papillion Transport'* was a mere figurehead, a 'ghost' as it were, just the name of a former French industrialist used to establish documents to provide legitimacy to the shipping firm.

"Monsieur Richelieu is not available. Could I take a message?" the receptionist asked, reading from her script of questions and answers for calls that came from overseas.

"Yes, please have him call 'Mr. Higgins' at the following number," Sean said. He was not opposed to playing the part of his boss, and on this occasion, did so by design. He read off the number to a 'clean' cell phone not associated with himself or 'Mr. Higgins' in Belfast.

"I will see that he gets the message," the young woman said as she took the information.

"Thank you and have a pleasant day," Sean said, ending the call.

On the floor above Sean Gilmore, his employer was reviewing his legitimate holdings for the company he managed. Looking up from one of his ledgers, 'Mr. Higgins' noticed that it was nearing nine in the morning and saw that the reminder on his computer was illuminated. Picking up the phone, he selected intercom and spoke to his receptionist, "Erin, could you please dial Mister Hunt of Glasgow and connect him to my office?"

"Yes, sir," the young woman replied.

Sitting back in his chair, 'Mr. Higgins' pulled out a yellow legal pad with his notes from the previous evening, detailing what he planned to tell and more importantly, not tell Alistair Hunt about his arms shipment. Looking through his notes, the intercom buzzer came to life.

"'Mr. Higgins', Mister Hunt is waiting on line three for you," the young woman announced.

Picking up the receiver, 'Mr. Higgins' greeted his caller, "Good morning, Mr. Hunt."

"Good morning, sir," Alistair replied to the still mysterious Irishman on the other end of the call.

"I'm calling to discuss the additional information for our second arrangement," he said, beginning what would be a ten-minute lecture regarding the security of a shipping container.

"Do you have any questions for me?" 'Mr. Higgins' asked the Scotsman.

"The security requirement you've outlined, where will it originate and where will it end?" Hunt asked the first of several questions running through his mind.

"Currently, all activity is planned to take place in Northern Ireland," 'Mr. Higgins' said curtly.

"And how much warning will I have to gather my staff before being in place?" Hunt asked. *I'll need to know so I can communicate this to Gordon Wallace.*

"You'll have a minimum of forty-eight hours to be in the place of my choosing."

Alistair sat in his office in Glasgow, wondering how much more information he could get from the caller before being rebuffed. "Will my staff need to be able to protect themselves?" he asked. *I need to know if the men will need to be armed and let Gordon know this as well.*

"Yes," was the quick and simple answer from the Irishman.

"And the first date I need to be planning for is when?" Hunt asked.

"You need to ensure you are ready to travel no later than the tenth of September at the earliest," 'Mr. Higgins' said, replying to Alistair's last question.

"Very well, and our next call will take place…?"

"You will be notified." The mysterious Irishman hung up.

Looking at the phone buzzing with the disconnected tone emanating from the earpiece, Hunt pushed the intercom and spoke. *I'll have Robert contact Gordon to set up the meeting for tomorrow,* the syndicate boss thought to himself. "Janice, please contact Mr. Burns and ask him to come see me at his earliest convenience," he said.

"Yes, sir," Janice responded, reaching for her file with Robert Burns' number on it.

***

Having spoken with Alistair Hunt regarding the security to his weapons shipment, 'Mr. Higgins' next began to write a few notes on his legal pad so when he called the weapons supplier, he would have his thoughts focused. Finished with putting his notes in order, 'Mr. Higgins' picked up the phone on his desk and pushed the intercom button for his receptionist for the second time this morning.

"Yes, sir," was the response from the young woman in the outer office.

"Please contact Mr. VanHoorst of *'Gazelle Transport'* in Cape Town, if you please. I'll wait for the connection," he said, giving the woman the necessary directions to place the call.

What seemed like an eternity, the call was placed through the international exchange in Dublin to a similar exchange in Cape Town.

" *'Gazelle Transport'*, how can I direct your call?" the voice answered with the predictable heavy Afrikaner accent.

"Mr. VanHoorst, please," the young Irishwoman said to her counterpart over eight thousand miles to the south.

"Just a moment, please," the South African woman replied.

After several moments, the strong, deep baritone voice came on the line. "This is Mr. VanHoorst, how can I help you?"

"Please hold for 'Mr. Higgins'," Erin said, quickly making the connection to her boss.

"Good morning, Kurt," the Northern Irishman said, hearing the connection being established.

"Good morning, Michael," the South African said, returning the greeting upon hearing his friend's voice.

"I was pleased to receive your confirmation dispatch the other day," 'Mr. Higgins' said, letting the arms dealer know they were to discuss business from this point forward. "I see we're to expect the shipment to originate from Tangier, is that correct?" he asked the South African, wanting to confirm that was still the plan.

"Yes, we'll have a single container of product," the arms dealer said, providing another answer to one of the notes on the Northern Irishman's legal pad.

"Very good, then we'll complete our transaction upon transfer of the container from your staff to my shipper?" 'Mr. Higgins' said, informing the arms dealer as to how and when he could expect to be paid for the weapons.

"Agreed, Michael," Kurt VanHoorst said, concluding the deal, knowing that the Northern Irishman would make the transfer of one point five million rand upon delivery in Tangier.

"Very well, my friend, please take care and we'll talk again soon," 'Mr. Higgins' said, concluding the call.

"And the same to you, my friend," the South African said just before he hung up, disconnecting the line.

*No sense to discuss how the transfer will take place until after I discuss this with 'Messier Remesy'.* He leaned back in his chair and sipped the chilled mineral water.

***

"So, the young lad is going to spend a few days with Sheila," Conor said, relating the budding romance between his young partner and the forensics technician.

"Well, good for him," Ailene said, putting the final touch to their evening meal of lamb kabobs and roasted vegetables. Coming to the doorway of the kitchen, she said, "Dinner is served."

"Aye, and smells delicious too," Conor said, stepping in the kitchen seeing the meal laid out on the table. "I was thinking since I'd be without Andrew for the weekend, that you and I could take in a wee bit of culture," he said, planting the seed for her to consider.

"And what might that be?" Ailene responded, hoping it was something more than lying about.

"I propose that you and I take in the golf tournament being held at Nigg Bay," Conor said proudly.

"A golf tournament, are you daft?" she asked with a serious tone but a comical look on her face.

"I'm *nae* daft, one of the young constables is giving it a go, and I thought we could go and give him a cheer or two," Conor replied.

Ailene considered the proposal. *The thought of the cool sea breeze sweeping the golf links is appealing, as long as the rain stays away while we are outside, and the sun on my face might add a wee touch of color too.* "Aye then, we'll go, only if it's *nae* raining," she answered, placing a smile on Conor's face.

***

Once again, Chief Superintendent Collingsworth found himself entering the *'The Bulldog Arms'*, which he surmised as his friend's favorite public house. Walking through the door, he spied his friend Thomas sitting at a high table next to the bar area and gave him a polite wave, acknowledging his arrival.

"Good to see you again, William," the investigator for Lloyd's of London said above the din of the growing crowd.

"Seems we are always getting in before the crowd arrives," William said, placing his coat across the back of the chair and taking his seat.

"Gentlemen, what can I start you with?" the young waitress asked, laying out two menus for them to look over.

"I'll have an Absolut and tonic with a lime twist," Thomas said.

"And I'll have a Heineken."

"I'll be right back with the drinks," the young woman said, turning away.

"So, you said your chaps in Aberdeen might have a link between the freighters and the workboats?" Thomas said, starting the conversation off.

"Yes, they found a freighter, the *Motor Vessel Joan of Arc* that rendezvoused with two of the service boats nearly one hundred fifty kilometers from any reasonable point of anchorage."

"Interesting," Thomas said as the drinks were served.

"To your health," William saluted his friend, picking up the cold bottle of beer.

"And to you as well," the gentleman from Lloyd's said, returning the salutation with a lift of his glass. "So, getting back to the vessels," Thomas continued, "do we know where each vessel docked after the encounter?"

"Based on the information from my two inspectors, they found that the freighter docked in Hamburg after being at station for nearly six hours," William said, recalling the details offered by Conor and Andrew. "The service boats then returned to Aberdeen."

"Well, luckily I still have a contact at the *'Küstenwache'* offices in Cuxhaven that owes me a favor or two," Thomas said, citing the German

Coast Guard responsible for amongst other things, border security and ship safety.

"If possible, we'd like to try and see who the registered owner of the freighter is to see if there's a connection as well," William informed his colleague, finishing the lager from Holland.

"I'll see what I can do in that regard," he answered. "How 'bout a quick supper?"

"Sounds fine," William replied, knowing he was going to order the *'Hunter's Rump'* steak dinner.

***

Sitting at their desks for most of the day, McDermott and Fletcher were busy trying to find additional links between the platform service vessels and the freighters sailing through the Channel that originated from the Mediterranean.

Looking at the clock, McDermott stood up and stretched. "On Monday, we need to go back to the docks and see if we can get a few words with those captains again," he reminded his colleague.

"All right, do you have information as to which vessel?" Fletcher asked, pulling the legal pad and pencil out from under the shipping reports. "Or are we going on your gut instinct?"

"Aye, we'll start with that captain from the *Nordic Supplier* first and then move on to your two," he said, referring to the *Standard-Hercules* and the *Standard-Apollo* vessels.

"All right," the younger inspector replied, writing down his notes.

# Chapter Nine

The noise grew as the evening shift of constables and detectives began making their way into the small duty room where the inspectors from Scotland Yard were working. "You and your young lass have an enjoyable weekend," Conor said to his younger partner as they both finished putting their things in order before leaving the office for the weekend.

"You sure you're okay with this?" Andrew asked, not wanting to upset things between him and the elder Scotsman.

"*Nae* worry, lad, *gae heid* and enjoy yer self," Conor said in his gleeful Scottish tone, ushering the young Londoner out of the office.

Walking down the short hallway to the front entrance, Conor and Andrew caught up with Sergeant Gordon at the sergeant's desk. "Enjoy your time," Conor said, sauntering past the young lass.

"Thank you, Chief Inspector, I will," she said in a joyful tone as Andrew joined her as they exited the building.

Walking to her car, Andrew opened the door for her to get settled into the passenger seat. Walking around to the driver side, he quickly got behind the wheel, a sense of excitement and trepidation beginning to course through his body. "You'll navigate?" he asked, turning to Sheila, starting the car, and putting the selector into drive, realizing that he didn't have a clue on where to go.

"Of course I will," she giggled. In the few minutes it took to walk from the office to the car park, Sheila had gone from constable to a teenager. Her emotions obvious at the thought of having the young man for the whole weekend.

And with that said, Andrew pulled the Ford Focus out of the police station parking structure and made his way through town, with Sheila's help, to the A95/A96 roadway to make their way to the resort she had booked. "What was the name of this resort again?" Andrew asked over the radio, quietly playing a popular Van Morrison song.

"It's the Ardmore resort at Colyumbridge," Sheila said, thinking of the chilled bottle of wine and fruit platter that she arranged for that would be greeting them as they entered the room. Not only did she arrange for the wine and fruit, she had also booked a private table for their first meal at the five-star restaurant located on the resort's grounds.

"So, how much is this little extravagant weekend going to cost me?" the young inspector asked, not wanting her to feel obligated to handle all the costs.

"I'll let you decide at the end of the weekend," she said, placing her hand on his and gently squeezing it as she looked at him behind the wheel.

*Is this really happening?* He and Conor had only been in Aberdeen for just over a month and yet here he was going to a resort with an attractive young Scottish woman he barely knew, but sincerely wanted to get to know better. *What if Chief Superintendent Collingsworth recalled us to London, then what?* He thought of the negatives instead of the positives. He continued to think through the various scenarios and how they would affect his growing relationship with Sheila when she suddenly cried out to him.

"Andrew, you missed the turn," she said in an excited tone.

"I'm sorry, I was thinking of something else," he said, apologizing for the error in his driving.

"It's *nae* worry really, we've got plenty of time," she said, knowing it only took less than three hours to drive to the resort.

After nearly ninety minutes of driving since returning to the proper roadway, Andrew found himself pulling into the resort entrance. Slowing down to enter the car park, he found himself behind an antique silver Aston-Martin DB5 coupe at the front of the valet station before bringing the car to a stop. Pulling up to the valet station at the resort entrance, two young lads stepped forward to assist the couple in gathering their belongings.

"Good evening," one young attendant said, opening the passenger side door for Sheila, allowing her to step out of the car.

"The bags are in the boot," Andrew said to the other attendant who stepped forward to take the keys to the car, accepting a twenty-euro note.

"Yes, sir. Thank you, sir," the attendant spoke, accepting the money and keys.

Walking around the front of the car, Andrew took Sheila by the arm and led her to the front entrance of the resort lobby, starting their weekend away from the hustle and bustle of police work. "Shall we?" he said, offering his arm to her.

"Yes, we should," she replied, slipping her arm through his and walking with him up the steps into the lobby.

Stepping through the entrance, they proceeded to the reception counter and the young female desk clerk who provided a cordial greeting to the resort.

"Good evening, we've a reservation," Andrew said, taking the lead on starting their time together.

"Yes, sir, the reservation is for…?" the receptionist asked when Sheila suddenly cut her question off.

"It's under *Fletcher*," she said proudly, answering the question for her beau.

"Thank you, miss," the receptionist responded, glancing quickly between the couple, and keyed the response into the computer.

Andrew turned to look at Sheila, who stood confidently at the counter, a beaming smile stretched across her face. "That was rather cheeky," he whispered into her ear.

"I see you're staying with us for the weekend," the receptionist announced, interrupting their brief conversation. "We have you in Room 327, facing the glen and river," she continued, pulling the registration documents from the printer. "Please initial here, here, and here and sign at the bottom," she pointed out to Andrew where he needed to show understanding for no pets, no smoking, and payment for any damages incurred.

"There you are," he exclaimed, placing the pen back in the holder on the counter and sliding the documents back to the receptionist.

"Here are your keys. You'll find the lift on your left," the receptionist directed them. "Have a pleasant stay."

"We shall," Sheila responded with a gleam in her eye that caused the young receptionist to blush.

Watching the young couple walk away, the receptionist stood shaking her head. When Andrew and Sheila were out of earshot, the receptionist blurted out, "More bloody newlyweds," to her co-worker.

***

In the early evening crowd of diners who had gathered in one of Glasgow's newest restaurants, two friendly rivals sat across from one another. "I was surprised to get the call from your barrister," Gordon Wallace said, putting his glass of Chardonnay down. He was sitting across from his friend as they dined at the new Brazilian restaurant located in Glasgow's business district in the center of town.

"I do appreciate you coming on such a short notice," Alistair Hunt said, placing his glass of scotch down, while the waitress came to the table.

"Good evening, gentlemen, may I start you off with an appetizer?" the young red-headed lass queried.

"Aye, that sounds appealing, Ali," Wallace said, looking at his friend.

"Aye, I'll have the tiger prawns and the *'Salada de vagens'*," Hunt spoke, selecting the salad with green beans, onions, and peppers, looking over the menu, "and the *'Cordeiro'* with the roast potatoes." He selected the Leg of Lamb entrée.

Seeing that his friend was not shying away from showing the depth of his hunger, Wallace spoke to the waitress as she finished writing down Hunt's order. "And I'll have the fried squid and the *'Vinagrete'* salad, and for the entrée the *'Contra filet'* with mashed potatoes," he said, pausing for the young lass to finish writing down the items he'd selected.

As the waitress walked away from the table, the conversation began anew. "So, now that we have that out of the way, why did I get summoned here tonight?"

Hunt looked at his friend across the table from where he sat, picked up his glass, and offered a toast. "Here's to a successful business venture, Gordon." As often as they crossed paths, the two men had a genuine respect for each other, and fact be known, both knew they would die for the other if it came to that.

The fellow Scotsman picked up his wine glass and replied, "Good health to you," in return to the offered toast, tilting the glass back and emptying its contents in one swallow. Placing his now empty glass on the table, he looked directly across the table and spoke.

"So, is this the need for some of my men you were discussing with me earlier?" Gordon asked.

"Aye, it is," Alistair said, retelling of his conversation with 'Mr. Higgins' from the other day. Within ten minutes, he had recounted everything he had been told by the mysterious Northern Irishman.

"And so, from what you have been told, the job requires everyone to be able to travel to Belfast within forty-eight hours, and we're expected to be able to 'protect' ourselves," Gordon said.

"Aye, you've nae worry, I've got that covered," Alistair said just as the servers were delivering their first course to the table. "You see, I've a vessel captained by a sympathetic soul who will be helping us transport what we need to Northern Ireland." He outlined the plan, pulling the head from one tiger prawn, and dipped it into the garlic herb and butter sauce.

"And this *'captain'* is being paid by you for this effort?" Gordon said, pulling one of the fried tentacles of squid from the pile on the plate in front of him.

"He's actually seconded to me by our joint employer," Alistair said, taking a bite of another quick fried crustacean from Thailand.

"I see. So, you've full and complete trust in this captain and the men on his ship?" Gordon asked, getting a feeling that he would need to caution his men on the support that they would have during this job.

"I do today, but tomorrow is another day with new surprises."

"And that we're providing 'protection' of an item that we know nothing about."

"I can't imagine it being something that would cause any concerns beyond that it has a very high value," Alistair responded to his friend, sensing the uneasiness growing between them.

"I'll have a chat with our gentleman of the first part tomorrow regarding the urgency of the matter, and I'll call you about the details," Alistair said, tossing down the empty tail of a prawn to his plate.

"Fair enough," Gordon said, beginning to attack his salad.

***

Maneuvering his vessel slowly into the estuary of the Aberdeen harbor, Captain Clive Duncan of the *PSV Nordic Supplier* began the demanding "Y" turn in the tight confines between the 'Commercial' and 'Albert' quays. With a deft touch on both the throttles and the helm, the captain executed the turn like a world-class rally driver, sliding his car through a slalom course.

"And that Seaman Carr is how you 'park' a seventy-five-meter vessel in tight quarters," the seasoned mariner boasted to the young deckhand standing by on the bridge.

"Aye, Captain, fine maneuvering 'twas," the young lass from East Lothian said, taking the readings from the engine gauges just past the helm.

Picking up the ship-based intercom, the captain called out, "Mister Spiers to the bridge," letting everyone onboard know that the vessel's second in command was wanted. Standing on the aft section of the vessel, the loudspeaker bellowed out the captain's call, which the first officer heard quite clearly.

"Make sure you tie her down smartly," the first officer directed the deckhands, who were in the process of securing the vessel to the pier. With his order to the deck crew, Malcolm Spiers made his way to the bridge. "Yes, Cap'n?" the young Scot from Inverness said, entering the bridge.

"I've some errands to take care of ashore before it gets too late. You'll have the ship for the evening," Captain Duncan said to his second-in-command, taking his charts and notes and locking them in navigation cabinet.

"Aye, sir," Spiers replied, trying hard not to show his displeasure in front of their newest crewmember. *I had plans to meet someone, as if you cared.* However, in fairness, he was learning quite a bit from the elder seaman on how to command the vessel and was looking forward to his exam date later in the year when he would try to apply his knowledge and skills in his attempt to obtain a captain's license of his own.

With the watch set, Captain Duncan left the bridge and made his way to his at-sea cabin to grab his duffle bag, which he packed earlier in the day. Nearing the edge of the deck, he looked up noticing Officer Spiers standing on the bridge wing and gave a salute to the first officer.

"Captain's off the ship," Spiers said, returning the salute, watching the elder Scot exit the vessel as nimbly as a gymnast doing a somersault. In less than two minutes, Captain Duncan was nothing but a shadow amongst a sea of growing darkness, strolling away from the docks to the street and the first available cab for hire.

Seeing the figure of the captain fade into the shadows, Spiers pulled his cell phone from the inside pocket of his foul-weather jacket. Thumbing the 'phone' button, he quickly selected his number list and after scrolling past several names stopped when he came to that of his lady friend's number. Selecting the number, he quickly received a dial tone. "Hello, Linda?"

"Malcolm, you're in early."

"Aye, but the Cap'n went ashore, so I won't be off the boat until he returns."

"Well, we'll just make the best of it then," she said rather disappointed in the fact she was going to spend another evening alone in bed. What made the feeling worse was knowing her man was only four kilometers away on the 'smelly barge' as she called the *Nordic Supplier*.

"I'll ask for a fortnight's leave when he returns," Spiers stated. "I'll tell him I need to study for my exam."

"You'll *nae* do too much studying, will you?"

"No, of course not," he said with a chuckle.

Standing on the edge of the street, Captain Duncan spied a vehicle that was seemingly out of place. Amongst the various work vehicles, trucks and miscellaneous ship-borne gear, the dark-colored sedan was backed in amongst the shadows of two buildings, attempting to remain hidden from view. In a moment, he knew why. One of the occupants brought a pair of field glasses to his face and stared directly at him, but more than likely at the vessels coming in and out of the harbor.

*So, Aberdeen's best is having a look about.* Looking in either direction of the roadway, he spied a cab with its occupant light illuminated, meaning it was available for hire. Waving down the car, the captain entered and gave the driver the address to his flat in West Aberdeen. *I think I need to give Mr. Gilmore a call as soon as I am settled. If the local police are getting nosey, I might have to secure another port to use for business.*

In less than ten minutes, the cab driver was pulling up to the nondescript building the captain called home when in port. Paying the driver for the fare plus a decent tip, he exited the vehicle and walked to the second-floor apartment. Unlocking the door and entering, he was hit with the musty smell of a room that had not been open to the outside air for several weeks. *Next time I'll need to give Miss Kennedy a visit and remind her to open the windows a wee bit before I get home,* he thought, opening the window in the front room.

Next, he walked into the small and sparsely furnished kitchen and opened the window to the rear alleyway behind the apartment complex. Soon a fresh breeze began to gently push the blinds about as the stale air gave way for fresher air to enter. With that done, Captain Duncan opened the refrigerator to find simple staples of his time in the apartment, greens for a salad that were past their prime, several pre-cooked meat pies that only require a short time to heat, and a couple of bottles of his favorite ale neatly stacked on the bottom shelf.

Taking one of the pies, he placed it in the oven, set the temperature for cooking, and set the timer, then opened one of the bottles and poured the golden liquid into a glass that he placed on the counter. After taking the first long refreshing swallow of beer in the last two weeks, he pulled his phone from his pocket and selected the number for his second employer's counselor, Mr. Gilmore.

On the second ring, the Irish barrister in Belfast answered the call. "Hello?"

"Good evening, Mr. Gilmore, it's Cap'n Duncan calling."

"Good evening, sir, I wasn't expecting your call till tomorrow morning at the earliest."

"Aye, we had a fair tail wind and a following tide allowing us to make port a wee bit earlier than planned."

"I take it this call is in regards to our earlier discussion?" Gilmore asked.

"Aye, we can discuss that, but I think it's important for you and your employer to know the local constables are stepping up their surveillance on the docks," Captain Duncan said, relating the scene from earlier in the evening where he spied the sedan at the quay.

"I see. I'll make note to inform 'Mr. Higgins' of this development," the counselor said.

"And just so you know, I'll be able to meet in Edinburgh, but for no more than an hour's time," the vessel master said, knowing he couldn't expect Officer Spiers to be held onboard more than a day or two without letting him know the reason.

"I'll inform 'Mister Higgins' then," Gilmore said. "Please plan on being at the Edinburgh Zoo's *'Asian Tiger'* exhibit at ten-thirty the day after next."

"Aye, I'll be there," the Cap'n said as the timer on the oven chirped, announcing that his supper was ready.

"Until the meeting then," Gilmore said, ending the discussion with the caller from Aberdeen.

***

One hundred kilometers to the north, a dying fire was providing nature's serenade to two prone figures lying on the bedspread laid across the floor of a room at the resort hotel in Colyumbridge.

"This has been a rather pleasant evening," Andrew said, tracing his hand across Sheila's breast, using his finger to circle her areola, recalling the events that led to the present situation. From the chilled bottle of Chablis and fruit and cheese, the young Londoner found out just how important the weekend would be to his companion.

"I'm glad you're enjoying it so far," Sheila replied, sliding her hand softly across the smooth skin of Andrew's hairless and barren chest. She was pleased to see the surprise on Andrew's face, from seeing the prepared room to their evening meal in the gourmet restaurant on the resort premises.

As the fire slowly died to a few glowing embers, Andrew rolled slightly to his side and gently placed a kiss to her lips and slid his hands across her thighs, slowly moving them apart and exposing the moist folds of skin, the dampness adding to his heightened arousal. He slowly worked his way to a point where they would be kindling their own fire for the rest of the night.

## Chapter Ten

Trying to focus in the darkened room that was black as the bottom of an oil well, Ewan rolled over in bed for what felt like the twentieth time this morning. Reaching across the nightstand, he found his cell phone and pressed a button that activated the device. *Bloody hell, it's only four-thirty in the morning.* Rolling onto his back, the young Scotsman stretched his arms over his head, banging his knuckles against the wall, which elicited a murmur in the next room where his friend Ian slept.

Slowly swinging his legs over the edge, he placed his feet onto the chilled floor of the bedroom, forgetting how sparsely the flat was furnished, not having a rug under his feet. Standing, Ewan reached for the light switch to help him gather some clothes to put on before he sauntered into the kitchen.

Filling the kettle with water, Ewan placed it on the stove's front grate and turned the dial to *'HIGH'*, igniting the gas burner under it. Walking back to the bedroom, he picked up his phone and returned to the kitchen. Sitting at the small kitchen table, he looked through his messages and was surprised to see one from Alistair Hunt.

*Next shipment is due in three weeks, inform Cap'n "D" today,* Ewan read, scanning the text message from Alistair Hunt's barrister in Glasgow. *I guess I'll be taking a wee walk about today.* As steam from the water started to sound the whistle built into the spout of the kettle.

Having finished eating, Ewan Sutherland stepped out of his friend's flat for the first time in three days. Walking down the stairs and onto the quiet street, he began to walk the three miles to the docks, hoping to meet with the captain of the *Nordic Supplier* before the activities around the port became too hectic.

In just under an hour, the young Scot found himself crossing the Victoria Bridge towards the docks, when his cell phone rang. Stopping in the middle of the bridge, he removed the phone from his pocket and looked at the number displayed on the screen.

"Mr. Burns, good morning, sir," the young Scot said as a lorry carrying two large containers roared past him, carrying goods to their next destination.

"Good morning, Ewan," Burns, barrister for Alistair Hunt said. "I take it this call didn't wake you," he said, referring to the loud diesel truck that drove past.

"No, sir, I was just on my way to see Cap'n Duncan based on the text message that was sent last night," Ewan replied, acknowledging the fact he was paying attention to his duties to Mr. Hunt.

"That's why I'm calling, Ewan," Burns said to the young man. "He's not onboard his ship. He is staying at his flat."

Ewan stood in the middle of the bridge, pondering how the barrister in Glasgow knew about a ship captain's whereabouts here in Aberdeen. "I've *nae* got his flat number, Mr. Burns," he said, referring to the flat's location, wondering if he was going to be given it over the phone.

"I'll send it to you by text in a moment," Burns said, letting Ewan know he would be expected to contact Captain Duncan as soon as possible.

"Aye, I'll be on my way," Ewan said, turning back to his friend Ian's flat to wake him so he could drive him to his meeting.

"I'll be in touch later today with more information for you," Burns said, realizing the young man had no idea that three syndicate 'helpers' had been dispatched to see that he was not apprehended by the police or roughed up by the crews on the docks.

***

The morning chill swept through the room as Andrew and Sheila lay intertwined under the bedspread. Feeling her companion shift slightly, Sheila slowly raised her head from the pillow to see Andrew reclined on his back, the bedspread covering part of his body, but not the best feature, she mused.

Slowly, the young woman slid her arm out from under the covers and placed it gently on his exposed thigh, causing a slight stirring in him, but not waking him. Moving her hand across his muscular leg, she came across what she had intended to find, flaccid for the moment, but capable of so much more. *I hope he's up for another go.*

Sensing something touching him, Andrew slid his hand to his leg where he encountered Sheila's arm draped across his thigh. Rolling towards her, he opened his eyes. "Good morning," he said, sleep still clouding his mind.

"Good morning," Sheila said, responding to his greeting with a firmer hold on him. "I hope you don't mind the *'wake-up call'*, do you?"

"No. Not at all, don't let me stop you," he said, lying back against the pillow, his eyes closed and allowing her to continue.

***

Having gotten up early for a weekend, Conor and Ailene were just finishing their breakfast as the announcer on the radio planned to speak about the weather after a commercial break.

"Remember, if it's raining, I'm *nae* going," the young woman said across the table to Conor, waiting for the announcer to give his report. *"Partly cloudy skies, westerly winds at ten kilometers and a high temperature of nineteen degrees Celsius,"* the voice on the radio said to those listening.

"Now, there's a bonnie forecast for ya," Conor exclaimed to his girlfriend, who didn't seem as happy to hear it like he was.

"All right, we'll go and cheer Trevor on since it'll be dry," she replied with a sheepish grin, knowing she was looking forward to being out with her man.

***

The early morning mist hung in the air like a grey shroud as Constable Taylor was walking his post outside the cargo terminal entrance at London's busiest airport hub, Heathrow. Every three minutes a jet would glide gently in for a landing from some foreign destination or begin its rolling take-off that culminated in a scream of the giant engines and stench of vaporized jet fuel.

*I guess it could be worse,* he thought, pulling the collar of his jacket higher around the nape of his neck in a vain attempt to keep the drizzle out. Nearing the end to his first week of duty, he had endured the harassment from several of the constables as the facts of his new assignment to the airport swept through the ranks. One of the senior constables called him a *'coward'* to his face when it was made known that he walked away from his post. What made it all the worse was the fact his post was a desk job that each of the Heathrow crew would gladly have, especially on mornings such as this.

"Constable Taylor, stand by for a shift change," his partner shouted above the din of an Aer Lingus jet beginning to take off, sticking his head out of the guard shack. This was more to alert Ethan that a vehicle would be approaching soon and to sharpen his focus at the task at hand.

***

Sitting in his office on a Saturday afternoon was not unusual for Thomas Sinclair, reviewing what seemed the fiftieth file that referenced the *M/V Joan of Arc* as part of its report. Each file contains information that Lloyd's would use for an insurance policy that a vessel might have written for it or its cargo.

In most cases, he found that the policies were written for the cargo but not the vessel. This would not be uncommon if the vessel was at the end of its useful service life, except that the vessel in question was still very much in service and not on its death throes as it were.

Turning the page, he noticed a reference to a parent company, *'Papillion Transport'*, it read. This was not the first instance that he saw that name, but he couldn't recall where. Turning to his computer, he typed in the name of the vessel under *'ownership'* and let the computer begin its search, pressing the 'enter' key.

After what seemed like ten minutes but was less than two, the computer stopped searching and displayed the results. The screen displayed *'Papillion Transport'*, which was listed as being based out of Marseille, France and the listed owner was *'Adrien Richelieu III'*. Looking over the other listings, it showed three other vessels, *'M/V Bonaparte, M/V De Gaulle, and M/V Cousteau II'* that made up the rest of the fleet. Leaning back in his chair, he considered the impact of his discovery. And more importantly, what it meant to his friend, Collingsworth at Scotland Yard.

Selecting the tab on his screen that read *'Other holdings'*, Thomas came across another nugget of information he hadn't expected, a listing for vessels sublet to *'Papillion Transport'*. Looking down the list, he saw that most were small vessels that plied the waters of the Mediterranean Sea between France, Italy, and Spain. Selecting the next page, he saw the name of two vessels William had mentioned before, *PSV Standard-Apollo* and *PSV Standard-Hercules*, showing their homeport as Aberdeen. The information also showed the boats being sublet to *'Papillion'* five years ago, on a fifty-year lease.

*That's rather odd,* he mused, knowing most vessels are lent to another company within their service life, which is normally five to ten years, but these were listed well beyond their usefulness. With the information at hand, he decided to take a chance and call his friend at Scotland Yard on his off day to pass along the information.

Closing the window of his computer search engine, he next opened his email program and selected *'Contacts'* and scrolled to William's name. Selecting it, he was greeted with his friend's information, which included his private mobile number. Picking up his office phone, he quickly dialed the number in hopes of not disturbing him on the weekend.

*'Hello, you have reached William Collingsworth, I'm not available…'* was what Thomas Sinclair's call was greeted by, hearing his friend's answering service take the call. As it ended and he heard the obligatory prompt, he quickly relayed to his friend that he should return his call and that he had important information regarding the Aberdeen situation.

With that done, Thomas quickly, but methodically, printed out the pages of the search that he had made for his records and so he had something to pass along to William when the time came.

***

Strolling through the grounds of the resort after dinner, the evening in the highlands came upon the couple as a cool and gentle breeze as they walked along the river by the resort. Andrew and Sheila had spent the better part of the day discussing their respective likes and dislikes as well as what each of them had thought of the other.

"I have to admit. I've rather enjoyed all this time and attention," Sheila said as they sat down on one of the benches overlooking the glen and river. Looking across the expanse of green foliage and hearing the gentle babble of the river flowing downstream, she felt very much at peace for the moment.

Looking at her, Andrew considered his response carefully. He too had enjoyed the closeness of the weekend and her company. His greatest fear was being separated from her now that they had become closer. "I've enjoyed it as well, and I'd like it to continue if you would?" he said, pulling her closer to him and placing a soft, passionate kiss on her lips. He realized that after all the women he had met and courted in the Royal Marines, he might have found the one he could be with for more than a just week or two.

"Andrew, I can't think of anyone else I want to be with right now." She sighed into his ear as she snuggled closer into his arms. She finally came to realize that this young man from London, *'the Sassenach'* might just be the one she had been looking for all along.

Sitting alone on the bench, embracing each other as two young people in love are seen doing, they didn't realize that the cool breeze from earlier had brought with it an early summer drizzle, which now was beginning to come down heavier.

"Best we get in and dry off before dinner," Andrew said, standing up and taking the hand of his newfound love.

"How about we call room service instead?" she responded, drawing him close, her mouth pressed against his with a passionate kiss, her tongue eagerly exploring his mouth, sparking a response in him he was becoming more accustomed to as his time with the young woman grew longer.

***

Sitting in the warm confines of the *'The First One'* eatery, Conor and Ailene were discussing the events of the day over a drink. As promised, they stood fast in the cool breeze that swept over the golf course and cheered the young constable from Victoria Station as he went on to a respectable finish, though his placement was out of any standing that would have paid back the entry fee.

"So, you're telling me Trevor could have done better if you were his caddie?" Ailene said with a hint of sarcasm to her delivery.

"Aye, I was the boys champion at *'King's Links'* back in my prime," Conor boasted to his lady friend, taking a sip of his scotch.

"And that makes you a better caddie than Trevor's friend?" she added, taking a sip of her coffee, which had been fortified with a quality brandy.

"He lost three strokes on his card just because he was talked into using the wrong club at the wrong time," the Scotsman said, thinking back to his youth when he played the game of golf.

As an only child growing up, Conor's parents did their best to try to have him get involved in all the popular sports; football, rugby, cricket, as well as golf. He found a sense of solitude and calm when he was on the golf course, which became close to his second home when not at school or busy with his studies.

Early on, he struggled with the true concept of the game until he met a young Irish pro named Padraig Cohan, who took a liking to the young lad and his golf game. Slowly, Padraig taught Conor the importance of knowing the land and the elements, as much as the swing when it came to the game. Soon, Conor was playing and beating golfing youngsters much older than him, and by several strokes each time. At one point, he was known to take a few schillings from members of the golf club, placing a wager on certain holes he'd become capable of mastering with the help of his tutelage from the young Irish pro.

"So, if I ever retire from the Yard, I think I would do quite well," he said, turning to Ailene but noticed she'd gotten up and left him alone, and that he was talking to an empty chair. *'Fancy that'* he thought to himself, taking the last swallow of scotch, feeling the warmth of the golden liquid burn as it cascaded down his throat.

***

"We hope your stay with us was enjoyable?" the clerk said to Andrew and Sheila as they proceeded to check out of their room. With the workweek looming, they decided it would be best to depart the resort early so that they would have time to return to Aberdeen and get things ready for their return to work the following morning.

"It was very enjoyable, thank you," Sheila responded, grasping the arm of Andrew, who collected the bill from the clerk and placed it in his trouser pocket. Realizing he wanted to spend more time with Sheila, Andrew took it upon himself to pay his fair share of the weekend. Based on his feelings, he reckoned that his next step would be moving into her flat when they returned to Aberdeen.

Reaching across his waist, Sheila said, "Give me that," alluding to the bill for the weekends stay.

"We'll settle this when we return to Aberdeen," Andrew responded, playfully pushing her hands aside with a Cheshire cat grin on his face. Contemplating the move into her flat, Andrew thought the first of his 'purchases' to help out would be a larger bed for the two of them, though he didn't mind the closeness so far in their relationship.

***

"I'll call you when I get myself settled," Ewan Sutherland said, planning to meet with the two *'police officers'* from Glasgow he saw on the train.

"Who are you meeting now?" Ian asked, handing his mate a cold beer.

Taking a quick drink of the offered beverage, Ewan said, "The two blokes from the train station."

"Are ya daft, man?" his friend asked, nearly spitting out a mouthful of lager in his friend's face upon hearing the statement.

"Turns out that Mr. Hunt had them dispatched to *'protect'* me if the local constables, the dockworkers, or deckhands on the boats tried to pinch me," he replied to his friend's question. "I'll be meeting them tomorrow outside the train station about nine or so," he added, letting him know he was going to keep his friend's flat location safe.

***

Having spent an eventful weekend or a quiet one depending on who you talked to, the two inspectors returned to their duties, considering the movement of illegal drugs through Aberdeen and the oilrig service boats.

"So, you had a good time?" Conor asked, looking across the desk at his young partner.

"Yes, it was quite nice," Andrew said, not wanting to let his true feelings for Sheila come blurting out to his partner. Recalling the last evening together after they came in from the rain, he called for room service and ordered a nice easy meal as they had difficulty keeping their hands off each other.

"And you had a quiet one as well, I take it?" he asked Conor, with the full knowledge that his partner had renewed a relationship with Ailene from the Maritime and Coast Guard Agency, which had started several years back.

"Aye, we went and cheered young Trevor from the Armory on while he competed in the local golf tournament at Nigg Bay," Conor replied, not wanting to divulge anything of a sordid detail about him and Ailene and the bedroom habits, lest he try them with Sheila and hurt himself or the young lass in the attempt.

"Can we get back down tae business? We know we've several vessels that we need to consider. How 'bout we take a stroll along the quays to start the week off right?" Conor said, looking at Andrew with a hint of playfulness in his eyes.

"All right, you warm up the car, and I'll go and check out the camera," Andrew said.

"You'll *nae* go and get a quick feel while on the job," Conor snapped back, knowing all too well that his partner was heading to the forensics lab for a quick hug and kiss from his lady friend.

Properly chastised, the young man from London shook his head, grabbing his coat from the back of his chair. "Fine, you win," he mumbled, grabbing the patrol car keys while walking out of the office.

After making the short drive from the police station to the docks on the east end of town, Fletcher parked the car near a small local eatery. From there he and McDermott could walk across to the waterfront and the service boats tied to the docks. Making their way amongst the containers stacked along the quay, they both began the task of looking for the thin blond chap from the previous week, or one of the dockworkers who had been to the meeting as well.

Having walked halfway down the length of the *'Albert quay'*, Fletcher noticed Ewan Sutherland talking to two men. Motioning to McDermott to go around the left side of a stack of containers, Fletcher proceeded along the right side, keeping a watchful eye on all three men.

Making his way closer to the threesome, the young inspector from London easily recognized the features of Ewan Sutherland as the man they saw meeting with the mysterious Arab from the previous week.

One of Stuart Ross' men finally caught on that Inspector Fletcher was walking towards them, and motioning to the other two, and began walking in the opposite direction. This move caused the two men to sojourn in the opposite direction, leading them to where McDermott was waiting.

As the two men from Glasgow moved away from Sutherland and closer to the safety of the containers, they began to relax more. After a few more paces, the two men finally turned the corner of a container stack only to collide with McDermott, as they'd lost sight of the second inspector. "Good morning, gentlemen," McDermott said loudly, surprised by the sudden appearance of the two men of the Glasgow crime syndicate, holding up his credentials and pistol motioning them to stop where they were.

With Conor confronting the two men working for Stuart Ross, Fletcher was seeing to Sutherland, who had turned and left in the opposite direction, placing him face to face with the Scotland Yard inspector. "I've a few questions for you, sir," Fletcher said, coming face to face with the tall blond-haired criminal.

"And who the hell are you to be questioning me?" Ewan replied defiantly, knowing the local police had no evidence that would allow them to hold him at the station.

"My name is Inspector Fletcher of Scotland Yard," flashing is identification at the young man.

"So, what do you want?"

Conor was having a similar conversation with the two men from the Glasgow syndicate, since this was the first encounter with them and he had no evidence to link them with anyone other than Ewan Sutherland.

"Last week you were seen with this gentleman," Andrew said, holding up a photocopy of the Arab from the previous week.

"Aye, what of it? He was lost and was asking for directions," Ewan said without a hint of nervousness to his voice.

"If that was the case, why were you seen leaving with him then?"

"He wanted a ride to the train station, so I obliged the chap," the young blond spoke with a sense of security, knowing the inspector had nothing on him.

"And the two gentlemen today, who are they?" Andrew asked, pointing to Conor and the two men sent from Glasgow to look after Ewan.

"Acquaintances' from out of town," Ewan said, which would turn out to be his first slip while talking to the Scotland Yard inspector.

"I see," Andrew replied, trying to think of how he could have the young criminal divulge the connection to the other two men.

As Andrew was questioning Ewan, Conor had finished his talk with the two men from Glasgow and had let them leave and walked towards his partner to see if he could assist in some way.

"You're free to leave," Fletcher said, seeing his partner walking toward him without the other men in tow.

"Good day," Ewan said, walking briskly away from the two inspectors, not wanting to be subjected to any more of the questioning lest he say something that would get him or the others in trouble.

Standing next to his partner, Conor asked, "Anything of consequence?"

"Seems the young man knew we might know something; but not enough to keep him," Andrew responded. "And it really hit him when I showed him the photo of the Arab."

"So, what was the young blond fella, who knows the mysterious Arab doing with two chaps from Glasgow?" Conor said, relating to Andrew what little information he had gleaned from Stuart Ross' men.

"It seems there might be more to just the Arab, and it might include someone from Glasgow now," Conor said. "Let's head back to the office and see if we can put a finger on the two chaps." He motioned his partner towards their parked car.

"It just might be our chance to expose the Irishman funding the drugs," Andrew said, alluding to the tip from the Portsmouth investigation.

***

Having checked off duty at Heathrow, Officer Ethan Taylor drove the twenty minutes to his apartment in the Fulham district of London, where he quickly shed his damp uniform and proceeded to take a quick shower, shaking off the early morning chill brought on by the drizzle and foggy conditions he endured while walking his post.

*How do I get the information on Gordon Wallace?* asking himself as he stepped out of the shower and began the task of drying off. Walking into his room, he pulled out a clean and dry uniform set and prepared it for his next shift. Having arranged his uniform and accessories for the next evening, Ethan proceeded to finish getting dressed, all the while considering his chances of getting the information his uncle had asked for last week. *I can't call Jones. He's too busy sniffing at Collingsworth's arse,* alluding to the portly clerk he worked with, but was a wizard with a computer.

Sitting at the small table in the kitchen, he recalled a former acquaintance was still working at the Hall of Records and decided to give her a call. Grabbing his cell phone, he quickly scanned his contact list until he came upon her name, Lena Boyd.

"Hello?"

"Lena? This is Ethan Taylor."

"Good morning," she said in a neutral voice, wondering why she was getting the unexpected call from her former date early on a Saturday morning.

"Lena, I was wondering if you could help me find a fellow who might've bumped my car by accident." Ethan asked.

"Lucky for you I'm at work. Give me the chap's name and I'll see what I can bring up."

"The gentleman's name is Gordon Wallace," Ethan said, adding, "I was re-assigned to Heathrow, and I think he might have been one of those harried travelers not paying attention in the car park." As he provided the name and brief lie to cover his request, Ethan could make out the tapping of fingers across the keyboard as Lena went about searching for the information.

Within moments, she was able to provide Ethan with some information. "My word, Ethan, you seem to have gotten nipped by a bad one," reading to the young constable the facts of the crime syndicate boss from Glasgow.

"Looking over the entries, it seems this fella has a history with Police Scotland. No outstanding warrants have been currently issued, but he's made several court appearances on accounts ranging from attempted burglary, money laundering, extortion, and one offence under Section 21. All of them have been documented in Scotland's High Court in Edinburgh," she said, reading off the accounts from her computer screen.

As Lena spoke of the issues she brought up during her search, Ethan quickly wrote them down to pass to his uncle. "I'm not sure you want to collect on the damages to your motor from this man," she said, ending what was currently in Scotland Yard's database for Gordon Wallace.

"I think you're right, Lena," Ethan responded, "but I do owe you a lunch sometime for helping me," he added.

"Give me a call next Saturday then," she replied, thinking of a posh eatery to have the young constable spend his money on her behalf.

"I will, *cheers*," he said, ending their conversation.

Looking at his wristwatch, Ethan decided it wasn't too early to give his uncle a call regarding the information found on Wallace. Selecting the correct number for Alistair Hunt's private phone, he pushed the phone icon and waited for the connection to engage.

"Good morn', Ethan," came the response from the man in Glasgow. "You're up early for a weekend, lad."

"Well, I've just finished with my shift at Heathrow as it were," the young constable said, relating how he was placed on the graveyard shift being the newcomer to the squad responsible for patrolling the sprawling facility, known as one of the busiest airports in the world.

"I've some news on Mr. Wallace," he continued speaking, relating to his uncle the details that his former date from Scotland Yard's Records Office had provided. "It seems Police Scotland has quite a write-up on him."

"Aye, I'm *nae* surprised at some of the events," the elder Scot said. "Thank you for getting that information for me," Alistair said. "Hopefully I won't have a need to ask you to place yourself at risk again."

"I'll do my best to help you," Ethan said. "I'm off to get a quick bite," he added, letting his uncle know that he was done discussing the matter with him.

"Fine, Ethan, I'll be in touch," Alistair said, ending the call.

# Chapter Eleven

Grasping her cup of tea with both hands, Ailene O'Leary dreaded the beginning of the workweek. All too often, she would have her desk cleared on a Friday afternoon, only to return to find a new stack of documents on a Monday. *No rest for the wicked.* She placed her tea down and grabbed the first folder from the pile.

Looking over the individual papers in the folder, they were comprised mostly of cargo handling, cargo storage, vessel docking, and fuel tax charges that each vessel was obligated to pay before the beginning of a new month, which was approaching fast.

Setting each folder aside in a methodical fashion, Ailene began to establish the order of action that she'd to be taking on each pile. One for each specific charge was soon laid out before her as she reached for the last of the twenty files for the morning.

Opening the folder, she noticed the billing document was for the payment of renewal for docking and fuel charges, but also listed a change of ownership for the vessel in question. Turning the first document over, she saw there was a sublet agreement for *PSV Oceanic-Ranger* to *'Callaghan and Higgins Limited'* in Belfast. She also noticed that the homeport for the vessel would be changed from Inverness to Upper Ingleston at Port Glasgow, on the west coast of Scotland.

Before placing the folder in the pile for payment, she made a note of the ownership change so she could pass it along to Conor, since he had brought up the name of the owners before. Now that she had her working order done for the morning, she took a break and went to the records room, where she retrieved the folder of the other platform service vessels that were listed under *'Callaghan and Higgins Limited'*, adding their information to the notes she made earlier.

Returning to her office, Ailene picked up the phone and dialed Conor's number at the police station. As the phone chimed in her ear, she gathered her notes in front of her, ready to pass everything to him.

"Hello, Deputy Chief Inspector McDermott, how can I help you?"

"How 'bout you treat me to a candlelight dinner, handsome?"

"Good thing Andrew did *nae* answer the phone now," he quipped, hearing her voice on the other end of the call.

"Aye, the young lad might have thought he had more than one lass chasing after him," she said with a laugh.

"Is that so? Now, what's the real reason for this call?" Conor asked.

"I've found something of interest for you," she said, spending the next few minutes going over the details of the report and the coincidence of the vessels having the same ownership.

"You've just earned another supper, lass," Conor said, writing his own notes. "I'll have to get back to you later, though, this needs to be called in down south," he said, referring to his supervisor at Scotland Yard.

***

Sitting at the desk reviewing completed documents from the weekend staff, Sergeant Gordon was hard-pressed to keep her concentration. Her thoughts continued to drift back to the time that she and Andrew had just shared at the resort in the highlands. Recalling the first night, she was surprised that Andrew was genuinely taken aback at the care and thought she had put into his comfort. Between the wine, fruit, and cheeses as well as the flowers, she could tell from his expression that everything was appreciated.

*I'm sure he appreciated the attention, since he showed it in many ways throughout the weekend. From the long thoughtful time spent pleasing me the first night, not worrying about himself, to his playfulness as we lounged in the lavender scented bath, it was nearly perfect.*

The silliest moment Sheila recalled was later in the evening as they were both lying in front of the roaring fireplace having a drink. It had never come up before then, but Andrew finally noticed the thistle tattoo on the right cheek of her butt. He playfully made a comment about the 'thorny bush' but then gently placed a kiss on the flesh around the artist's rendition of Scotland's national flower.

In moments, he was working his way to more intimate areas, nearly causing her to pass out from the orgasm he brought her to. Soon, they were both engaged in a tantric session of sex lasting longer than the fire, finishing in the dark, the embers dying well before they had reached a zenith of pleasure.

"Sergeant Gordon, answer the phone, will you!" one of the lab techs, shouted from the front counter of the forensic lab.

"What?" she asked, not realizing she'd allowed her thoughts of Andrew to partially render her deaf to her surroundings. "Sergeant Gordon," she said, picking up the receiver on the fifth ring.

"Good morning, Sergeant Gordon, this is Constable Ames at the district office. You're being summoned to the Administrative Supervisor's office at three o'clock today," the clerk on the other end of the phone said.

"Yes, certainly, three o'clock," she answered back to the other officer. "I'll be there."

Looking at the clock, she saw that it was nearing ten o'clock, so she'd have five hours before she would find out what the fuss was all about. Looking back at the front of the lab, she quickly offered her apologies to her colleague for not answering the phone.

"Devin, I'll need to leave 'bout two-thirty. They want to see me at district," Sheila said to her follow technician.

"Aye, I'll be fine," the young Scot with carrot-colored hair, said to his senior technician.

*What did I do?* asking herself, having never been summoned to the main police station before. *I'd had better let Andrew know at lunch that he's on his own till I'm done,* was her next concern as they had returned from their weekend and they'd agreed that he could stay with her for the time being.

***

Having discussed her appointment with Andrew over lunch, which she hardly touched, Sheila found herself sitting outside the Administrative Supervisor's office. Looking at her watch, she saw it was a minute to the top of the hour, and just as she pulled the sleeve of her uniform jacket down, the door of the office swung open.

Stepping out of the office was the Supervisor, Mr. Campbell, and noticing Sheila sitting in the hallway, he spoke, "Sergeant Gordon, we'll see you now."

Standing tall and setting her uniform squarely on her shoulders and hips, Sheila walked purposefully into the center of the office and to the front of the table set off to one side of the room.

"Sergeant Gordon, reporting as directed," she said, saluting the officers present.

"As you were," the senior constable directed her, allowing Sheila the chance to stand in a less rigid manner before them.

"Sergeant Gordon, you've been summoned to this hearing on the recommendation of your supervisor at the Victoria Road Station," Supervisor Campbell said, reading a prepared statement that sat in front of him.

"With the retirement of Inspector McCready, there's been a vacancy in the forensics lab here at headquarters, and you've been nominated to fill the post," he continued speaking.

Sheila heard the words from the supervisor, but had a hard time comprehending the significance behind the announcement. "Sir?" she asked, a slight tremble in her voice.

"Sergeant Gordon." It was the chief superintendent's turn to address her. "You're being promoted to the rank of inspector, with placement here in the district office."

"I'm not in any trouble?" she asked, the sudden realization beginning to hit her that all was well.

"No, you're most certainly not in trouble," Chief Superintendent (CS) MacCallum said, rising from his chair and walking around the table to congratulate her.

"Thank you, sirs," Sheila finally said, a tear of joy forming in the corner of her eye.

"You'll be required to report to district headquarters next week to begin processing and orientation," Supervisor Campbell said, bringing the proceedings to a close.

"Yes, sir. Thank you very much, sir," she replied, saluting them prior to leaving.

"Before you run off, I'd like to introduce you to the senior officer you'll be reporting to," Chief Superintendent MacCallum said, walking with her out of the office and towards the lab area.

Walking through the halls, Sheila began to sense the magnitude of the promotion, as there were three times the number of officers and offices than what she encountered at Victoria Road. Entering one of the offices opposite the lab area, the senior inspector began the introductions with the two officers sitting at their desks.

"Sergeant Wallace, this is Inspector Gordon," he introduced Sheila with her new rank to the officer coming to his feet first.

"Welcome, Inspector," Logan Wallace responded, shaking her hand.

"Good afternoon," she replied, hoping to remember his name when she returned next week.

"And this is Chief Inspector McIntyre, head of the facilities whom you'll report to," the chief superintendent pointed out.

"Pleasure to meet you, Inspector Gordon," McIntyre said, extending his hand to hers.

"Inspector Gordon, since being at Victoria Road, have you worked with the two chaps from London?" Sergeant Wallace asked.

"Not directly, no," she replied, surprised at the sergeant's request. "Why do you ask?"

"It's nothing. I was just curious what working with the *big city* types from Scotland Yard would be like," the sergeant said.

"Oh, well, I've…" she said.

Looking at his watch, CS MacCallum motioned her towards the door. "Shall we inspector?"

"I look forward to seeing you both next week," Sheila said, leaving the room with the senior inspector leading the way.

Walking back to his office, the chief superintendent pulled Sheila to one side of the hallway and away from the passing officers who were walking from one space to another. "Inspector Gordon, have you discussed your relationship with anyone in regards to Inspector Fletcher?" he asked, looking her straight in the eyes.

"How do you know about me and Andrew?"

"I'm made aware of many things, Inspector, but I need to know if you've said anything in an 'official' capacity," the senior officer asked.

"No, no one outside the station, sir. They all seem to know that Inspector Fletcher and I have been seeing each other," Sheila responded, surprised at the fact the chief superintendent knew of her relationship with Andrew.

"You should know that other than the Chief Inspector at Victoria Station, myself, and you, no one else knows of there being two inspectors here from London. Or the case Scotland Yard is working on here in Aberdeen," he related to her.

Hearing this news sent a cold shiver cascading down her back and beads of sweat began to form on her forehead. "How would Sergeant Wallace know then, sir?" she asked, having a genuine fear for her newfound love interest.

"I'm not sure, but I will find out," MacCallum spoke, "and I need you to keep mum on this as well."

"Yes, sir," she replied, hoping he didn't notice her hands trembling at her side.

***

After receiving the news about her promotion, Sheila Gordon rushed back to her flat to let Andrew know the good news. Sitting in her car outside the flat, she took several deep breathes to calm down from hearing of a potential informant knowing about Andrew.

Entering the small apartment, she smelled just finished roast pork coming from the kitchen. Pulling her uniform coat off, placing it over the couch, and tossing her purse on the cushions, she entered the small kitchen. Andrew was leaning over the stove, mixing the butter, milk, and freshly boiled potatoes that were meant to accompany the roasted loin of pork that sat resting on the counter when she stepped through the doorway.

Turning as she entered the room, he said, "Hope you don't mind, but I thought it best to have something ready for when you came home."

"It smells wonderful," she replied, wrapping her arms around his neck and placing a passionate kiss to his lips. The excitement of her promotion and seeing her lover cooking made her senses spike higher than she had ever felt.

"I would ask what that was all about, but I'm not going to bother as it seems you are rather happy about something," Andrew said after she broke off the kiss.

"I was granted a promotion," she responded. "I'll be working at the district office beginning next week."

"That's fantastic," he said, returning the kiss from earlier with one of his own.

"We'll have to figure out our arrangements, but I know we'll manage," Sheila mentioned, going to the refrigerator, and pulling out the leftover bottle of wine from their weekend getaway.

As Sheila opened the bottle of wine and poured two glasses, Andrew finished mixing the potatoes and heating the vegetables for dinner. He next took out a small carving knife, sliced the roasted pork, and placed it on the plates sitting out on the counter.

Sitting at the table, Andrew raised his glass. "A toast, to the most attractive forensics technician in the Aberdeen police force," he exalted.

"Thank you," Sheila replied, carefully touching her glass with his in acceptance of the offered toast. *"Slainte."*

***

Returning to Aberdeen from his meeting with 'Mr. Higgins' in Edinburgh, Captain Duncan went about gathering his things he'd need while at sea. Stopping at the local market, he purchased some items for dinner and made a stop at the local liquor shop to buy a bottle of scotch and several bottles of ale.

Entering his apartment, he quickly placed the food and drinks in the small icebox, then went to his room and began to pull his clean clothes together before packing his weathered and worn duffle bag that lay on the floor.

Returning to his kitchen, Captain Clive Duncan opened a leather-bound notebook and selected the first available blank page.

As he had done before every voyage to sea, whether it was for a day, a week, or months, Duncan wrote out his instructions in the event he should be injured or killed for the disposition of his belongings. Ever since his first voyage as a deckhand on an older WWII-era freighter out of Portsmouth, he'd learned that having one's affairs in order before departing was the safest means of sailing with a clear mind and conscience.

Finished writing the notes, he closed and tied off the notebook and placed it on the small nightstand in the front room, where Miss Kennedy knew of its location. Returning to the kitchen, he pulled out his evening meal and a bottle of ale, and once again took the pen to paper, but this time, he outlined his plan to meet with the French merchant ship.

Recalling the instructions passed on by Ewan Sutherland and from his meeting with 'Mr. Higgins', Captain Duncan noted that he'd need his senior deck crew present as they transferred an empty container from the deck of the *Nordic Supplier* to the freighter. Then reverse the process by taking the fully laden container from the freighter and securing it to their deck.

*Can I trust Malcolm with the information about the cargo?* He took a bite of his mince-meat pie. Knowing that as the first officer, Malcolm Spiers had every right to be made aware of what they were going to attempt; Cap'n Duncan had yet to confide in the young Scot as to what they were involved in when it came to the contents, the shipping of illegal narcotics. "I'll worry 'bout that tomorrow," he said to the empty room, taking a long swallow of beer from the bottle.

***

Rising before the sun crested the horizon was a common practice for Captain Duncan, and today was no exception. After showering and getting dressed, he quickly prepared and ate a small breakfast, remembering to clean the small pile of dishes in the sink. Making sure the gas was turned off at the stove, he called the local taxi service for a car while gathering his duffle bag and proceeding to the door.

Standing outside his flat, it was not but a few minutes before the taxi arrived and he climbed in. "*Albert quay, please,*" he announced to the driver, who quietly obliged the patron in the back.

In a short ten minutes, the taxi had arrived at the head of the docks, slowly becoming bathed in the golden amber glow of the rising sun. "Two quid, fifty," the driver declared, looking at his meter, letting the ship captain know what was owed.

Pulling a ten-pound note from his pocket, he handed it to the driver. "Keep the rest," he offered. Pulling his duffle behind him as he stepped out of the taxi, Captain Duncan began the short walk to his boat and the sleeping crew. Nearing the side of the boat, he looked up at the bridge wing and saw the silhouette of a crewmember pacing back and forth.

*Glad to see Spiers knows well enough to keep one member up.* He recalled the need to have one of the ship's crewmember up and alert to any dangerous situation always, even in port. Stepping over the side, he skillfully mounted the ladder leading up to the bridge where he encountered Seaman Carr standing her first bridge watch while in port.

"Morning, Captain Duncan," she announced excited, not expecting anyone entering the bridge at this early hour.

"Good morn', lass," the captain said, greeting her in a personal manner that was not usually the way most ships' captains addressed the crew, especially a junior seaman such as herself.

Just as the captain was preparing to enter his sea cabin located off the bridge, First Officer Spiers entered from the opposite side of the bridge. "Good morning, Cap'n," he said, acknowledging the vessel's master.

"Mister Spiers, you're relieved for the next forty-eight hours," Captain Duncan said. "Make a note in the logbook Seaman Carr to that effect."

This order caught the ship's first officer, Malcolm Spiers, off-guard.

"Yes, sir," he replied, walking to the navigation table and the ship's log, writing the captain's orders down as well as the date and time they were executed.

"Mister Spiers, when you return, we'll begin preparing the crew for an 'at-sea transfer' evolution," he directed at his first officer.

"Yes, sir," Malcolm replied. "Will it be pallets or a container?"

"It'll be a container, at least a twenty-footer. Moreover, we'll need to prepare the deck to receive one before we set sail. It'll get transferred for another." He noted that he was taking a risk by telling his first officer that much detail of what was to take place.

"Yes, sir." First Officer Spiers heard what the task was to be but wondering about the why.

"Enjoy your liberty," was the last thing he heard from the Captain Duncan, entering his cabin and shutting the door.

"You look a wee bit worried," the young female seaman said to her first officer on the bridge.

"It's nothing," he said. "Everything'll be just fine, I'm sure."

# Chapter Twelve

Having spent a wonderful weekend with his wife, Camille, in Dover, Chief Superintendent William Collingsworth walked back into his office at Scotland Yard to begin another attempt at ridding the British Isles of illicit drug traffickers. As was their custom, both he and his wife swore off using their cell phones one weekend a month, and so William missed the call from his friend at Lloyd's, which he was prepared to correct upon entering his office.

Sitting behind his desk, he leaned over and pushed the 'on' button to bring his computer to life, allowing him to see his calendars and appointments to determine when he could make the call to Thomas Sinclair. In a few moments, he was reviewing the various entries listed for the day and saw he had a space between a meeting with the other chief superintendents, which ended at eight forty-five and another meeting at nine, so he had fifteen minutes available.

Just so he wouldn't forget, William placed a reminder notice on the calendar, then sent an email to his colleague, letting him know about his availability. With that done, he settled down to review the morning dispatches and outstanding items he'd left from the past week.

"And that, gentlemen, is the conclusion of today's brief," the deputy chief constable said to the gathered staff members, which included William. Looking at his watch, he noticed the briefing finished ten minutes earlier than scheduled, so he knew he had time to contact Thomas as arranged. Walking back into his office, William picked up the phone and dialed the number for his friend.

Shortly after the second ring, the investigator for Lloyd's answered the phone, "Thomas Sinclair, can I help you?"

"Thomas, its William Collingsworth returning your call from Saturday."

"Ah yes, William. Sorry for trying to call on the weekend, but I thought it important to let you know what I found. After a little digging, I believe I found a clue to your two chaps' mysterious ship ownership," he said, pulling his notes out from the center drawer of his desk. Over the next ten minutes, Thomas filled in his friend on the ownership of the *Joan of Arc* being that of *'Papillion Transport'* of Marseille, France, but also the connection of the two platform service vessels as well.

"It seems there are at least three other freighters listed under *'Papillion Transport'* as well, but we've only encountered the one based on what your inspectors identified in their report," Thomas said.

"Is there a way to track down the owner?" William asked.

"We have what is on record, but if this company is involved in illegal activities, the chances are very small that it would be accurate, I'm afraid."

"So, from a legal standpoint the two PSVs had a reason to meet up with the freighter."

"Yes, they did, but the question could still be asked why the vessels met when and where they did," Thomas said, referring to the rendezvous a hundred and fifty kilometers from any other known anchorage point.

"Thank you for the information, Thomas. Next chance, the first round of drinks will be on me," William said.

***

Because of the search for a common link between the drug trafficking by their chief superintendent, the two inspectors now had additional information to investigate. Having learned of the owner's relationship between the PSVs and the French freighter they had identified, Inspectors McDermott and Fletcher began conducting another surveillance of the waterfront in Aberdeen.

"So, we know that the two PSVs have not left port based on what I gathered from Ailene," Conor said, preparing documentation for potential arrests they might make.

"And we know that this young Scot, Ewan Sutherland, was seen with an unknown Arab and several dockworkers in a possible drug transfer," Andrew added, finishing the document information on one of the arrest warrants.

Gathering up the necessary documents in a folder, Conor grabbed his field jacket as Andrew went to the lab to check out a camera and field kit used for testing drugs. Both inspectors knew it was better to be prepared in the event they apprehended someone with illegal drugs like hashish in their possession.

Entering the lab, Andrew quickly caught the attention of Sheila, who walked up to the counter and asked, "Can I help you, Inspector?"

"Yes, Sergeant," he replied. "I need to check out a camera and a drug kit."

Looking slightly perplexed, she reached under the counter and handed her lover a custody form to fill out for both items. "Might I remind you, Inspector, that I've recently been promoted in rank? I'm not a sergeant anymore," correcting Andrew with a smirk on her face.

"My apologies 'Inspector' Gordon," he said with a sour but playful look.

"Please remember to bring everything back in good order, won't you," she quipped, watching him fill in the necessary blank spaces on the custody form.

"You sound a wee bit like the technician who makes gadgets in those spy movies," Andrew replied to his companion.

"You don't want me to report your *'poor performance'*, now, do you?" she quickly chided the young man from London, knowing how well he could perform.

With that comment, Andrew slid the form across the counter to her. "I didn't think I ever had a *'poor performance'* that you're aware of," he replied to her barb at his bedroom activities and sexual prowess.

***

Driving to the same parking area near the *'Albert quay'*, the two inspectors once again took to their customary role of watching the activity take place on the various docks making up the Aberdeen harbor.

Walking along the southern access road of the quay, McDermott quickly noticed Ewan Sutherland standing amongst three dockworkers beside a row of containers. Continuing to walk along the access road, he also spied the two gentlemen from Glasgow that he had encountered the other day, but this time they were acting more as 'observers' rather than lost citizens.

Bringing his gaze back to where Ewan was standing with the dockworkers, McDermott noticed two of the burly seamen grabbing Ewan, while the third took a swing at the young Scot with what seemed to be a pipe. The swing caught the former football player a glancing blow to the side of the torso, but still caused him to double over in pain.

Pulling his service weapon from his side, Fletcher quickly ran towards the four men, his reaction just a second quicker than McDermott. At the same time, the two men dispatched from Stuart Ross also sprang into action to come to the young Scot's defense. "Police, drop the pipe!" Andrew shouted, pointing his weapon at the stevedore holding the rusted length of metal in his hands.

Just as his partner was drawing his weapon on the dockworker, McDermott was rushing from the other side of the quay, his weapon drawn and held low to his side, coming upon the two men from Glasgow. "Hands where I can see them!" he yelled at the two crime syndicate members, who each had pulled out weapons of their own. Outnumbered by the criminals, McDermott pulled his cell phone from his pocket, quickly calling the station for help, as he and Andrew were in this game of cat and mouse.

Looking over at Andrew, Conor could see he had the three dockworkers standing against the container, hands placed against the side and their backs turned toward him, allowing him to keep his weapon trained on them in a precarious balance of abduction. He also noticed the young Scot, down on one knee clutching his side and struggling to breathe, the result of two broken ribs.

As all this was taking place, the faint sound of sirens could be heard echoing across the harbor as more police arrived at Conor's summoning to provide their assistance. Also, an interested bystander was watching the proceedings from the deck of his vessel, as Captain Duncan noticed his contact from Glasgow take the hit from the stevedore and then fall to a knee, clutching the point of impact.

As constables were responding to the call from Conor at the *'Albert quay'*, the three suspects were quickly subdued and placed in separate vehicles and taken to district headquarters. The notable exception to this being Ewan Sutherland. Several members of the responding medical crew were preparing him for transporting to *'BMI-Albyn Hospital'* for treatment under the watchful eye of Inspector Fletcher.

As Sutherland was wheeled into the hospital, nurses began preparing him for an examination by the doctor on call. As they removed his personal belongings from his clothes, an odd-looking package fell to the floor.

"I'll take that," Inspector Fletcher told the lead nurse, holding out an empty evidence bag in front of her. Looking at the small package through the clear evidence bag, it was evident to the young inspector that this was not a common substance.

Sutherland was still in an extreme amount of pain, but the look on his face seeing the nurse deposit the 'balloon' of hashish in the evidence bag was enough for the inspector to realize he'd caught the young Scot with a portion of illegal drugs for sale.

"Ewan Sutherland, on behalf of His Majesty and under the Authority of the High Court of Scotland, you're under arrest for possession of illegal drugs," Andrew said. "You have a right to trial and representation, do you understand?"

"Aye, I understand," the former mid-fielder said, dropping his head onto the pillow, resigned to his fate with the police.

"Nurse, could you please sign this as witness to Mr. Sutherland's acknowledgement," Andrew said, addressing the lead nurse in the room.

"Aye, with pleasure," she responded, signing the police document where Fletcher was pointing towards.

"Thank you," he said, looking down at the suspect lying in the bed being treated. Looking at the document, Andrew asked, "I'm sorry, but what's your first name? I can't seem to read your signature?" He requested the nurse for clarification on her name.

"It's Catherine, with a 'C' and no middle name," she said, turning her attention back to the patient.

While Inspector Fletcher was dealing with Ewan at the hospital, Chief Inspector McDermott was at district headquarters questioning one of Stuart Ross' men about his involvement at the dock. To the chief inspector, the interrogation room felt like a broom closet compared to the one in London.

"I told you. I was paid by the young one's uncle to look after him," the felon said, answering McDermott's questions.

"Aye and you just happen to have a loaded pistol on you to help, as you say, 'look after' the lad," the inspector replied. Looking down at his notes that he took while questioning the first of the men from Glasgow. *Their stories matched in that they both said they were looking out for Ewan,* he mused as he read the notes from his earlier interrogation. As McDermott was preparing to ask another question, there was a knock at the door. A brief look of disgust came over his face, since he hated interruptions while questioning suspects, especially if it was for a minor matter, but this was not minor.

"Excuse me, Chief Inspector; can I have a brief word with you?" the senior sergeant, John Giles, asked, sticking his head in the open door.

Closing the folder that was in front of him, McDermott rose from the table and walked out the door as the sergeant closed it behind him. "You have something for me?"

"Aye, sir, Inspector Fletcher thought it'd be important to tell you he found drugs on the suspect being treated at the hospital."

With this piece of information, McDermott now needed to tread lightly in his questioning of Stuart Ross' men so as not to give away his advantage that was just handed to him.

"Thank you, Sergeant Giles."

"Mr. Smith, your young charge is being detained on suspicion of assisting in the act of drug trafficking," Conor stated, standing in front of the man from Glasgow.

"I don't know of any drugs. I was hired to just watch the lad."

"Well, the court will decide what you were really doing. On behalf of His Majesty and under the jurisdiction of the High Court of Scotland, you're under arrest for harboring and aiding a felon in the transportation and distribution of illegal drugs," Conor stated. "You've a right to representation before trial, do you understand?"

"I do, and I want to contact my barrister right now," Mr. Smith said, looking at Conor with a look of smug indignation.

This same scene was played out with the other member of Stuart Ross' syndicate as Mr. Brown was also read the charges being brought before him and his rights under Scottish law, which he too acknowledged, also requesting a visitation by his barrister.

***

Shortly after finishing his meal at his favorite eatery on Jamaica Street, Stuart Ross' cell phone chirped loudly as a texted message was delivered. Looking down at his phone, he noticed that the text message was coming from Angus Dunbar, so he opened the message and read it.

*Brown and Smith in custody. ES hurt at docks,* was the body of the message, and the meaning sent a chill down the seasoned syndicate member's back as it foretold that he was in for a long night.

Closing the message, Stuart quickly scrolled through the contact list until he came across the private number for Alistair Hunt. Knowing he was going to endure the most of what was to come from the syndicate leader, he selected the number and allowed the phone to auto-dial the number for him.

"Hello?" Alistair said.

"*Good* evening, Mr. Hunt, it's Stuart Ross," he said in response to his employer's greeting.

"What can I do for you at this hour, Mr. Ross?" Alistair asked. *It's late for him to be calling me. It's nearly half past seven in the evening.*

"I've just received a message regarding some activity in Aberdeen," he said, "and it's not good."

"What is it that you've heard?" Hunt asked, listening with his full attention.

"It seems both of my men, Brown and Smith, have been detained by the police," Ross explained.

"Go on," Alistair directed his associate to continue explaining the situation.

"It also appears that young Ewan was injured in an altercation at the docks today," the syndicate associate added.

"Do you have any further details?" Hunt asked, knowing he needed to contact Gordon Wallace as soon as possible.

"No, sir, but I'll be leaving for Aberdeen shortly to see if there's anything I can do," was Ross's only response in hopes of avoiding the wrath of the syndicate boss.

"Fine," Hunt answered, ending the call.

Sitting in his front room, Alistair Hunt quickly thumbed through his contacts list until he came across the number for his counterpart in the Glasgow crime world, Gordon Wallace. Picking up the receiver of his desk phone, he quickly dialed the number and waited for the call to be answered. On the third ring, a familiar voice answered his call.

"*Good* evening," the booming voice of Gordon Wallace filled the earpiece as he spoke.

"Gordon, it's Alistair Hunt."

"Aye, Ali, what can I do for you?"

"I have an associate in Aberdeen who was hurt in a scuffle and by chance was pinched by the authorities. The young lad knows a few things and I need to find out what he's being charged with, so I know what assistance I can provide," he said.

"Aye, Ali, I've got a man I can call. Give me a few hours," Gordon said.

"Thank you, Gordon, I'll be waiting for your call," Alistair said.

***

He knew his friend was asking for a repayable favor, but Gordon was always reluctant to involve his cousin by calling him directly, but tonight he would make an exception. Getting up from the chair in the front room of his house, Gordon made his way to his study where he kept a separate phone used when calling certain numbers and his cousins was just such a number.

Sitting at the antique roll-top desk, he pulled out a card file where he kept family information. Thumbing through the myriad of three by five cards with the various names and family relationships on them, he finally came across the one he was looking for. Pulling it out, he turned and began dialing the number written on it.

After the second ring, a woman's voice answered the phone, "Hello?"

"Good evening, Maggie, it's Gordon," he replied, letting his cousin's wife know who was calling.

"Good evening, Gordon. I take it you need to speak with Logan?" the woman said with a touch of sarcasm to her voice.

"Aye, if you please."

"Aye, Gordon, how are you?" the young cousin asked, taking the phone from his wife.

"I need information on Ewan Sutherland tomorrow, everything you can," Gordon said.

"I'll try and make it to the match. What time should I be there?" Logan asked.

"As soon as possible, and call me directly," Gordon said with a terse and abrupt response.

"Aye, I'll see you then, cheerio," Logan answered before hanging up the phone.

"And what was that all about?" Maggie Gordon asked her husband.

"Gordo has a free seat for an upcoming football match and was asking if I would like to attend," the sergeant responded with a clever lie.

"Well, if he's paying the bill, then you can go," she said. "Come on, yer dinner's getting cold." She ushered him to the table, unaware of the illegal act her husband was just asked to perform for his cousin.

# Chapter Thirteen

In the aftermath of making their arrests at the *'Albert quay'*, McDermott and Fletcher were both busy finalizing the mountain of paperwork associated with the arrest of multiple suspects. This was a task that McDermott took to with distain, hating the use of the computer, less his awkward two-fingered typing skill be revealed.

One item that had to be completed was the signing of the evidence log by Andrew for the drugs confiscated from Ewan Sutherland while being treated for his injuries. Walking through the district building, Andrew stopped one of the constables for directions to the forensics lab.

"Two doors down and to your right," the constable said, directing the inspector from Scotland Yard.

As he entered the doorway, he spied the familiar outline of his love interest's voluptuous, round ass under the lab coat, bending over an open filling cabinet returning documents to their proper folder.

"Excuse me, Inspector Gordon?" Andrew asked, clearing his throat in the process.

Looking around from her compromised position, Sheila blushed with surprise, seeing Andrew at the counter staring at her backside, holding a custody form in his hand and a sheepish grin on his face. Gathering her wits about her, the new inspector stood up and walked the few paces to the counter. "What can I do for you?" she asked, a motherly scowl on her face, letting him know she was not amused at his boyish manner of staring at her backside.

"I'm here to complete the chain of custody for the evidence brought in yesterday."

Reaching under the counter, Sheila pulled out the logbook from yesterday's activities and turned to the section marked "Narcotics."

Preparing to turn the book towards Andrew, Sergeant Logan Wallace walked in with an armful of documents for filing. Noticing the inspector, he greeted the young man. "Great work earlier today by you Scotland Yard-types, Inspector Fletcher. Getting the goods on the young chap at the docks."

Caught off-guard, Andrew's only response was, "Yes, quite right, I suppose," having finished signing the custody log for Sheila. "I'll be in touch if there is anything else to attend to," he said, walking out of the lab area.

"How do you know the inspector, Sergeant Wallace?" Sheila asked.

"Well, the news is all over the office about him and his partner nabbing the druggie at the dock," the desk sergeant said, placing the documents in their proper slots for filing.

"Oh, I suppose it is," she responded, knowing she was having a conversation with a possible police informant to a criminal organization. Turning away from the counter, she returned to her desk where she quickly made a note about the conversation and time, having been instructed to do so by Chief Superintendent MacCallum.

Returning to the office used by the other district inspectors, Andrew caught Conor's eye and nodded for him to meet outside the space.

"Aye, what's buggin' ya, lad?" Conor asked, glad to have a break from typing out the reports, seeing the concerned look on his face.

"I was just completing the log for the drugs found on Sutherland and one of the desk sergeants called me out by name," Andrew said.

"By name?"

"Yes. I think he might be the one who the chief superintendent had mentioned to me the other week."

"Well then, let's you and I go and bid farewell to Chief Superintendent MacCallum and let him know what happened," Conor said.

***

"I'm out for a wee bit of fresh air," Sergeant Wallace said to the constable working the administrative office.

"Aye, *nae* too long," the police officer sitting opposite him said, hoping she would have a chance at a smoke soon, her craving for nicotine hardly suppressed by the silly patch on her arm.

Walking through the double doors at the front of the district office, Sergeant Wallace quickly turned and walked out toward the car park and the promise of privacy, pulling his cell phone out to call his cousin, dialing the number to a phone located one hundred fifty kilometers to the southwest in Glasgow.

"Hello?"

"Gordon, its Logan and I've bad news."

"Go on, what is it?" the older Scot asked, prompting his cousin to divulge what information he had.

As the police sergeant spoke, he failed to notice the approaching inspectors walking up behind him. Continuing to describe the situation that Sutherland and the two men from Stuart Ross had been caught in, Conor and Andrew stepped in front of him, causing the sergeant to stutter his final statement to his cousin.

"What the hell is going on?" the sergeant demanded to know, seeing his superior walk up from behind a parked car.

"Sergeant, for the moment you are being placed into custody for conduct unbecoming of an officer of the Crown," Chief Superintendent MacCallum said as one of the constables stepped behind the sergeant and directed him to return to the station.

"I'll take that," Conor said, grabbing the cell phone from the sergeant's hand.

"That's private property," the sergeant said.

"That's okay. I know the inspector working forensics. She'll see that it is documented as belonging to you," Andrew quickly replied to the sergeant's protest.

As the constables led the sergeant away to the interrogation room, Conor turned to the chief superintendent and asked, "What will he really be charged with?"

Chief Superintendent MacCallum thought for a moment since he didn't want the informant released on a technicality. "Providing information that could have compromised an ongoing drug investigation is the first item. We'll have to see where the number from his recent phone call leads us before we do anything else." He walked back to the district office to prepare the incident report to his superiors in Edinburgh.

Walking back into the district office building, Conor and Andrew made their way to the forensics lab. Walking in, they found Sheila standing at the counter with an empty evidence bag and custody form waiting.

"Word spreads fast," Andrew said, reaching for the form, filling in the appropriate boxes with the information regarding Sergeant Wallace's cell phone.

"Aye, almost as soon as he walked out of the building the chief superintendent notified Chief Inspector McIntyre," she related to the two inspectors.

"Well, it's now a matter of finding out who he was talking to and how much was discussed," Conor said, handing the phone to Sheila for placement in the evidence bag.

"Here you go," Andrew added, holding out the custody form to her.

"Thank you, inspectors. I'll handle it from here."

Looking at Andrew, she added, "And I'll see you this evening."

***

Returning to the office at the Victoria Road police station, the two Scotland Yard inspectors were greeted with a warm welcome as word had reached Sergeant McCord from his counterpart at the district office. "On behalf of us constables," the sergeant said, "you've our deepest appreciation for finding out that bad apple."

"The likes of him hurt us all," McDermott said, shaking the hand offered from the desk sergeant in the lobby.

Entering their office, he and Fletcher found a message from Chief Superintendent Collingsworth hanging from their desk lamp.

"Call as soon as possible," Andrew said.

"Well, I guess we call."

***

"Your report will be filed later today," the chief superintendent said to his colleague, who was requesting assistance with an issue with one of his subordinates. Just as the fellow inspector had left Collingsworth's office, the phone rang. "You'll excuse me." He picked up the receiver.

"Hello, Chief Superintendent Collingsworth."

"Afternoon, William," Conor said.

"Conor, I'm glad you called back when you did," the senior officer said, pulling a file from his desk drawer.

"What seems to be the issue?" Andrew asked.

Conor just looked at this partner and shrugged his shoulders in a sign of not knowing.

"I need you and Fletcher to return to London for a briefing tomorrow morning," Collingsworth said.

"With all due respect, William; what the hell for?" Conor asked.

"I can't discuss the topic over open lines, but it does directly pertain to your current investigation," Collingsworth said, not wanting to divulge any more information than necessary. "You and Fletcher are booked out of Aberdeen on the British Airway flight that leaves at six o'clock tonight, and I'll have a car waiting for your arrival."

"Aye, so much for my dinner date," Conor quipped. "We'll see you in the morn' then," hanging up the phone.

"What did you mean by *'see you in the morning'*, Conor?" Andrew asked.

"We've been summoned, lad. The chief superintendent needs us in London for a briefing in the morning." *How am I going to break the news to Ailene?*

"Both of us?" *How in the hell do I tell this to Sheila?* He thought of his companion, with whom he was just beginning to develop a comfortable routine.

"Aye, so we best get our bags packed. We have a seat waiting for us on the six o'clock flight," Conor said.

Grabbing the phone from the center of the two desks, Andrew quickly dialed the direct number to the forensics lab at district headquarters to talk with Sheila about the latest orders from London.

After two rings, the phone was answered. "Forensics. Inspector Gordon speaking," she said.

"Sheila, it's Andrew."

"What is it, Andrew? You were just here an hour ago, what's on your mind now?"

"Conor and I were just called back to London, and we leave on a flight tonight," Andrew said.

"For how long?" *I was just getting used to having him in my bed, now he's packing his bags?*

"I'm not sure. Conor just said the chief superintendent needs to have us present for a briefing tomorrow morning."

"Well, give me a call when you know you're returning," Sheila said.

"I will. As soon as I can," Andrew said. *She doesn't seem pleased hearing this news, but it's not my fault, it's the chief's.*

Standing in the car park, Conor was explaining the same situation to his lover, Ailene. "I'm sorry, hen, but I need to go," Conor said.

"And you'll be coming back when?" Ailene asked. *I hope this isn't some ploy to move out. I'm getting rather fond of his touch again.*

"I dinnae know now, but as soon as I do I'll give you a call." *I don't know how long. It was William calling me and Andrew to London. I did nae plan this.*

"You do that or I'll have yer guts for garters, laddie!" she exclaimed, making sure he fully understood her displeasure at the sudden departure. *Another lonely night in bed, isn't it, hen?*

***

"Chief Superintendent, I've run the report that you requested," the sergeant from administration, said entering the senior constable's office at the Aberdeen district HQ.

"Thank you, Sergeant Giles, that'll be all," MacCallum replied to the desk sergeant.

Reviewing the printout, he read each line of information. *How in bloody hell did we miss him being an informant?*

Looking at each entry, he scrutinized the information, hoping to discern something out of the ordinary. *Nothing in the printout seemed out of the norm from any other constable's record. Place of birth, next of kin, living relations, schooling, financial status, marital status, it all seemed to be in place.*

Sitting back and looking out his window, Chief Superintendent MacCallum saw several of his officers walking through the car park heading home, and most had their cell phones out doing something. That was what struck him as he pushed his intercom button, asking Sergeant Giles to return to his office.

"Yes, sir?" Sergeant Giles asked.

"Can we get a printout of all the calls, coming and going, mind you, from Sergeant Wallace's phone?" he asked.

"Certainly, sir. It might take a wee bit, but we'll get it."

"Have the night watch put it all together, and then you head home. Let them know I'll expect it in the morning," MacCallum said.

"Aye, sir," Sergeant Giles said, glad to know he could pass the request to his relief and head home for the evening.

*Rest assured, I'll find out who you talked to, Mister Wallace.* He knew he needed to do it for his officers, as well as for himself.

***

"Please bring your seats to their full and upright positions as we prepare to land," the flight attendant exclaimed as the British Airways Airbus A319 slowly began its descent into Heathrow Airport.

"Fancy yourself a rock star, Andrew?" Conor asked. *He does nae realize someone would be at the terminal with a sign just for them.*

"Not really." *I'm just realizing how much I'm going to miss squeezing into that small bed with Sheila tonight.*

With a jolt, the pilot touched the aircraft onto the tarmac and began the process of slowing the craft down to a controllable speed as they taxied off the main runway, allowing a Lufthansa A380 to begin its long and laborious roll-out as it was beginning its journey to Cape Town, South Africa.

Within minutes, they had arrived at the gate, where Conor and Andrew used their credentials, allowing for a quick exit from the aircraft and the brief stroll down to the arrival lounge and baggage claim. Riding the escalator downward, Andrew was the first one to spot the sign held by the attractive red-headed constable that read *'Fletcher & McDermott'* standing behind a group of students from a local boarding school from the look of their attire.

"I'm Inspector Fletcher," Andrew said. "And this is Chief Inspector McDermott." He pointed to the scraggily Scotsman in the rumbled field jacket.

"Good evening, gentlemen. I'm Constable Harris. I've been assigned to escort you to the hotel, as well as to the Yard in the morning," the young police officer said, her tone being a matter-of-fact fashion to the two men who stood before her.

"Aye then, best we get moving," Conor said.

Stepping through the doors of the terminal, Constable Harris walked directly to the driver's door of the unmarked BMW X5 parked at the curb, its blinkers flashing in annoyance to the other drivers being ushered about by the local security details, one of them being Constable Taylor.

"Conor, I was wrong and you were right," Andrew said, getting in the back seat of the SUV.

"Aye, and what was that?"

"Did I miss something?" Constable Harris asked.

"I do feel like a rock star," Andrew said, looking through the dark-tinted windows at the passing crowds.

## Chapter Fourteen

Sitting in the lounge of the St. James Court hotel, Conor and Andrew were in the process of finishing their breakfast as Constable Harris walked into the lobby. Seeing the two inspectors from last night sitting in the lounge, the bubbly young redhead, dressed and pressed for another day in uniform, made her way to the table.

"Good morning, gentlemen," she said, standing tableside.

"Good mornin'," Conor said.

"Good morning, Officer Harris," Andrew said, standing as did his partner but also offering a chair to the young woman to sit in.

"You have but a few minutes before we need to depart for your meeting."

"Aye, come on, Andrew, finish your tea," Conor said, quickly finishing his own cup and last bite of toast.

"You can pay the bill," Andrew said, pointing to the server who just exited from the kitchen.

***

"So, your investigation has turned up an interesting situation," Chief Superintendent Collingsworth said as his two officers sat on the opposite side of the conference room table. In addition, sitting at the table was Thomas Sinclair from Lloyd's, who was going to provide them with another piece to their puzzle.

"You see," Thomas said, "the *M/V Joan of Arc* is part of a fleet for *'Papillion Transport'*, which is the shipping firm owned by *'Adrien Richelieu III'* of Marseille."

"And that means what tae me?" Conor asked. *I left Ailene to be lectured by this grumpy old fella?* He felt he could have been told this over the phone.

"It means that you have uncovered a *'ghost corporation'*, I'm afraid," Thomas said. "The owner doesn't exist. Well, actually he did at one time. You see, Adrien Richelieu was a French industrialist in the 1800s who legitimately owned a small fleet of vessels that sailed the Mediterranean.

He eventually sold his interest in shipping and settled in Marseille where he became a lucrative banker and a member of the regional parliament, and from what can be found in the records, neither he, his brother nor any other family member ever restarted the business. However, the transport company also lists control of your two service vessels that you have under surveillance," he concluded as he added a new twist to the plot.

"How does that help us?" Andrew asked. *Sheila will not be happy to hear I left her to listen to a history lesson by a Lloyd's adjuster.* He wanted to be back in bed with his lover.

"You pointed out that the service vessels met with the freighter," Collingsworth said, adding to the conversation. "This, from a legal standpoint is for all intents and purposes, very legitimate."

"But the question that still needs answered is why they met, when they did," Thomas said. "There's still the possibility they made some transaction while at sea."

"What we need to do now is begin considering the support vessel activities themselves," Chief Superintendent Collingsworth said. "You'll also need to look at the activities of the crewmen while onshore, as well as where the vessels are going when at sea."

"And how do we go about getting them to cooperate, William?" Conor asked. "It's *nae* likely they'll greet us with open arms."

"With the help of Thomas and information held by Lloyd's of London, we've secured a vessel changing its homeport from Inverness to Aberdeen. You'll have the services of Captain Thomas Kinkaid and his vessel the *Oceanic-Talisker* when you return," Collingsworth said, sliding a folder in front of Conor. "Your task is to work with the captain and determine what the other PSVs are doing after they contact the freighter," the superintendent said.

"My counterpart in La Havre has told me that two of the freighters in the fleet, *M/V De Gaulle* and *M/V Bonaparte* have recently set sail from Marseille, so we suspect that one will make its way north into the Channel in the coming days," Thomas said.

"There you have it. Best get moving. You have an eleven twenty-five flight back to Aberdeen," Collingsworth said. "And, by the way, good job on apprehending the suspect last night," wanting to make sure he showed his appreciation for their effort.

"How did you find out so quickly?" Conor asked.

"Oh, did I forget to mention. Bruce MacCallum and I were cadets in the academy together," he replied, letting the inspectors know how the senior officer in Aberdeen could be trusted with their identities so easily.

***

Pulling up to the departure gate for domestic flights at Heathrow, Constable Harris was preparing to discharge her passengers that she'd only picked up the previous evening. "There you are, gentlemen," the young police officer announced, placing the vehicle next to the red painted curb and engaging the hazard flashers.

"Service with a smile," Conor said, opening the passenger door of the SUV, just as Constable Taylor walked up from the rear of the vehicle.

"You can't park here," Taylor said.

"Is that so, Officer?" Conor asked, looking at the young police officer standing in front of him, pulling his credentials out from his jacket pocket.

"Sorry, sir," Ethan blurted out, reading the credentials and realizing whom he'd just confronted.

Turning back to the open car door, Conor said, "Thanks again, hen, be safe," to Constable Harris, shutting the door and walking around the front of the vehicle where he joined Andrew standing at the curb, who watched the pander back and forth between Conor and the constable. Stepping onto the curb, Conor watched as Constable Harris pulled the BMW back into traffic and disappeared amongst the other drivers circling the airport thoroughfare.

"Shall we get on with it?" Conor said to his partner as they entered the terminal to catch their return flight to Aberdeen and their assigned task from the chief superintendent as well as their significant others.

***

Pacing back and forth in his office on Argyle Street in downtown Glasgow, Alistair Hunt was nervous at the thought of facing his friend Gordon Wallace this day. Just last evening he'd learned that not only did Stuart Ross' men and Ewan Sutherland get pinched at the docks in Aberdeen, but he also learned that Gordon's cousin, a sergeant with the police, was detained as well.

"Mr. Hunt? Mr. Gordon just called. He'll be late for the meeting by a few minutes because of traffic," Janice said, sticking her head into the office.

"Thank you, Janice," Alistair said, looking down Brown Street at the sliver of waterway that was the River Clyde. *Is there a chance that Gordon would be implicated by his cousin? I can't recall ever taking a call from Gordon's cousin, but did Janice? And what about Robert Burns, did he ever talk with the policeman?* Looking out the window, he caught the reflection of himself in the glass, a worried look etched on his face, contemplating the effects of what has transpired over the last forty-eight hours.

Entering the outer office of Alistair Hunt, Gordon Wallace not only had exhibited the mannerisms of a man who had not slept the previous night, but he also had the appearance to match. Disheveled hair, red blood-shot eyes, and a growing stubble of an unshaven face were the indicators of the troubling night the Scot had just endured.

"I'll show you in, Mister Wallace," Janice said politely, seeing the troubled look on his face. Escorting the burly man to her employer's door, she opened it, announcing the guest's arrival. Stepping through the door, Gordon's look of a once proud man was more of one who had just taken a severe blow, like that of a heavy weight boxer.

"Good morning, Gordon," Alistair said. "Please take a seat," motioning him to the couch.

Both men took a moment to collect their thoughts; one not wanting to say something that would aggravate the open wound that had just been made; the other not wanting to show his vulnerability by asking for the help he desperately needed.

"So, Alistair, do we have any more news about our next effort?" Gordon asked. *I don't need to dwell on Logan or his pending incarceration.* He wrung his hands instinctively.

"Aye, we'll be providing security for a container being shipped in from off-shore," Alistair said, "to the port in Belfast, and then to a place I've not yet determined or been told about."

"Does your contact have plans to provide us with vehicles?"

"I'm *nae* sure, but I'll make a note to ask him during our next meeting," Alistair said, writing down the question regarding the vehicles as well as the location to be guarded.

"Is there anything I can do to help out?" Alistair asked.

"You mean with Logan? He knew what he was getting involved in," Gordon said. *Alistair has every right to ask that question, and I'm sure he's concerned for the family, as well as his own organization.* He recalled how his cousin offered to help him after his posting in Police Scotland's force.

"I've already heard from Ross. He'll be sending his barrister to argue the case of 'innocent bystanders' to the magistrate for his two men," Alistair said. "But with Sutherland, I'm not sure I can help him since they're considering him the drug dealer."

"You can't get it pinned on one of the dockworkers?" Gordon asked.

"Aye, but only if I can be assured that their fingerprints are also on the drugs that were being passed," Alistair said. *So many of issues to deal with, plus those surrounding the possibility of that the seamen being implicated were mounding quickly.* He wondered about the impact to his current operations.

"We'll get through it, lad, we always have," Gordon said, seeing the concerned look on his friend's face. "So how 'bout a wee dram to settle the nerves, heh?"

"Aye, it's *nae* too early, is it?" Alistair said. Walking to the cabinet, he pulled out the ever-present bottle of single malt scotch and two of the lead-crystal tumblers.

***

Arriving back at Aberdeen from their brief trip to London, Conor and Andrew were met at the terminal by Sergeant Giles of the district headquarters staff, advising them that they were to meet with Chief Superintendent MacCallum.

"Pleasant trip?" MacCallum asked as they were shown into his office by the sergeant.

"Aye, it was *nae* bad for BA," Conor said. *British Airways at times is known to be delayed for some of the silliest reasons.* He shook his head.

"Well, I've got good and bad news to share," MacCallum said. "The two chaps from Glasgow have a barrister submitting for a dismissal, while your young Mister Sutherland did not sustain any *'life-threatening'* injuries, just two fractured ribs."

"And that's the good or the bad?" Andrew asked.

"That's the good news," MacCallum said. "The bad news is that CI McIntyre found several sets of fingerprints on the baggie of drugs you recovered and none of them belong to the two chaps from Glasgow."

"So, the person we thought was the drug dealer is really who we thought. As long as he doesn't argue that the drugs were planted on him," Conor said, sitting back in the chair, rubbing a hand across his face.

"I'm afraid so," MacCallum said. "That will be something for the courts to decide as well. On a more positive note, I've been asked by William to place several of my constables at your disposal for your investigation."

"Do we have a sense of their loyalty?" Andrew asked. "I mean, we've just uncovered one bad apple from the current ranks."

"You will have my guarantee that the officers who work with you know their duties and their loyalties to the crown, Inspector Fletcher," the chief superintendent said, snapping back at Andrew.

Sensing the tension, Andrew replied, "I didn't mean to be disrespectful, sir."

"I know you didn't, young man, but it pains me to find out that this informant was in my command and I was unaware of it," Chief Superintendent MacCallum exclaimed, speaking of Sergeant Wallace and his betrayal to his command and that of the men and women serving it.

"*Nae* worries, Chief, we'll see to it that the department shines again," Conor said, standing to leave the office.

"Thank you, gentlemen, that'll be all," MacCallum said.

Andrew glanced at Conor as they left the office.

"Before we head back to the station, can I have a minute?"

"Aye, lad, let her know you're *hame*," Conor replied to his young partner, knowing the importance of a relationship.

Within a few moments, Andrew covered the distance from the admin spaces of the district headquarters building to the forensics lab, hoping he could catch his love interest by herself.

"Hello, Inspector," he said, entering the spaces, his face flush from hurrying to her office.

"Oh, hello, Inspector Fletcher," Sheila said, trying desperately hard not to show an overabundance of emotion at the sight of her lover. "And how was your trip to London?"

"Too long," he said, gazing into her eyes, realizing he was falling in love with the young woman standing before him.

"Well, I'm off at three-thirty if you'd like to get a quick bite to eat." *God, if I could just grasp him by the shoulders and show how much I missed his company, even though it was for just the one evening.*

"I'd like that, but Conor and I need to go back to Vic Station for a wee bit," Andrew stammered, not wanting to waste a minute away from the young lass.

"I'll be there just after four o'clock then to pick you up," Sheila responded, leaning over the counter and placing a long-awaited kiss on her lover's lips. "Go on, I'm sure Conor's waiting."

***

Sitting in the ornate and well-appointed office in the Belfast high-rise, the barrister and his employer discussed future transactions. "Is there anything I need to be particularly stern on?" Sean Gilmore asked 'Mr. Higgins', discussing his upcoming visit with the drug dealer *'Louis Remesy'*.

"Make sure he's aware that I won't tolerate any mistakes or delays in getting this shipment on the vessel," the Northern Irishman declared. He didn't want to delay providing the weapons promised to his comrades preparing for an Irish version of the 'French Foreign Legion' arranging to outfit the thousand-strong militia being planned for and assembled outside Northern Ireland's largest city.

"What assurance do we have from Mr. VanHoorst and the delivery time?" the counselor asked, wanting to make sure the timing matched the requirements laid out by his employer.

"I trust Kurt. He's promised delivery in Tangiers on the tenth of September and that's what we'll plan for," 'Mr. Higgins' said rather forcefully, the events from the last few days beginning to take their toll on him mentally.

Realizing the tone of his delivery, 'Mr. Higgins' said, "I'm sorry, Sean. I'm just tired of having what appeared to be well prepared plans go awry," the executive verbalized. *My legitimate business cannot cover the costs for the weapons.* He was beginning to show a sense of doubt on continuing the drugs for money scheme with the Glasgow syndicates after the latest fiasco that occurred in Aberdeen.

Seeing his employer sitting in thought gave Sean the reason to end his query regarding his trip, since he had several days to discuss things with his boss before leaving. "I'll see that an action plan is ready for your review by tomorrow evening," the counselor said, rising from his seat.

"Thank you, Sean." *I need to get my thoughts straighten out. These doubts are clouding my ability to think clearly and effectively.* He felt the onset of a headache brewing behind his temples.

As his counsel left the office, he realized he needed to detach himself, even if it was for a brief period from the current situation. Lifting the receiver of the phone, he pushed the button for the office intercom and spoke. "Erin, please have Geoff bring the car around and re-schedule my remaining appointments to tomorrow at the same time if possible," he instructed the young receptionist on the phone.

"Certainly, sir," the young woman said.

Soon, Geoff was pulling the Jaguar sedan along the curb, just as 'Mr. Higgins' stepped out of the elevator and into the lobby. Stepping through the door, he was greeted by his driver, who stood holding the rear door of the vintage automobile open, allowing his boss to enter.

"Geoff, take me to the golf club," he said, feeling the need to take his aggressions out on the innocent golf balls at the driving range.

"Yes, sir," the young man answered, sliding behind the steering wheel and setting the car in motion.

***

Chief Superintendent Collingsworth was just finishing the last details of his request to contact his French counterpart, Superintendent Marcel Chevallier at the Central Directorate of the Judicial Police (DCPJ) to discuss a collaborative effort in determining who was responsible for the influx of the drugs.

Pulling the finished printout of his two-page request for Commander Lewis' review and signature, the alarm on his computer chimed, letting him know he had five minutes before the scheduled meeting with his superior. Placing the two sheets of paper into a clean folder, he strode confidently out of his office and down the hall, just as the previous meeting was adjourning.

"Ah, William, do come in," the senior officer said, greeting the chief superintendent. "Your timing seems as precise as ever."

"Thank you, sir," he answered, stepping into the room ahead of his supervisor and standing in front of the desk. "Sir, I've prepared a request for submission to Superintendent Chevallier of the DCPJ for their assistance in helping determine who the individuals operating the vessels are that have become subjects in our investigation," he spoke rather hurriedly.

"I see. May I please look at the letter?" the commander requested, holding his hand out for the folder. Having the folder handed to him, he opened and pulled the two sheets out and looked them over for errors or omissions.

"Looks like all is in order," he said, taking his gold-plated fountain pen from its holder and signing the document, rocking the old-fashioned plotter across his signature to soak up the excess ink. "See that it gets placed in the courier's pouch before noon."

"I'll see to that. Thank you, sir," William said, taking the folder back from Commander Lewis. He quickly walked out from the office and headed straight to the dispatcher's office where the folder would be logged in and become one of the many documents being sent to Scotland Yard's sister agency in Paris.

# Chapter Fifteen

The morning light crept through the thin curtains covering the window in Sheila Gordon's bedroom and shone directly in the eyes of her lover, Andrew. Last night had been a whirlwind of sexual frenzy, the likes she'd not experienced with her past lovers or in the few weeks since she and Andrew had been together.

It was well after midnight when they had settled down, each one bathed in perspiration from the tossing and turning, trying their best to gain the 'upper' position as it were, but ultimately succumbing to a compromised position each, laying together, their limbs intertwined.

With the bright ray of sunlight directly in his eyes, Andrew rolled to one side and nearly made a comical exit from the bed as he clung to the bed sheet with but a few fingers. "If we're doing that again," he exclaimed, "we need a bigger bed."

Awakened by the sudden shift of weight on the bed, Sheila propped herself on her elbows and looked at him with a sheepish grin. "Well, if you did *nae* let go of what you were holdin' earlier, we'd have no need for a bigger bed." She alluded to the fact that he'd been handling her left breast before rolling toward the bed's edge.

"True, but then you'd need to explain the bruise to your doctor," he said, leaning in and kissing her good morning.

"Shall we squeeze into the shower?" she asked.

***

Sticking to his routine, 'Mr. Higgins' was up as the sun rose in the eastern sky, jogging at a steady pace along the shoreline, his heart pounding in cadence with every step, but his mind calm and focused at the coming tasks at hand.

Turning back to his home, he contemplated his pending discussion with Captain Duncan regarding the shipment of narcotics making its way from Marseille. He'd normally allow his counselor, Sean, to conduct such discussions with the captain and make the arrangements for transport to Glasgow. However, it had been decided to have the counselor travel and meet with the French-Algerian drug supplier,

*Monsieur Remesy* to initiate discussions surrounding the need to assist in the weapons shipment from South Africa.

Nearing the entrance to his estate, 'Mr. Higgins' slowed his pace and began his cool down period before entering the residence and getting cleaned up for the coming day's activities. Walking down the driveway towards the front door of his home, he saw that his driver Geoff had already arrived and was waiting dutifully in the front seat of the Jaguar sedan.

"Come in and have a cup of coffee, Geoff," the executive said, waving to the young man.

"I'd like that, sir," he replied, keying the window switch to shut the driver side window before closing the door behind himself. Following his boss inside, he thumbed the remote, setting the security system to the vintage motor car.

***

Gathering the folders in her arms, Erin had just finished preparing the daily reports for her boss' review when he entered the office's outer door. "Good morning, sir," she said, watching him hurry past towards his private office.

"Good morning, Erin," he said, entering the office. "Please prepare some coffee and ask Mr. Gilmore to join me straight away."

"Certainly, sir," she said, walking back to her desk to make the call, summoning the counselor. After making the call, she went about fixing her employer a pot of his 'special' coffee, a Jamaican Blue Mountain blend that he only drank on occasions when conducting serious negotiations.

Walking the five hundred meters from his office to that of his employer, Sean Gilmore strolled into the outer office as Erin was pouring the coffee into a serving urn complete with cream and sugar held in Waterford crystal.

"You wish to see me?" Sean asked, entering his boss' room followed closely by the young Irishwoman.

"Yes, Sean," 'Mr. Higgins' said, hesitating while Erin placed the coffee service down and left. "I want to pass a few ideas to you before I speak to Captain Duncan." For the next twenty minutes, 'Mr. Higgins' explained his plans to cease having the narcotics transferred from the derricks to Captain Duncan's vessel and to have them transferred directly to the support vessel from the freighter and then onto Glasgow and Belfast for distribution.

"The key point will be making sure that the containers are identical, I would think," Sean said.

"That's where I will impress upon the good captain to make sure he selects the men with the utmost care; or I must ask that Mr. Hunt make an example of the untrustworthy souls who can't insure a successful transaction," the Irishman said, taking a sip of his coffee. "Ah, just like old times."

***

"We need to finish or we'll have nothing but cold water left," Ailene exclaimed, squeezing next to Conor's lathered up torso, trying to rinse her hair. Tilting her head back to rinse shampoo from her hair, Conor cupped her breasts in his soaped-up hands, sliding them smoothly across her damp flesh. With water and shampoo cascading down from her hair, Conor used his thumb and forefinger to tease her nipples, gently squeezing and pulling the flesh taunt until he noticed that she stopped rinsing her hair and was bracing herself against the sides of the shower walls.

"We'll be bit late if I keep on, you know that," he said, his cock, swollen and erect, resting upright directly against her abdomen, letting his hands drop from her breasts. Squeezing past Ailene, he quickly turned the valves to shoot a stream of cold water against his chest and allowed it to cascade downward across his groin, with desire results of causing him to lose his erection as the cold water made the blood swollen flesh contract.

"Damn you, Conor. Next time, give me a warning, will you," Ailene gasped, stepping away from the residual spray of cold water, causing her flesh to stiffen, creating goose bumps that rivaled her erect nipples from Conor's foreplay just moments earlier.

***

As with every vessel in port, mornings began by checking that nothing shifted in the evening and that the mooring lines were still secure. F/O Spiers walked aft to the edge of the service deck checking the lines, looking for any telltale signs of damage or looseness.

Walking forward on the 'wet' side of the vessel, he looked for anything that was floating in the water that could cause damage to the propellers or rudder once they began to get underway when leaving the dock for open water. As he entered the bridge, the ship-to-shore phone chimed that an incoming call was being made to the vessel.

146

"*Nordic Supplier*, first officer speaking," he said, taking the incoming call.

"Is Captain Duncan available? This is 'Mr. Higgins' calling," he replied to the seaman's greeting.

"Stand by please," the young Scot said, knowing his captain was in the small galley having his breakfast. Walking through the center hatchway and down the short stairwell, the young officer entered the crews' galley and motioned to Captain Duncan that a call was pending for him on the bridge.

Seeing his first officer motion to him, Captain Duncan took a last gulp of coffee, making his way to the bridge but a few paces behind the young Scotsman who took the call. "Captain Duncan, can I help you?"

"Cap'n, this is 'Mr. Higgins', can you speak privately?"

Turning to his first officer, Captain Duncan said, "Clear the bridge," expressing his desire to have the bridge emptied for a private conversation.

With the request made, F/O Spiers and the young seaman standing watch exited the bridge wing, closing the door behind them as they made their way to the galley for breakfast.

"Go ahead, 'Mr. Higgins', we're alone for the moment," Clive Duncan said, sitting in his chair situated on the bridge.

"I have two questions that I need answered this morning if possible. The first one, do you have the capability to secure a container, void of any shipping or ownership markings? And the second one is if you can provide me with the name of a captain, someone like yourself who operates in the Irish Sea, someone who can be trusted?" 'Mr. Higgins' asked.

Taking a moment to ponder the questions, Clive Duncan contemplated the results of his answers and that of his vessel and crew. Neither question seemed to pose a great threat. However, if he gave an answer that seemed contrary to what 'Mr. Higgins' wished to hear, it could mean the end of their working relationship.

"Aye, I can get a clean box if need be," Captain Duncan said. "I just need to know what color I'm matching it to."

"All right then, I'll see what I can provide. I'll have that information to you later today or tomorrow," the Irishman said, making a note for later.

"As for the second question, I've got someone in mind, but I'll need a day, maybe two to discuss your request with him," Clive said, thinking of his fellow captain and protégé, Brodie Fraser of the *PSV Oceanic-Ranger,* working out of the Port of Glasgow at Greenock.

"I'll give you two days, Captain, then I'll expect an answer," 'Mr. Higgins' said, "at which time, I'll have your answer regarding the container color."

*Aye, you'll have the answer in two days.* He hung the receiver in its cradle behind his captain's chair.

***

Looking over the printout from the local phone company, Conor and Andrew searched for Sergeant Wallace's phone number so they could begin building the case against him.

"Bloody hell, Conor," Andrew said, pouring over the six-inch stack of computer-printed paper. "There must be thousands of numbers listed just for this past Monday alone."

"Aye, and this is just a two-week printing, mind you," Conor said. "There's more where this came from."

Being reminded of the monumental task didn't make it any easier for the two inspectors. Since they'd made the initial arrest of Sergeant Wallace, they were showing the other officers in the station of their willingness to do the 'dirty work' of scouring the mounds of documentation that comes with every investigation, just part of being a policeman. As each of them turned their respective page over to a new section, the desk phone rang, providing a much-needed break to their task.

"Chief Inspector McDermott," Conor said, answering the phone.

"CI McDermott, this is Chief Superintendent MacCallum," the senior officer said. "I've got good news for you and Inspector Fletcher."

"I'm certainly happy to hear that the news is good, sir."

"I've 'deputized' a class from the academy to assist in the searching of the phone records for you and Inspector Fletcher," MacCallum said, relating the information regarding the local police cadet council needing to be kept busy.

"Aye, so what do you want us to do?" Conor asked. *I've nae time to 'baby-sit' young cadets with runny noses or dirty diapers on their arse.* He bristled at the thought of twenty-somethings asking too many questions and calling him 'sir' all the time.

"You and Andrew just need to make a note where you are now, and I'll have one of the constables come by the station and pick up everything," CS MacCallum said. "And we'll have them work here in our extra room next to the forensics lab."

"Andrew will be most disappointed in knowing that, sir. He's gotten quite fond of looking at all the numbers."

"I'm sure he'll overcome the disappointment," the senior officer said, ending the call.

***

Sitting in his office overlooking Churchill Gardens, Chief Superintendent Collingsworth was reviewing the reports being developed by Conor and Andrew, recounting the drug seizure and the arrest of the one constable. *I wonder if the French are tracking this closer than we are?* He read the lab report on the chemical make-up of the hashish and cannabis resin cocktail. The findings from the analysis were showing a potent mixture that solidified their findings from the autopsies from the three poor souls who succumbed to the drug in Portsmouth.

Beginning to review the results of the inspector's surveillance of the workboats, his desk phone rang. "Yes, Chief Superintendent Collingsworth," he said, answering the call.

"Inspector," Officer Jones said, "you've a call from Superintendent Chevallier on line four."

"Thank you, Jones," the senior officer said, switching lines from the internal intercom to the extension his caller was waiting on.

"Hello, Superintendent Chevallier," CS Collingsworth said, greeting the caller from Paris.

"Please call me *'Marcel'*," the senior French officer mentioned to William.

"Certainly, and please, you may address me as William."

"Very well, William," Marcel said. "It's a pleasure to finally have a chance to introduce myself and begin discussing our mutual problems."

"I was hoping we could pool our resources and combine the efforts to tackle this challenge together since it seems to be plaguing both our countries," William said. "It appears that what may have originated in France under your authority is now ending up here in England under mine."

"Yes, based on the information you provided, we've begun checking our records and I've passed it to my detectives in Marseille. Because of their efforts, they've uncovered a possible connection we're willing to share with you and your inspectors working this case."

Hearing this revelation made William hopeful that they would be able to end this scourge quickly, allowing his inspector to focus on other events. "Do you believe it is possible for our agents to meet and exchange information?" he asked, hoping Conor and Andrew could be given something new to add to their investigation into the drug trafficking.

"Most certainly, William. I'd be happy to make the arrangements," Marcel said, he too wanting his agents, Detective Benoit and Senior Detective Lemieux to meet and work closer with the members of Scotland Yard.

"I propose my inspectors meet with your agents in Marseille then, and I believe the sooner would be better," the chief superintendent said, not wanting to waste any more time than needed.

"Agreed, William, I will contact you as soon as everything is ready to receive your inspectors," Marcel said. "And I hope you'll be willing to attend the meeting with them as well."

"I would be glad to make the trip and meet with you and your staff," William said. "I won't keep you any longer, Marcel, since we both have things to attend to."

***

The barrister that Stuart Ross had sent from Glasgow to Aberdeen to defend his two men was having a difficult time preparing his case due to the evidence against them. Both men were arrested in a city where their firearm permits were not valid and they'd no written notice from Alistair Hunt or from Stuart Ross as to their 'assignment' protecting young Ewan Sutherland.

Along with those issues was the fact that Ewan Sutherland was being held for drug trafficking, which gave the prosecutor the ability to argue that Mr. Brown and Mr. Smith were also involved in the drug trafficking business.

"Mr. Mason, my clients had no affiliation with the narcotics you are alleged to have linked to Mr. Sutherland," the defense counsel said, meeting with his counterpart in the case.

"The Crown has evidence to the contrary. We've fingerprints on the narcotics being transferred," Mr. Mason said. "In addition, the young man has already been convicted in the past in other jurisdictions."

"But they haven't been identified as those of Brown and Smith. And if that's the case, I'll be making a motion that the trials be held separately," the barrister from Glasgow proclaimed, hoping to force a concession from the senior court official.

"As you have the right to do," Mr. Mason said, closing his portfolio, ending the discussion.

Knowing he was not going to get any further with the prosecutor, the barrister for Stuart Ross' men closed his portfolio as well, preparing to return to Glasgow empty-handed and discuss the situation with his employer.

***

CS Collingsworth had just finished discussing how the collaborative meeting between the Scotland Yard inspectors and the French Justice Department's Central Directorate investigators would be conducted with Commander Lewis when he was handed a message by Constable Jones at his office door.

*Have lead on person of interest in Glasgow,* the message read and it was from his good friend Bruce MacCallum in Aberdeen. "Thank you, Jones." he read the note, walking into his office. "Oh, Officer Jones. I need you to make travel arrangements for Inspectors' McDermott and Fletcher. They'll need a flight to and from Aberdeen to Marseille, France," the officer dictated to the constable before he had a chance to return to his desk.

Picking his phone up, William dialed the number to the office that Conor and Andrew were sharing at the station in Aberdeen to give them their orders for the meeting. *How much do we press the French when it comes to handing over information?* he mused as the phone rang for the third time.

"Victoria Station, Sergeant McCord speaking."

"Sergeant, this is Chief Superintendent Collingsworth, Scotland Yard. Is CI McDermott in the area?"

"I'm sorry, sir, but he's gone tae meet with a vessel captain at the docks," the sergeant said.

"Very well. I'll give his mobile number a try," William said. "Thank you, Sergeant."

Pulling up his contact list, William searched for Conor's information to obtain the cell phone number. As soon as it appeared on the screen, the senior officer quickly dialed the number in hopes of catching his inspector before his meeting, assuming it was with Captain Kinkaid.

The ringing of his cell phone caught Conor off-guard as he walked to the parked car with Andrew. "Hello?" he asked, answering the call, but not recognizing the telephone number of his supervisor's desk phone as it appeared on the screen.

"Conor, Chief Superintendent Collingsworth here," William said at the surprised response to his call.

"Aye, William, what can I help you with?" Conor said, standing in the middle of the car park.

"I've arranged a meeting for you and Inspector Fletcher with several French detectives in Marseille," he said. "Flight arrangements are being made as we speak."

"Aye, that's just fine, but what are they going tae talk about?" Conor asked, with Andrew standing close by, attempting to hear the conversation.

"I've convinced them that they're at the beginning of the drug trafficking that we've encountered and it's their flagged vessels leaving Marseille with the drugs," CS Collingsworth said. "As soon as I have the information on the flights, I'll pass it along."

"Aye, thanks for the warning," Conor said. Ending the call, Conor looked at Andrew and asked, "Did you learn any foreign languages in the Royal Marines?"

"Why do you ask?" Andrew replied.

"Because we're going to Marseille to discuss the drug trafficking with the French," Conor said.

***

Sitting in the assembly hall, decorated with images of past activities from of the police station, Trainee Constable Howe looked over his third stack of digital printouts for the day, looking for the matching numbers as prescribed by Sergeant Giles in his earlier instructions.

"Sergeant Giles," the trainee said, "I've got something of interest here."

**Sergeant Giles** rose from his place at the head of the room. *Thank the heavens for a wee break.* He too studiously reviewed the reports, doing his part in the attempt to find the person behind Sergeant Wallace's betrayal to the force. "What have you got, lad?" the officer asked.

"I've noticed a pattern with the same two numbers, this one originating from district headquarters and this one that is relayed from a cell tower in downtown Glasgow," the young constable explained, pointing to the established routine he found.

"I see. Is there any other sequence you've come across that's similar?" the sergeant queried the young man, wanting to make sure the cadet wasn't overlooking something.

"None that's this specific, sir," the cadet said.

"Very well then. Make your notes clear and I'll pass that to the chief inspector. Good work, Constable Howe," Sergeant Giles said, loud enough for the cadet's fellow classmates to hear the praise for a job well done.

***

Andrew was looking at the notes created by the young cadet earlier in the day, as Conor drove out to the Regent Quay to meet with Captain Kinkaid of the *PSV Oceanic-Talisker* to discuss a surveillance plan.

"It seems that one of the cadets found an excessive amount of calls from the district office to a cell phone number used in downtown Glasgow," Andrew said as Conor maneuvered the police car through the traffic circle leading to the harbor area.

"That would make it seem the two blokes we apprehended were being helped from Sergeant Wallace," Conor stated, pulling the car into an empty space on a side street near to the dock area.

"That's what it appears. We'll need to have the cell tower number identified to determine where in the city to begin looking, though," Andrew stated, thinking he'd be able to work closely with Sheila, since she'd be involved in that part of investigation.

"Aye, but that could lead to a very large neighborhood to search," Conor said.

As they began walking towards the *PSV Oceanic-Talisker,* they could make out the brilliant white superstructure against the deep blue hull, its name emblazoned in just below the railing of the top deck.

Making their way across the busy thoroughfare, the inspectors could see several of the vessel's crew operating a fire hose, already engaged in the daily routine of keeping things in order. This chore along with others was being done under the watchful eye of what seemed to be the first officer.

Reaching the vessel's lower deck railing, Conor hailed the first officer. "Is Cap'n Kinkaid aboard?" he shouted over the din of the whooshing water emerging from the hose being manned as the deck was being cleaned.

"Aye, come aboard, but mind yer feet," First Officer Gerard King shouted back at the two inspectors with a wave.

As the two inspectors walked across the short gangway bridging the chilly waters of the harbor and onto the vessels working deck, F/O King directed the crew to cease their clean-up momentarily, allowing the officers to make way to the forward stairwell. By the time Conor and Andrew covered the short distance to the stairs leading to the bridge, Captain Thomas Kinkaid had already made his way to the working deck to greet his visitors.

"Welcome aboard," the skipper said, holding out his hand that could be mistaken for a bear's claw.

"Thanks for seeing us," Conor said.

"Let's get out of the way of the crew, shall we."

Walking through the opening, Andrew was impressed at how clean and orderly the vessel's interior looked as opposed to the British and America Navy ships he had been on during his tour with the Royal Marines. "It never seems to amaze me how clean a ship can be, yet still smell like a machine shop," Andrew said.

"Oh, and you've experienced working onboard boats?" Captain Kinkaid asked.

"Six years' service as a first lieutenant in the Royal Marines with three ship-board deployments," Andrew said, ducking instinctively through an open hatch. *And I still get queasy from the rocking of the damn waves.* He steadied himself against one of the bulkheads.

Entering the galley area, Captain Kinkaid directed his guests to take a seat as he sat down at the head of the table as a matter of habit. "So, gentlemen, I understand that Scotland Yard has recruited my vessel and crew," he said, responding to the telex that came from his home office the day before.

"Yes, in a matter of speaking you've been 'deputized' as it were," Andrew said.

"Captain, we've been tracking the movement of drugs coming north through the Channel, but there's *nae* solid evidence of it coming onshore in a 'bulk' form," Conor said. "You see, we believe that one or possibly two service vessels operating here in Aberdeen are being used to transfer the drugs from cargo ships and then somehow distributing smaller quantities afterwards."

"So, if that's the case, what role will the *Oceanic-Talisker* have in assisting you?" the captain asked, wanting to know the risk to his crew and vessel.

"As it is now, sir," Andrew said, "we'll need your vessel to shadow selected vessels as they transit from the harbor to the North Sea, possibly out to the platform areas."

"That's a mighty big area for one vessel to keep track of, young man," Captain Kinkaid said, knowing the extent of the area that vessels ply while servicing the various oil and gas derricks.

"It would be if we did *nae* already have a list of the vessels to track," Conor said. "We believe the PSVs *Standard-Hercules* and *Standard-Apollo* are involved in the drug trafficking because they've 'questionable records' on file with the Maritime and Coast Guard Agency."

"Aye, I'm familiar with one of the captains. His name's Captain Bernard McIntosh if I recall. Hails from Inverness originally," the captain spoke. "He's a bit rogue with an ego to match when it comes to conning his vessel. He's shown a bit of recklessness at times when entering or exiting the harbor."

"If that's the case, then the maritime office should have record of his actions," Andrew said.

"They should, young man, but not all actions submitted as offenses are being recorded at the Coast Guard's office when reported," Kinkaid said. "I know, since I've made reports myself that haven't been acted on."

"We'll make a note to check on that," Conor said. *I'll have to inform the chief superintendent of a possible security issue within the Coast Guard and Maritime office and tell Ailene tae mind herself if what Kinkaid is saying to be true.* He knew he'd be placing his love interest at risk. "For now, we appreciate the time discussing this and we'll get back to you tomorrow with our timetable," he said.

***

Returning to the district office, Conor and Andrew spent the next hour finishing their reports on the meeting with Captain Kinkaid and preparing for their next travel. With the information provided by the chief superintendent, Andrew walked into the forensics lab to discuss his abrupt travel plans with his love interest. "Good day, Inspector Gordon."

"Good day to you too, Inspector Fletcher."

"I wanted to let you know Conor and I are being directed to meet with the French on this drug trafficking case, and we are heading to Marseille." A disappointed look was evident on his face.

"I see. And this'll be for a night or two, I suppose?" *This is getting ridiculous. I'll never get into a routine with this man if he keeps leaving.* She tried to gain a sense of normalcy in her life.

"Probably two days, but not more than three, I would expect," Andrew said.

"Aye then, go on and hurry back. I'll still be here," Sheila said, resigned to the fact having an affair with a fellow officer was going to be tumultuous at times.

***

Sergeant McKee pulled the police car up to the departure terminal, where Conor and Andrew got out. As Andrew went to grab their bags from the boot, Conor spoke with the sergeant.

"Do us a favor, Annie," Conor said. "Can you get this note to Ms. Ailene O'Leary at the Coast Guard and Maritime Office for me?" He handed over an envelope.

"Aye, I'll swing it by first thing in the mornin' if that's okay?"

"That'll do," he said. "Thanks again for the lift, hen."

"*Nae* worries, Inspector," Sergeant McKee said, smiling at Conor, finding his rogue-like features appealing to her eyes.

"Thank you, Sergeant," Andrew said, stepping around from the back of the car.

"Same to you, Andrew," she said. "And Sheila wanted me to remind ya that you can look, but *nae* touch."

"I'll keep that in mind." Andrew blushed at the remark.

"Come on, lad," Conor said, "we've got a few stops in between to keep."

With a wave of their hands, they grabbed the bags off the curb, both inspectors entering the terminal to check in for the flight to Marseille and the rendezvous with their French DJSE counterparts, Detective Geneviève Benoit and Senior Detective Claude Lemieux.

## Chapter Sixteen

The fading light of day crept over the *M/V Bonaparte* as it sailed into the English Channel, on its way to the rendezvous with *PSV Standard-Apollo*. As the vessel maneuvered through the Straits of Dover between Canterbury and Calais, First Officer Pierre Bellamy took note of all the shipping traffic making its way through the bottleneck, his captain, Henri Levet looking on in silence.

*In twelve more hours, we'll be rid of the container.* Henri scanned the horizon forward of his vessel. Off in the distance he saw the distinctive silhouette of a British warship sailing off the starboard bow and moving away from his intended path. "Pierre, keep your distance from that patrol boat. We don't want to give them a reason to board us," Captain Levet spoke to his first officer. A boarding party at this stage of the operation would be disastrous for his ship and crew.

***

In the gathering darkness, the *Nordic Supplier* glowed under the lights spaced along the docks. "Mister Spiers, prepare to get us underway, if you please," Captain Duncan said, beginning his part in the plan to retrieve the drugs from the French vessel making its way through the English Channel.

"Aye, Captain," the first officer said. "Engine room, stand by to get underway."

"Aye, we're ready for normal operations," the engineer said over the ships intercom.

"Let go of the aft lines." With that command, F/O Spiers began the delicate balance of maneuvering the vessel away from the dock and the other ships tied alongside. "Three degrees' right rudder, steerage way on the engines Seaman Carr," Spiers said in a steady and calm voice, not wanting to show any signs of nerves before the captain.

"Aye, sir," Seaman Carr said, acknowledging the order. "Three degrees' right rudder and steerage way on the engines."

Sensing the shifting motion of the ship, F/O Spiers ordered the bow lines to be released as the tide began to take hold and move the vessel farther from the docks. "Bring your rudder six degrees to port," Spiers

157

ordered the young woman manning the conn, this act bringing the bow away from the dock and setting it towards the harbor entrance and the open sea beyond.

"Very good, Mister Spiers," Captain Duncan proclaimed, having seen and heard his first officer's actions. "The same goes for you as well, Seaman Carr."

With the vessel now clear of the dock and the other ships, F/O Spiers now had the task of taking the vessel out past the breakwater and the open waters of the North Sea. "Bring your engine speed up to one quarter," he directed.

"Aye, speed to one quarter," Carr replied to the order, bringing the vessel's forward speed up from a crawl to a purposeful stride in walking terms.

With the delicate task of taking the vessel away from the docks completed, the *PSV Nordic Supplier* was underway for its rendezvous in the English Channel.

***

Sitting in his office in Belfast, Sean Gilmore was reviewing his discussion points for the upcoming meeting with *Louis Remesy* when his employer walked into his office. "Evening, 'Mr. Higgins', I didn't expect you to still be in the office."

"I need you to make a call to Scotland Yard," the Irishman said, "proclaiming knowledge of a possible drug shipment onboard the *PSV Standard-Apollo*. Inform them that the parties are using gas cylinders to hide the narcotics in." He set his plan of deception in motion.

"And if they ask for any additional information, what should I tell them?" Sean asked.

"Let them know that you heard about the transactions between two dockworkers and a crewman while at a pub near the quay's in Aberdeen," 'Mr. Higgins' declared. "The dockworkers appeared to be wearing BP overalls and the crewman was outfitted in *'Chevron'* livery." Pulling out a package from under his arm, he handed it to the counselor. "This is a new cell phone. Use it to make the call and then dispose of it on your way home," 'Mr. Higgins' said, knowing the police would attempt to track the call using the cell phones location software against it.

"Very well, sir," Mr. Gilmore answered, taking the package from his boss.

Exiting the building, 'Mr. Higgins' walked directly to his car, with Geoff standing by dutifully with the rear passenger door open, allowing for his quick entrance. Sitting in the back of the Jaguar, 'Mr. Higgins' pulled out his own cell phone and selected the saved number for the *Nordic Supplier* and thumbed the 'call' button to begin the dialing. "Maritime and Coast Guard Agency. What vessel do you wish to contact?" the man's voice announced as the call was answered.

"The *Nordic Supplier*, if you please," the Irishman said.

"Stand by," the operator replied as the switch was made to the maritime system for shore-to-ship communications.

"*Nordic Supplier*, Captain speaking," 'Mr. Higgins' heard as Clive Duncan answered the call.

"Captain, 'Mr. Higgins' calling," he announced. "The transaction will take place as planned."

"Understood," the captain answered, knowing he was now committed to making an at-sea transfer of a container from the French vessel sailing up the English Channel. Just a week earlier Captain Duncan had met with the mysterious Irishman in Edinburgh, who quickly outlined the plan to transfer the drugs being shipped at-sea instead of using the oil and gas derricks as before.

Unbeknownst to the vessel's captain, this was to be a trial run for a more daring plan to conduct a similar transfer in the Irish Sea, only the next container would be a shipment of five hundred Belgium-style FN SCAR 7.62 assault rifles supplied by Kurt VanHoorst, instead of hashish.

With that call completed, 'Mr. Higgins' next located the number for Alistair Hunt and selected the call button to confirm the next step in the transfer of the drugs. After three rings, his call was answered by Janice Gordon, Mr. Hunt's receptionist.

"Good evening," the older woman replied, answering the call that had interrupted her departure from the office for the evening.

"Good evening, ma'am," the Irishman spoke. "Is Mr. Hunt in this evening?"

"If you don't mind holding for a minute, I'll see if he's available." She placed the caller in telephone limbo. Walking to Alistair's office, she quietly opened the door and saw her boss studiously working on a document laid out upon his desk.

"Yes, Janice, what is it?" he asked.

"You've a call on line two." She pointed to the flashing light on the phone console.

Picking up the handset, Alistair pushed the button flashing red on the console. "This is Mr. Hunt."

"Good evening, Mr. Hunt, this is 'Mr. Higgins'," the Irishman said matter-of-factly to the Scotsman, "calling to confirm that the arrangements are in place for receiving my parcel?"

"Aye, I've got assurances the lorry and driver will be standing by in Aberdeen," the syndicate boss answered. Alistair recalled the conversation he had with the Irishman several days earlier where they discussed moving a bulk container to Glasgow.

"Very well." *He doesn't need to know I've changed plans when it came to moving the drugs piecemeal from the gas derricks. The Scotsman just needs to ensure his arrangement for a lorry to move the entire shipment from Aberdeen to Glasgow is in place. And he's being well paid to keep this part of the plan quiet from the Frenchman, 'Mister Remesy'.* "Please contact Mr. Gilmore upon receipt of the parcel," *'Mr. Higgins'* said.

"Aye, I'll make the call," Alistair said.

"Thank you," 'Mr. Higgins' said, ending the call.

***

Heading out of the harbor, Captain Duncan gave F/O Spiers orders to set his course to make the scheduled rendezvous with the *M/V Bonaparte* and that he'd be taking the morning shift at the helm. Before heading to his cabin, Captain Duncan went onto the weather deck, making one last check of the container to ensure that it was still chained securely.

It took some convincing on his part to persuade Alistair Hunt he could obtain the 'clean' shipping container, since one was needed devoid of all markings. Once this was delivered to the docks, Captain Duncan supervised the unloading from the truck and onto the deck of his ship, making sure the chains and binders securing the large metal box were placed in the proper locations.

Satisfied that the container was still secured, Captain Duncan made his way to his cabin where he removed the fake documents from his shipboard safe that 'Mr. Higgins' counselor had prepared. Along with the documents, there were markings and decals that had to be placed on the container before they returned to port, ensuring that they matched the documents for the customs officials to check against.

***

Finishing his plans for the trip to Algiers, Sean Gilmore donned a pair of surgical gloves he kept in his desk drawer and unwrapped the cell phone that 'Mr. Higgins' had provided him earlier in the evening and made the call to Scotland Yard.

"Scotland Yard, how can I help you?" the constable asked, answering the call from the counselor.

"Yes, I'm calling because I've overheard some workers discussing the purchase of narcotics earlier this evening," Sean exclaimed, beginning the dialogue.

"And where did this take place?" the officer asked, beginning the task of gathering information.

"Outside a pub near the Albert quay in Aberdeen," the Irishman said, recalling the specifics that his employer wished to have translated to the police. "There were three chaps, two in a BP uniform and the other wearing overalls, with *Standard-Apollo* stitched on the back."

"And what were you doing when you heard this?" the constable asked.

"I was outside getting a bit of fresh air," Sean stated. "One of them said the drugs would be hidden in oxygen cylinders, or something of the sort."

Over the next five minutes, the constable repeated his questions and Sean Gilmore provided the answers back to make sure that the call was taken seriously. At the end, the constable asked for his name and phone number that he was calling from, and the counselor gave the operator a fictitious name, but the genuine cell phone number since this could be verified by the call logs.

Having collected the information from the caller, the constable staffing the switchboard now routed the information from his station in London to the district headquarters in Aberdeen for the local officers to begin their investigation.

***

Looking over the results of the laboratory results of the narcotics, Inspector Sheila Gordon saw how the deadly cocktail had been scientifically altered between the hashish and cannabis resin. The introduction of the chemically-enhanced and purified resin to the already potent hashish added to the psychoactive nature of the THC levels,

161

which would have contributed to a user's impaired motor skills, the lab technician knew. *Nasty stuff this is,* she thought to herself, closing the file and placing it into the cabinet behind her.

Picking up the notes from the cadets who were providing their assistance in searching the cell phone logs from Sergeant Wallace's deceptive practices as an informant, she began to scan the list of common numbers.

Running through the notes, she came across a series of numbers that seemed vaguely familiar to her. Turning another page, she realized why the number series were recognizable to her, reaching into the desk drawer and pulling the cell phone from her purse.

Scrolling through the names in her phone, she came across the one she was looking for and saw the number matched one of the two she had listed in the phone. Not wanting to accept the possibility of a family member being involved, Sheila looked through the notes of the cadets for a second time, and she found the same number listed six times on five different occasions.

Seeing the possible evidence before her, her heart began to ache at the thought of what she could do with the information and knowing what she must do as a sworn officer of the police force. Gathering the notes from her desk, she placed them back in the folder they had come in and picked up the phone, dialing the number for the chief superintendent's office.

***

Sailing into the night onboard the HMS *Tyne*, the deck watch was scanning the horizon, keeping a watchful eye out for small boats that their radar would have difficulty picking up in the choppy seas. The glowing green image outlining the face of one young petty officer slowly searching the waters along the port side of the patrol craft, while an able seaman, a young woman, was similarly doing the same on the starboard side, the only sign of their presence on deck.

Lieutenant Smythe stood stoically on the bridge, watching the parade of merchantmen fade away in the dark as they sailed in all directions of the compass, making their way to the various ports situated on both sides of the channel. "Helm, make your course two-nine-zero degrees," the officer announced, bringing the small craft onto its next heading for this patrol.

"Aye, sir. My heading is two-nine-zero degrees," the petty officer manning the vessel's helm exclaimed, following the order.

The shift in the patrol craft's heading would bring it on a parallel course with the *M/V Bonaparte*, which was steaming at twelve knots through the congested waterway. The normal routine of the patrol craft was to monitor the activities of the vessels transiting the channel and assist when needed. As the French freighter loomed larger, Lieutenant Smythe could make out the containers stacked high against the superstructure as well as the two gantry crane control suites as they protruded above the multicolored boxes.

***

Ailene sat alone in her flat, looking over the note Conor had left her before making his way to Marseille. *Have information regarding a possible informant in your office. Take care when discussing with me or Andrew*, the note read.

Looking down upon the paper, she closed her eyes, attempting to filter out possible suspects. Knowing Conor was investigating drug traffickers, that meant more than likely the informant could see vessel movements, both commercial and private, including military ships moving in the area.

Taking a sip of tea, she pulled a small writing tablet from her purse and started to list the names of possible people for her to pass along to Conor. Most of the names she knew would come from the Operations office, but there was always the possibility of someone outside Operations who could access information and pass it along. After ten minutes or so, she looked at her list consisting of sixteen possible candidates who might need to be questioned by the local constables. *I'll leave it up to the authorities,* she said to herself, sliding the list into her purse and going to bed, wondering what the next few days would bring.

***

Onboard the *M/V Bonaparte*, F/O Bellamy was looking over the navigational charts when the seaman assigned to the radio room came onto the bridge with a telex.

"From *PSV Standard-Apollo*; make way to rendezvous at the following coordinates 54-8916 by 02-0470," the first officer read back to the radioman. "Is this correct?"

"Yes, Mister Bellamy."

Turning to the navigational chart he'd just pulled out of the desk, he quickly took his straightedge and placed it on the map, looking for both the longitudinal and latitude markings to determine the place they were to meet the support vessel.

Finding the navigational point, he made a note of distance and speed from their present location and calculated the time it would be for their arrival. *At our current course and speed, this will have us there at 'nautical dawn' or close to it. Just dark enough to make it hard to see what's going on, but with enough visibility to get the container moved.*

What the young French first officer didn't know was that Captain Duncan of the *Nordic Supplier* had been given the radio frequencies used by *Standard-Apollo* as well as *Standard-Hercules* by 'Mr. Higgins' for use in deceiving the French merchantman into thinking they were rendezvousing with their normal vessel.

On the bridge of the *Standard-Apollo*, Captain Dillan McKenzie was looking over his own navigational chart, preparing to meet the *M/V Bonaparte* to take possession of a container that would be transferred to an abandoned gas derrick on the southern edge of the 'Erskine' gas fields.

The Scottish captain didn't need to contact the freighter as he'd already undertaken this journey once before with its sister vessel, *M/V Joan of Arc*, just six weeks earlier, transferring three pallets from the French vessel and then making his way to the gas derrick. Having already been contacted by the German consortium working the derrick, he knew he was just twenty-four hours from receiving another healthy fee for transferring the drugs.

***

Sean Gilmore sat in the outer office of his employer 'Mr. Higgins', chatting politely with Erin as she went about filing the various documents from yesterday's board meetings. "You'd think there would be an easier way to handle all the files?" he said, making yet another attempt at small talk with the young and attractive Irishwoman, something he always seemed to struggle at.

Erin Malone was by all appearances, your typical young Irish woman. Sporting a slim figure, like that of a swimmer, she carried herself with a sense of grace without privilege. She always kept her deep auburn hair pulled back and wore fashionable but sensible clothing in the office. Today she was wearing a mid-length tartan skirt and a complementary blouse, both of which did little to hide her feminine features from the counselor in the room.

"Well, 'Mr. Callaghan' is rather set in his ways," she replied, alluding to 'Mr. Higgins' business partner. "He likes to feel the pen slide across the paper when he signs something, as he puts it."

"There is something tangible in having something firmly in your grasp, I suppose," Sean said, hoping not to give the young woman the wrong impression to what he was thinking. *Ah, to have my hands on those legs.* He watched her walk between file cabinets.

Just as Erin was preparing to express her opinion to the counselor, 'Mr. Higgins' entered the office, followed closely by his driver Geoff Brennan. Exchanging pleasantries, he walked through and into his private office, Sean rising from his seat and following him closely behind, shutting the door as asked to by his employer.

Geoff wearily took the now vacated seat that the counselor had occupied earlier. "Feck, I'm knackered," he exclaimed to the receptionist.

"Getting to be a bore, is this?" Erin asked the driver, but already knowing his reply.

"I'm not getting my necessary beauty sleep," the young Ulsterman joked, reaching for the carafe of coffee sitting in the middle of the table before him.

"Don't let the master hear you or you'll be out on your arse," she pointed out to Geoff that he could be in worse condition.

***

Shortly after F/O Bellamy of the *M/V Bonaparte* read the telex from what he thought was the *Standard-Apollo* but was *Nordic Supplier* instead, a similar message was received in a personal account for the president of *'Papillion Transport'*, letting him know the service vessel would be making the rendezvous with his freighter to exchange the container of narcotics.

Unknown to the principal running the shipping company was the deceptive plan put in place by 'Mr. Higgins' to have the drugs taken directly to Aberdeen instead of the gas derrick. It was on the derrick where a group of German workers would normally be waiting for the container, tasked to prepare the drugs for transfer to countries such as Denmark, Germany, and other northern continent buyers as well as Scotland.

***

Sitting in the Business Class section of the British Airways jet, Conor and Andrew kept most of their thoughts to themselves while

165

sipping on their drinks. Andrew's thoughts were of his reunion with Sheila, hoping to have more than just a few days' time to 'reacquaint' himself with the shapely young lass.

Conor, on the other hand, couldn't shake the sight of the Arab from their surveillance in Aberdeen from his mind, wondering why he was walking through the terminal in Marseille. Self-doubt lingered heavily on his thoughts, knowing he should have said something to the French detectives, Lemieux and Benoit, before he boarded the aircraft.

Closing his eyes, he recalled the man at the terminal. *Once again, the Arab looked comfortable in his surroundings, but also somewhat nervously out of place, just as he did when I saw him in Aberdeen.* As the flight bore on, he replayed the image in his mind, noting his attire and mannerisms specifically. Pulling out the tattered moleskin notebook from his field coat, Conor jotted a few notes, making sure to list things of importance to pass along to his French counterparts.

"Something bugging you, Conor?" Andrew asked, seeing his partner writing a few things in the notebook. *It's about damn time he started keeping his own notes.* It was out of the norm for him.

"Aye, I think I saw our Arab friend whom we spied in Aberdeen," Conor said, filling his partner in on what he observed in the airport just ninety minutes previously.

"Sounds like something for Detective Benoit and Detective Lemieux to investigate," Andrew said.

"Aye, something for the French," Conor muttered, finishing off the can of Newcastle Ale and motioning to the flight attendant for another in the same instance.

## Chapter Seventeen

As the glow of the rising sun began to paint the horizon in shades of orange and yellow to the east, Captain Duncan maneuvered the *Nordic Supplier* into position, beginning the delicate ballet between the two ships, transferring the empty container from his vessel to the French freighter *Bonaparte* while succumbing to the ebb and flow of the current. "Stand by working deck," the captain bellowed at his crewman on the bridge, who immediately relayed the message to the deckhands and F/O Malcolm Spiers leading the crew.

"Stand by to release the shackles," Malcolm declared, seeing the gantry crane begin to move over the side of the freighter, its hook, and the container components swinging precariously in the air over the deckhands on the service vessel.

Perched dangerously on top of the empty container was Seaman Fiona Carr, the ship's gaff hook in one hand, the other hand grasping a safety line tied to the ship's railing, watching the swinging gear begin to lower in her direction from the gantry crane.

"Fiona, stay clear as best as you can," Malcolm exclaimed, seeing her inching closer to the center of the container, attempting to snag the swinging cable and container locks on the first try.

In but a few minutes, the crane operator had successfully lowered the gear onto the waiting service vessel where Fiona quickly made the necessary connections at each corner with the twist lock components.

Shimming down from the container like a performer from the French-Canadian circus troop *'Cirque de Soleil'*, Fiona was quickly clear of the container and standing next to the first officer. "Aye, that'll get yer blood moving," she exclaimed, her face flush with excitement, her breathing coming in gasps as if she just ran a one-hundred-meter sprint.

Seeing that all was ready, F/O Spiers gave the command to release the shackles securing the container to the *Nordic Supplier* at the same time he signaled for the gantry crane operator to begin hoisting the container skyward. In a well-choreographed act, the container was lifted off the deck and placed onto the freighter in the open space against the superstructure.

In what seemed like an hour but was just three minutes, the freighter's crew had secured the empty container and prepared the one with the drugs for hoisting onto the service vessel's deck.

As the container was swung over the side, Captain Duncan deftly used the controls of the bow and aft thrusters to keep the vessel in position, to allow securing the container easier for his first officer and crew when it hit the deck.

With a dull thud and a screech of metal on metal, the container contacted the deck of the *Nordic Supplier*, which put the deckhands into motion, quickly lashing chains through the lower eyes and ratcheting the shackles snug to keep the loaded metal box from sliding about.

As she had done before, Fiona made her way to the top of the now secured container to release the twist locks, allowing the crane operator to retract the hook and cables. Just as she approached the last lock, a rogue wave caused the *Nordic Supplier* and *Bonaparte* to encounter each other and the sudden jolt sent the free-swinging locks in her direction. Seeing them out of the corner of her eye, Fiona deftly dodged the chain and locks by diving away from them, grabbing the handle of the last lock, disengaging it from the container.

Just as he saw his crewman diving for the lock, Malcolm Spiers ran to the corner of the container, hoping to catch his young seaman and break her fall as they both tumbled to the deck.

"That'll leave a mark," she exclaimed, rubbing the spot on her ass cheek, rolling off the first officer as they both lay sprawled on the wet deck of the service vessel.

"Aye, and I'll have a hell of a time explaining it to Linda, won't I," Malcolm groaned, feeling the growing welt left by the deck chain he landed on, knowing it would leave a bruise the size of a cricket bat.

As all this was taking place on the weather deck, Captain Duncan could only stand and watch as he saw the action of his newest deckhand as well as his first officer and the care shown by both, one for the sake of the cargo and the other for the individual crew member.

***

Several hours earlier, the same morning *Louis Remesy* was meeting with his mentor, Sean Gilmore boarded an 'easyJet' flight in Belfast that would take him first to London, where he would catch a British Airways flight to Algiers. He braced himself for the torture of nearly eight hours of travel by booking a seat in business class, thus allowing for a bit more room during both flights.

Looking over his notes as the flight attendant poured him a cup of coffee, he felt there was something he was missing that needed to be discussed. *Mr. Higgins mentioned that he needed to gain reassurances that the container would be safe until loaded.* Looking out the window of the Airbus A319, he could see the shoreline of the Isle of Wight passing below, and he recalled his last visit to the island was to see a pop festival that highlighted the surviving members of the rock group 'Queen' in one of their last concert outings.

Sitting back and closing his eyes, Sean began to wonder where his youth had gone and what his future held, since he didn't foresee remaining with 'Mr. Higgins' till he was old and grey. *I might need to start making plans for myself.* He thought of the possibilities still available to him. *I wonder if Erin would fancy a go with me?* He envisioned the young Irishwoman with the wavy brown hair and soft blue eyes standing before him.

"Please bring your seat forward," the flight attendant declared as they prepared to make the landing at Heathrow, which startled Sean, who realized he had drifted off to sleep thinking of his boss' receptionist.

***

Opening the *'London Times'* to the crossword section, William Collingsworth prepared to begin his day as he always did. Looking at the clue for '1 across' he contemplated the possibilities. *Another word for deception*, it read. *Four letters*, he thought to himself, tapping his finger against the fountain pen sitting on his blotter.

"Ah-ha, it's a *ruse*," he exclaimed, the precise moment that Officer Jones knocked on the doorframe, looking in at the senior officer.

"Excuse me, sir, but what's a *ruse*?" Jones asked before he proceeded any further into the office.

"Oh, I'm sorry, Jones, it's the answer to the puzzle," the chief superintendent said, pointing to the open newspaper on his desk.

"I see, sir. By the way, you have a Captain Julien Duval from Marseille calling for you on line three," the constable announced, backing out of the doorway.

Picking up the phone set on his desk, William selected the flashing number "3" on the console to speak with his counterpart in the French

DJSE. "Hello, Captain Duval," William said. "To what do I owe the pleasure of this early morning call?"

"Hello, William," Julien said. "I've good news on the investigation into the *'Papillion Transport'* ownership."

"That is good to hear," William said, pulling a legal pad and pencil from the center drawer of his desk.

"It seems that the business of *'Adrien Richelieu III, LLC'* was actually begun by two former Legionnaires," Julien spoke, reading from his notes.

"So, you know who these men are then?" William asked in the hopes that the information would lead to something more substantial.

"Yes, one is Emilio Carbone and the other is Claude Guerini. We're looking at their last known residence now," Julien said. "It's rather auspicious that their surnames are the same as two rather notorious criminals that were incarcerated in the 1980s. It's also possible one is associated with a Corsican mafia family."

Little did the French and British officers know was that the partners of *'Adrien Richelieu III, LLC'* were names of two dead French Foreign Legionnaires, dispatched at the hands of two fellow legionnaires while on a training exercise in the jungles of French Guiana, who were both very much alive and living in Marseille.

***

Having returned from their visit with their French counterparts in Marseille, Conor and Andrew were back at work, armed with the information from their supervisor, Chief Superintendent Collingsworth and his associate Thomas Sinclair regarding the British platform support vessel's ownership and the French freighters.

Walking against the cool sea breeze that ebbed down the length of the quay, Conor and Andrew were heading towards the *Standard-Hercules* to question her skipper, Captain Bernard McIntosh.

"Damn this Scottish weather," Andrew said, pushing his hands deeper into his jacket. *I might need to convince Sheila to move to a posting in the Bahamas if this shit keeps up. And it's fucking summer right now.* He noted he needed to buy a heavier coat if he stayed in Aberdeen any longer.

"What are you complaining about? This is summer," Conor replied. "Wait till winter comes."

"Don't remind me." *It's never this cold in London.*

Walking toward the support vessel, its red and white structure a stark contrast to the gathering grey skies above, the Scotland Yard inspectors moved aside for a lorry unloading pallets of goods.

"Mind ya, they *dinnae* know we've got details on the vessels," Conor instructed his young partner as they neared the fantail of the vessel tied to the quay.

"I'll let you do all the talking then," Andrew replied, slightly miffed at the thought he wasn't trusted to know what should or shouldn't be discussed.

Seeing a deckhand near the back of the looming superstructure, Conor waved to gain the young man's attention. "Is the captain aboard?" he asked, one foot against the rail of the ship, the other firmly planted on the quay.

"Aye, give me a minute," the seaman said, walking through the hatch leading into the vessel's interior.

Shortly thereafter, a short robust figure walked through the hatch, followed closely by a second figure, this one slightly taller and of average build.

"I'm Cap'n McIntosh. What can I do for you?"

Stepping over the rail, Conor and Andrew approached the two gentlemen and displayed their police credentials for the men to observe. "I'm Chief Inspector McDermott, Scotland Yard and this is Inspector Fletcher," Conor said, pointing to Andrew. "We've a few questions to ask you and your crew regarding some activities from last month."

"Doesn't seem like anything I do onboard me own vessel would involve the Yard," Bernard McIntosh said, suddenly taking a defensive stance before the two inspectors.

"We believe that there might have been some illegal activity taking place that you or your crew observed while at sea that pertains to an investigation here in Aberdeen," Conor said, getting the sense that McIntosh was not going to be cooperative.

"Let's go into the crew's mess where we can sit and discuss the issues, shall we," Bernard said, a stern stare being made at the two police officers.

Conor turned to Andrew. "Go and see if you can locate the *Standard-Apollo*, and while you're at it, contact Chief MacCallum to have a couple of constables at the ready." He sensed something being withheld by the captain.

"Blake, go see that we've the mess available," Captain McIntosh directed his first officer, who had been standing silently behind him the entire time.

As each of the subordinates took their leave, Conor and Bernard looked like two contestants preparing to compete in tossing cabers in the highland games, neither flinching nor wavering from the other.

"This way, Inspector." Bernard motioned to Conor, leading him towards the open hatch he had come from just minutes earlier.

Walking back to the parked car, Andrew withdrew his cell phone and made the call to Chief Superintendent MacCallum as directed to by Conor.

"Hello?"

"Chief Superintendent, this is Inspector Fletcher."

"What is it, Inspector?" CS MacCallum queried. "I thought you and McDermott were questioning the vessel crews this morning."

"We are, sir, but Conor asked that I contact you to request several constables be sent over to the 'Albert Quay' where the *Standard-Hercules* is tied up," Andrew said, standing outside the parked car.

"Is there a problem?"

"I'm not sure, sir, but Conor seems to think we might need to have a few extra hands ready if things get out of control," Andrew said. *Conor is not one to ask for help, but when he does, it's normally for a good reason.* He learned as each week passed a sense of his partner's concerns the more they worked together.

"I see. I'll have Sergeant Giles head over with a crew to your location in a few minutes," MacCallum said. "Keep me informed as best as you can, Andrew."

"Yes, sir, I'll do that," Andrew said.

As Andrew was making the call back to the district headquarters, Conor was sitting down in the crew's mess room across from Bernard McIntosh and his first officer, Blake Young.

"So, what is it that you need to discuss?" Bernard asked, his hands placed on the table and his gaze straight at Conor.

"Records show that on the morning of the thirteenth of May, your vessel and the *Standard-Apollo* were at station keeping at the following coordinates: 55.94 and 0.56. This is well over one hundred fifty kilometers from your intended destination in the 'Erskine' gas fields," Conor disclosed to the two seamen. "At the same time, there're records that show a French-flagged vessel, *M/V Joan of Arc* in the same location, but we've no record of her docking in a British port."

"If I recall, we were rendering assistance to Captain McKenzie. He thought he had a fouled prop and began to drift," Captain McIntosh said, recalling the events like a well-rehearsed part of a play.

"I remember we got a signal from the French vessel that they were attempting to render aid as well," F/O Young added to the conversation, speaking for the first time.

"So, does our rendering of aid answer your questions?" the vessel's master asked, a hint of distain in his voice.

"There's an ongoing investigation regarding drug trafficking that we believe stems from activity on this French vessel," Conor replied, "which as you know, carries with it a penalty of losing your master's license and vessel if you're found to have aided in the movement of drugs."

The accusation that Captain Bernard McIntosh heard from the inspector sitting across from him began to make his mind reel in the fact that what he had considered was a good plan and executed well, could all begin to unfold if he didn't choose his next words wisely.

"I see. And Scotland Yard has evidence to support its line of questioning?" Bernard asked, fighting the temptation to reach across and throttle the inspector for making the accusation.

"We have information that supports our need to ask all possible parties involved what they know," Conor said, in a quiet, resolved tone, making every attempt to keep control of the situation.

"Very well then, Inspector," Bernard said, standing up from the table. "I'd appreciate it if you would be so kind as to leave my vessel."

"I can come back with the necessary documents to conduct formal questioning of you and your crew," Conor said.

"I look forward to seeing you in the company of my barrister then," the vessel's master said. "Mister Young, see the inspector off the boat." And with that, Captain McIntosh left the crew's mess and headed toward the bridge, leaving his first officer to escort Conor off the ship.

As his first officer was seeing the Scotland Yard inspector off the ship, Bernard McIntosh went to the communication suite of the ship to have his radio operator prepare a telex to his employer in Marseille. *What do they know?* He prepared to dictate the message to the '*Papillion Transport*' offices in Marseille.

"Mister Boyd, take a message, if you please," the captain announced, entering the small radio room. With that, the young radio operator turned to his computer and prepared to type the dictation from his captain.

"Scotland Yard investigating activity with *M/V Joan of Arc* from May. Stop. Request legal counsel to be made available. Stop. Request guidance on how to proceed with next shipment. End message," Bernard said to the young operator.

"See that it's sent to *'Papillion Transport'* by encrypted means and get confirmation of receipt back to me and make sure you include Captain McKenzie on the *Apollo* in the transmission too," Bernard said, leaving the radio operator to finish sending the information.

"Aye, sir," the young man responded.

Shortly after Captain McIntosh had dictated the message to the young radio operator, it was received at the offices of *'Papillion Transport'* as well as the communication suite of the *PSV Standard-Apollo* as it sailed through the English Channel to make its scheduled rendezvous with the *M/V Bonaparte*.

***

As the message was delivered to the account for *'Papillion Transport'* offices, an alert prompt was flagged on the lead receptionist's computer. Upon seeing this, she immediately forwarded the message to the email account of the president of *'Papillion Transport'*.

Sitting in the office situated in the *'La Cabucelle'* district near the bustling docks of Marseille, he saw the alert flash across his cell phone that he had a waiting message. Turning to the desktop computer, he logged onto a public email site, accessing his private account to view the message.

As the message opened, he saw that it had been originated from Captain McIntosh on the *Standard-Hercules* in Aberdeen and included Captain McKenzie of the *Standard-Apollo* as well.

Reading the brief but powerful message, he stopped for a moment to think. *So, Scotland Yard has information on the 'Joan of Arc' from the May shipment.* He also saw that Captain McKenzie was asking for a legal counsel to be made available as well. *This will need to be handled carefully.* He didn't want to expose himself or the operation needlessly to anyone.

As he sat in the office alone, he contemplated asking for assistance from the mysterious Irishman 'Mr. Higgins' to provide his counselor to help in alleviating the potential criminal charges that could be levied against the captains.

***

Captain McKenzie looked at the printed message sent by his fellow-captain, Bernard McIntosh for what seemed to be the hundredth time. *How in the hell did the Yard find out about the transaction?* He stood braced against the wind while out on the wing of the bridge. Looking out along the horizon, he strained to see the outline of the merchantman sailing towards him and his ship. Before he entered the bridge, he took one last drag on the cigarette he had just lit before flicking it over the side and into the churning water below. It would not be much more than two or three hours and he would be coming alongside the *Bonaparte* and begin the transfer of the container carrying the drugs to his vessel.

Little did Captain McKenzie know, but six hours earlier, the *Nordic Supplier* captained by Clive Duncan had already made the transfer of the container, replacing the one with the narcotic cargo for an empty one he had loaded on his vessel in Aberdeen. And with the transfer complete, the *Nordic Supplier* had made its course correction and was on its way back to deliver the container to a lorry for its new destination in Glasgow.

***

Standing outside the Fisherman's market with the three constables and Sergeant Giles, Andrew caught sight of his partner being 'escorted' off the service vessel. Seeing Conor walking along the quay and away from the *Standard-Hercules* made Andrew wonder what was wrong.

"How did things go?"

"He knows he's caught, but he's *nae* daft either, asking for a barrister he did." Looking at the young man, Conor asked, "Any luck with questioning the *Standard-Apollo* crew?"

"The vessels at sea per the harbormaster records," Andrew said, "heading to the 'Erskine' gas fields as it were."

"I believe we need to contact Captain Kinkaid to see if he could tail her," Conor said, stepping into the parked police car and out of the biting North Sea winds.

With that, Andrew thanked the sergeant and his officers, dismissing them, allowing them to return to their normal patrols. Getting behind the

175

wheel, he quickly turned the engine over and opened the heater up to try and stave off the cold the wind had brought.

"Let's get to the Maritime office and see if we can contact Captain Kinkaid," Conor said, watching Andrew vigorously rub his hands together, attempting to bring some warmth back to his fingers.

Entering the Maritime Merchants and Coast Guard Agency building, Conor knew where he was going from his time visiting as the communications officer in the Royal Navy, so he and Andrew hurriedly walked past the receptionist and made their way to the communications hall.

"Can I help you?" the watch officer exclaimed as the two inspectors came through the door with a clatter.

"Aye, you can," Conor said, catching his breath. "We need to contact Captain Kinkaid onboard the *Oceanic-Talisker* immediately," he said, showing his credentials to the communications operator.

With a few keystrokes on the computer the operator brought up the shore-to-ship number for contacting the service vessel while at sea, and immediately set to dialing the number on the telecommunication system.

As the operator was making the connection to the vessel, she motioned to Conor that he would need to pick up the handset of the phone located at the end of the counter. "*Oceanic-Talisker*, this is Aberdeen, stand by for traffic," the operator said as First Officer King answered the call.

"Mister King, this is CI McDermott. I need to speak with Captain Kinkaid," Conor said, looking over at Andrew standing by the doorway to insure no one else entered during the call.

"Just a moment," the young officer said, placing the handset into his captain's weathered hand.

"Aye, this is Captain Kinkaid."

"Cap'n, this is Conor McDermott, I need you to take on a task," the inspector said, hoping the vessel's master would be able to accommodate him.

"Aye, what is it, lad?" he asked.

"I need you to locate and track the *Standard-Apollo*, but do not interfere with any action they undertake," Conor disclosed to the captain.

"And when I find her, then what?" Captain Kinkaid asked, knowing his fee would be sent to Scotland Yard.

"Contact me at the Aberdeen district headquarters," he answered, knowing it could be nearly twenty-four hours before the service vessel returned from its scheduled voyage to the gas fields.

"Aye, I'll let you know. *Oceanic-Talisker* out," the captain said, terminating the transmission.

With the call done with the inspector from Scotland Yard, Captain Kinkaid put his crew into action. "Helm, make your course one hundred eighty-five degrees, speed twelve knots," he ordered the crewman manning the deck console on the bridge, sending his vessel on a course headed south.

Captain Kinkaid had taken the liberty of making a search pattern right after his talk with Conor when his vessel was tied to the docks in Aberdeen, so he was already prepared to begin his part in apprehending those responsible for the drug trafficking. *Where, oh where are you, Dillan?* He stared out over the bow at the growing seas.

***

As the *Oceanic-Talisker* was completing its third search leg of the day, F/O King saw the faint outline of a service vessel emerge along the horizon to the starboard side steaming north. Taking his 'big-eye' binoculars, he stepped outside onto the bridge wing to try and gain a better look at the ship as it sailed closer.

Just as Gerard King was beginning his attempt to identify what was the *Nordic Supplier*, First Officer Malcolm Spiers was essentially doing the same, following the orders of his captain to track and identify every vessel since they retrieved the container from the *Bonaparte*.

As each vessel sailed closer to the other, it was but a matter of minutes until each first officers recognized the other. Stepping back into the warm confines of the bridge, F/O Spiers directed the seaman at the helm to maintain course and speed as he lifted the ship-to-ship radio and signaled an acknowledgement to his counterpart on the *Oceanic-Talisker*.

"Copy, *Nordic-Supplier*, safe sailing," Bernard King replied to the hail coming from the passing vessel as it made its way back to Aberdeen. "Brings us left to two hundred forty-five degrees," he instructed the helmsman as they continued their search for the *Standard-Apollo*, not knowing that the *Nordic-Supplier* was the vessel carrying the illegal narcotics within the container lashed to her deck.

***

Sitting in their new offices at the district headquarters building on King Street, Conor was busy dialing the number for Geneviève Benoit, remembering he needed to pass along the sighting of the Arab from the airport in Marseille. After the third ring, the police officer sitting in her office thirteen hundred kilometers away finally answered.

"Detective Benoit, how can I help you?" she answered quickly in French.

"Aye, you can, lass, if ya *nae* speak so fast," Conor said, trying his best to understand the language.

"Conor, I'm sorry," Geneviève said, embarrassed for assuming every caller understood her. "What can I do for you this morning?"

"I think I saw our mystery drug dealer at the airport yesterday," he said. "But he wasn't dressed like a Westerner, he had traditional Arab clothing on."

"I see. Where did we happen to be standing in the terminal when you saw him?" *Claude and I will need to get our hands on the surveillance tapes from the terminal.* She prepared to make notes of what the Scot said.

"It was just a few meters from the check-in counter and I was looking toward the departure gates and the security checkpoint," Conor said, talking with his eyes closed, trying to provide her with as much detail as he could.

"I'll get with Claude, and we'll look at the tapes from yesterday," Geneviève said, taking down notes as Conor described the scenario from the airport.

***

Completing its eastern most patrol leg, the HMS *Tyne*'s watch officer brought the patrol craft about and prepared to set course for home in Portsmouth. As the patrol craft made its turn, the radar operator notified the watch officer of an odd signal to the north.

"What do you make of it?" the officer asked as he looked over the sailor's shoulder at the image cycling every two seconds.

"I could swear that I'd two vessels and now just one at these coordinates," the young petty officer said, handing the officer a slip of paper with the last known location written for each vessel.

"Helmsman, come north to three hundred forty degrees and bring our speed to sixteen knots," the officer declared, unsure of what they might encounter when they arrived at the position of the vessels.

***

At the time the watch officer was being notified of the vessel's location, Captain McKenzie was busy maneuvering the *Standard-Apollo* alongside the *Bonaparte,* preparing to receive the container that was to be swung over the side of the freighter.

Entering the bridge, the first officer exclaimed, "We've got a problem, Dillan."

Letting the slip of proper shipboard protocol slide for the moment, the captain asked his first officer to catch her breath and then explain the situation to him.

"The French crew said they've already made the transaction," Alison said. "There's no container to be transferred."

Walking over to the radio, Dillan McKenzie selected the frequency for the *Bonaparte* and asked to speak with Captain Levet.

"This Captain Levet," he replied, taking the handset from his first officer.

"Captain Levet, this is Captain McKenzie. We're here to retrieve a container of cargo. Could you please verify?" he spoke as calmly as he could, considering the circumstances.

"The cargo has already been transferred per instructions from our office," the French skipper replied.

"The container was transferred, to which vessel?" Dillan asked, beginning to let his frustration show.

"I assumed it was the correct vessel as they had communicated on the proper frequency and had a replacement container prepared," Henri said. "I didn't notice the vessel name as we did the transfer at night."

He was beginning to suspect that he and the other captain had been used as pawns in an elaborate chess game. Earlier in the voyage, Henri informed his home office that the switch of the container had taken place but didn't understand the second vessel's appearance or the need to undertake the action a second time.

Dillan McKenzie looked at his first officer at hearing about an 'empty' container being used for the transfer and all he got in return was a shrug of her shoulders, her look just as perplexing as his at this new revelation.

As the two captains discussed the validity of the container and its cargo, a lookout on the *Bonaparte* sounded the alarm of an approaching vessel, this one flying the colors of a British warship.

"Captain, the French can see a patrol boat making its way up from the south, speed about sixteen knots," Alison said, listening in on the French radio frequency used for transferring the container.

"Captain Levet, we'll contact our office for clarification. Safe sailing," Captain McKenzie declared, turning his attention back to the helm, turning the engine speed actuator to full speed.

Taking the ship's intercom microphone from the console, Captain McKenzie announced, "All hands, prepare for rough seas," taking command of the ship, preparing to take every action to avoid being boarded by the naval patrol craft. "Mister Reed, contact the gas derrick and instruct them to have the previous shipment ready for transfer upon our arrival," he said.

Seeing the service vessel make its way to the north at increasingly higher speeds, Henri Levet turned to his first officer. "Pierre, get us back on course for Hamburg and let's make the best of a bad situation," he directed him to their port of call. Seeing that his ship was not at risk for the moment, Henri went to the ship's radio room and drafted a message to the home office of the second vessel and what appeared to be an elaborate deception to gain access to the drugs meant for the gas derricks.

On the patrol craft *'Tyne'* the watch officer was informing Lieutenant Smythe of the situation regarding the two vessels that were directly ahead of them. "One moment we had two sightings on radar, and then just one," the senior enlisted man said to his 'captain' of the ship. "Then after about fifteen minutes of having just one signal return, there began a second return as if they were split in two."

"Seems we might have one vessel rendering aid to another," the lieutenant said. *What else are you two up to? Considering all the possibilities of two vessels coming together.* Sensing they were closer to the freighter than the service vessel, Lieutenant Smythe directed his radio operator to hail the *Bonaparte* to ascertain the cause for their apparent need to have contact with the second ship.

"*Motor Vessel Bonaparte*, this is HMS *Tyne*, come in," the operator declared over the international shipping frequency monitored by all merchantmen sailing the English Channel.

"HMS *Tyne*, this is the captain of *M/V Bonaparte* speaking," Henri Levet replied to the operator's query.

Lieutenant Smythe took the radio handset from the bridge console so he could speak directly with the French captain. "Captain, we've noticed your station keeping and have concerns for your safety. Are you in need of assistance?" the British officer asked.

"HMS *Tyne*, we are safe. There are no issues or concerns to address now," Henri replied to the officer standing on the patrol craft now only three kilometers from his stern.

"Please account for the second vessel at your location," the British officer directed the Frenchman.

"We had a crewman that was not unaccounted for and we feared he'd fallen overboard. The second vessel was in the vicinity and offered to assist in the search, but our missing crewman has since been found onboard," the captain of the *Bonaparte* said, lying to the British officer, trying to avoid being boarded.

With no sense to suspect any wrongdoing and a reasonable explanation for the two ships being near each other, Lieutenant Smythe bid the French captain farewell. "Officer of the watch, make a log entry to account for our contact with the freighter. Helmsman, make your course three hundred forty-five degrees and your speed twenty knots," he commanded his sailors to action. "Officer of the watch, as soon as we have a radar sighting on the second vessel I want to know," the lieutenant spoke, making his way to the galley suite for a fresh cup of tea and some shortbread biscuits.

# Chapter Eighteen

With the soft crackling of a burning log on the fire and sitting in the leather wing-back chair in his study, 'Mr. Higgins' looked over the message on his computer from Clive Duncan. *Container secured, returning to Aberdeen,* it read. With a wry smile on his face, he began to think he was finally going to gain the upper hand with the French-Algerian drug dealer.

It had taken some doing to convince Captain Duncan that he could transfer the container from the French freighter. The good captain had shown genuine concern about the safety of his crew as none of them were experienced in handling a container while at sea, nor able to defend themselves if the merchantman were armed.

Looking at the mantle clock, he saw it would be too late to call upon Alistair Hunt, informing the crime boss in Glasgow that his part of the deception was soon to take place, beginning in Aberdeen. His other concern was for his young counsel, Sean, who was in Algiers negotiating the security of the weapons' shipment with *Monsieur Remesy.*

***

"Keep a sharp eye out, Fiona," Malcolm Spiers said, reminding the young woman of the dangers that lay before the ship while sailing the open waters in the dead of night. As the first officer, he had the most exposure with the crew on the *Nordic-Supplier* and he'd taken a liking to the young woman from the moment she signed on as a deckhand. From her spunky, happy-go-lucky attitude to her near fearlessness of the elements while working the deck, she was proving to be a valuable member of the crew.

It wasn't just her work ethics that made her easy to be around. She was also *'easy on the eyes'* as the other crewmen had described her. From her short, fiery pixie-style red hair, cut like the American gymnast Dorothy Hamill, it was also the tight and well-proportioned figure that filled out her work overalls that caught everyone's attention as she made her way about the ship.

"I've got a glimpse of the outer buoy ahead," she declared, seeing the flashing beacon set in place to denote the beginning of the sea lane for entering the Aberdeen harbor.

Looking out over the bow, F/O Spiers could also see the marker as it bobbed up and down with the waves. Glancing at the clock set against the bulkhead of the bridge, Malcolm calculated the remaining distance to cover before entering the harbor against the speed the vessel was currently sailing at and determined they would be tied along the dock within the next hour or so.

"Mind the store," the Scotsman proclaimed, disappearing down the inner stairwell that led to the captain's cabin. Gently rapping his knuckles against the door, Malcolm announced, "About an hour from dockside, Captain."

Hearing his first officer's knocking, Clive Duncan sat up in the bunk where he had been sleeping. "Aye, thank you, Malcolm," he replied. Reaching over and turning on the small light next to the desk, he carefully stood up before shuffling to the loo where he quickly relieved himself.

Getting his clothes on, Clive Duncan had a sense of accomplishment come over him, safe in the knowledge that he was soon to be rid of the container without mishap. This almost came to fruition as he saw Seaman Carr tumble off the container, but for First Officer Spiers' quick action to catch the young lass at the last moment.

Walking back to the crew's mess, he saw that Malcolm had kept a fresh pot of coffee brewing, which he poured into his cup before making his way back to the bridge. As he approached the top of the stairwell he could hear Fiona's voice clearly using a less than lady-like description for Malcolm's bruised torso.

"I see we're having a 'show-and-tell' session," Captain Duncan exclaimed, entering the bridge.

"My apologies, sir," Fiona replied. "I hadn't seen the extent of F/O Spiers' bruises since he caught me."

"Let's get back to manning this vessel then if we're all done," the vessel's master extorted, looking scornfully for a brief instance at his first officer, sending the disapproving message.

Seeing the look on his captain's face told Malcolm everything he needed to know about the captain's feelings regarding what he had just seen between the two members of the crew.

"Based on our current position and speed, I make our arrival alongside to be in an hour or so," the first officer declared, preparing to turn over control of the ship to his captain.

"Very good, Mister Spiers," Captain Duncan replied, sitting in the conning chair situated on the starboard side of the bridge. Reaching over, he slid the small window open and pulled his pipe from its holder on the console in front of him. "You've no objections, Seaman Carr?" He stuffed a pinch of tobacco into the weathered briar pipe and lit it with a match.

"No, sir, no objections," Fiona replied. *Who am I to tell the captain whether he could smoke his own bridge or not?* She stood, manning the helm.

***

Stuart Ross sat quietly, dozing on and off in his car that was parked along the M80 thoroughfare as he waited for the arrival of the lorry and driver that would pick up the container from the docks in Aberdeen and return it to Glasgow. It was a rather strange request from Alistair Hunt because they had never delved into any activity that required the use of a large truck or an individual not considered a member of their syndicate to act as driver.

In a few minutes, the sharp hiss of escaping air as the massive Volvo tractor and trailer pulled next to his car woke Stuart up. With a startled look, Stuart glanced at the passenger side of his Ford and saw the outline of a figure dressed in a workman's coverall and holding a flashlight in his hands.

Getting out of his car rather cautiously, Stuart walked around to the back until he could see the driver more clearly. It was at this point he could see that the driver was of Hindu or Sikh descent, as he wore the traditional turban.

"You Mister Ross?"

"That's right."

"I understand I'm to retrieve a container in Aberdeen and deliver it to Glasgow."

"That's correct. And no questions are to be asked."

"Understood."

"Two-thirds payment now, the balance when you deliver the container safely to the destination in Glasgow," Stuart said, handing the brown envelope to the driver. "The location for the pick-up and the delivery address are in the packet."

With the exchange completed, the driver nodded politely at the syndicate member and walked back to his lorry, when Stuart noticed that there was a second occupant sitting in the passenger seat.

"I've got to be more careful," he said, getting back into his car, realizing he could've been easily dispatched by the second person and robbed of the thirty-three thousand pounds he held in the envelope.

***

The kitchen clock in Ailene's flat ticked loudly in the early morning hours, the darkness kept at bay by a light from above the stove, Conor sitting quietly at the table, contemplating the actions from his time on the *Standard-Hercules* and seeing Bernard McIntosh face-to-face.

Tilting his head forward, he took a sip of tea. *He knows he's doing something illegal. But does he know enough to implicate the next bloke on the ladder?* He tried once again to place together a puzzle with out of shape pieces.

Rolling onto her side, Ailene realized she was alone and got out of bed and made her way to the dimly lit kitchen. Walking in, she saw Conor leaning back in the chair, his eyes closed momentarily in deep thought.

Sensing the presence of his lover, Conor sat up and opened his eyes to see Ailene in the doorway.

"*Kin ya nae* sleep?" she asked, walking over to him, wrapping her arms around his head and placing it against her bosom.

"I'm *nae* closer to finding these druggies as I was three months ago," he declared, taking in the softness of her breasts and the faint aroma of her Obsession perfume.

"Well, if it's any consolation, I've got a list of possible folks at the office you can have Andrew check on," Ailene said, pulling away from him.

"I told you not to take any chances, hen," he said, thinking that she had gone to her supervisor to ask about the workers.

She held out the list that she wrote earlier.

"I see that you list someone from nearly every department," Conor said, reading the names. "It'll keep Sergeant Giles busy."

"You're not going to have Andrew work on this?" Ailene asked.

"No. He's helping me with the questioning of crews from the service boats," he said, standing and placing the now empty tea cup in the sink.

Leaning against the sink, he thought about Captain Kinkaid and his crew, wondering if they had any luck in locating the *Standard-Apollo* and what they possibly could be doing while at sea other than providing services to a legitimate oil or gas platform.

***

As the *Nordic Supplier* was approaching the outer entrance to Aberdeen harbor, a non-descript Volvo truck and trailer was pulling into the holding area near the *'Commercial quay'* in Aberdeen. Looking back in the sleeper unit of the cab, the driver saw that his companion was still fast asleep, undisturbed by the trip of nearly three and a half hours.

Easing off the throttles, Captain Duncan maneuvered the seventy-five-meter service vessel into the channel of the River Dee. Looking at both the port and starboard buoys, he could see exactly what his senses were telling him. The outbound tide was lessening and it would shortly start to flow up the channel from the sea, making his passage simpler.

Keeping a close eye on the south jetty, Clive Duncan made his way into the protected waters of the harbor and slowed his vessel's movement to a crawl. His vessel's normal berth in the harbor would have been at the *'Regents quay'*, but because he had a container to be lifted from the deck, he needed to dock his vessel on the southern side of the *'Commercial quay'* where a mobile crane would be waiting to lift the load from his deck.

All of this had been pre-arranged by himself and Alistair Hunt, who was making the lorry for the container available for the trip to Glasgow. Easing slowly into the channel along the quay, Captain Duncan deftly used the maneuvering thrusters to place the ship between two other vessels already tied to the dock.

"Mister Spiers, secure the bow and stern," he said into the ship's intercom. Once secured around the bollards, F/O Spiers directed two of the crewmen to use the deck winches to snug the vessel against the pier and the heavy rubber fenders.

As soon as the *Nordic Supplier* was tied to the dock, the mobile crane moved alongside to off-load the container. As the crane lowered its cradle to be attached to the container, the lorry appeared from behind the cargo building at the end of the dock.

As the container was attached to the cradle and secured by the longshoremen working with the crane operator, F/O Spiers directed the deckhands to release the chains and shackles that had been used to keep it in place during the voyage.

Watching the container being lifted off the deck gave everyone onboard a sense of relief, as well as pride, as they had once again delivered their cargo without a mishap. Observing the activity from the rear facing bridge position, Clive Duncan lifted the ship-to-shore phone from its cradle and placed a call, leaving a message that would inform 'Mr. Higgins' that this part of his operation had been completed.

***

Sitting comfortably in his captain's chair on the bridge of the *Oceanic-Talisker*, Captain Kinkaid kept a keen eye on the speck outlined on the horizon. After nearly eighteen hours of searching, he located the vessel requested by Conor McDermott. It was the Captain Dillan McKenzie and the *Standard-Apollo* sailing back towards Aberdeen.

Captain Kinkaid's first officer, Gerard King, was the first to spot the vessel as it left the vicinity of an abandoned derrick near the *'Erskine'* gas fields. Upon their initial observation, they couldn't make out anything that would be considered as suspicious or out of the ordinary for the vessel being at a derrick.

It wasn't until they had closed the distance to within two kilometers from the derrick that they observed activity taking place. F/O King reported seeing numerous men occupying the derrick and milling about several containers that were placed on the heliport deck. Heeding the inspector's warning, though, they kept their distance and followed the vessel on its return voyage to Aberdeen, unsure if anything illegal ever took place.

***

Having made a valiant attempt to close the distance on the service vessel they had seen with the French freighter the day before, Lieutenant Smythe ordered his patrol boat to break off the pursuit as they had burned through most of their fuel in the chase.

What they could do was make a report of seeing the service vessel as it entered a group of derricks situated on the outskirts of the *'Erskine'* gas fields, and that the vessel failed to respond when hailed by the naval vessel.

"Helm, come about to two hundred seventy degrees and make your speed ten knots," the naval officer commanded the seaman who stood at the controls of the patrol boat. "Navigator, set your course for Newcastle and alert them that we are low on fuel," he directed the petty officer manning the navigational charts and radio. As they turned away from their prey, he mused, *I'll find out who you are and make amends for this embarrassment.* He knew he would have to explain his action to his superiors in the squadron, and that they would have to make a report to the Admiralty in Portsmouth.

***

Heading west on the M9 motorway out of Edinburgh, which leads to the M80 into Glasgow, the lorry driver was thinking about completing the delivery of the container and receiving the last part of the payment for his efforts.

Looking out the front window of the lorry, Angus Dunbar sat stoically, hoping that this trip would end as it began, with little fanfare and no bloodshed. He knew Alistair wanted assurances that the delivery would be made as directed and without incident, and he had every intention of doing just that. It took an extra thousand pounds out of his pocket to convince the driver that he would be a 'silent' passenger on the trip and would not cause any problems.

***

Sitting in the comfort of their car, Inspector's McDermott and Fletcher were quickly reviewing the plan to search the returning support vessel *Standard-Apollo* as soon as it had completed being secured to the dock.

"Reviewing the vessel manifest. She normally sails with a crew of fourteen, and that doesn't include the captain," Andrew said, reviewing the ship's records provided by his partner's love interest. "However, the report from the crew of the HMS *Tyne* could only account for six crewmembers on deck."

"So, we need to ensure we can account for a possibility of eighteen members in total?" Conor said more as a question than a reply to the young inspector from London.

"Yes. The captain, the first officer, engineer and his engine room crew of four, the cook and two galley-types, and eight crew members who work the decks," Andrew said, reading off the positions for a crew serving onboard the vessel.

188

Closing his eyes, Conor tried to envision the possible scenarios that could unfold as he and his partner boarded the support vessel with the half dozen constables in their attempt to search for the illegal narcotics reported to be stowed away. "We need to remind Sergeant Giles not to be too anxious about going below," he said, prompting the young inspector to take notice of the perils involved.

"Looking over the report, it doesn't give much detail about the interaction of the *M/V Bonaparte* and the PSV," Andrew pointed out to his partner. "Based on the sightings, it says the lookout lost the *Standard-Apollo* as it sailed amongst the gas field derricks."

Reaching forward from the driver's seat, Conor took the back of his sleeve and wiped the growing layer of condensation from the windscreen of the police car, trying to capture a glimpse of the vessel as it slowly made its way into port.

***

Just as she was bringing the service vessel past the inner channel marker, Alison Reid heard the familiar voice of the ship's captain bellow behind her. "Captain has the conn," he exclaimed, taking the controls of the seventy-seven-meter long service vessel from his first officer. The captain relished this part of his duties, showing off his mettle of seamanship to the other captains watching from their respective bridges. Slowing his vessel to a mere steerage speed with the touch of his right hand, Captain McKenzie swung the wheel slowly in his left hand until he sensed the rudder biting the water and swinging the ship around.

As the vessel swung about in the tight confines of the inner harbor, Captain Duncan took in the maneuver from the bridge of his supply vessel *Nordic Supplier* with a less than approving look on his face. Turning away from the bridge window, Captain Duncan saw the gathering of constables and the two inspectors from Scotland Yard standing by for the *Standard-Apollo* to finish getting tied to the docks, a concerned look crossing his face.

***

Shortly after watching the *Standard-Apollo* enter the harbor at Aberdeen, the *Oceanic-Talisker* followed suit, with F/O King maneuvering the seventy-eight-meter vessel into position along the northern side of the dock at 'Albert quay' while Captain Kinkaid prepared his notes for Inspector McDermott.

"Set the bow lines," Bernard directed over the ship's intercom to the deckhands below. Sensing the bow coming to rest against the fenders, he

189

then directed for the aft lines to be set. "Cinch up all lines. Prepare to set the harbor watch," he declared. With that order given, the enginemen below began the task of powering down the huge marine diesels and securing them until the next time they would be called upon to put the vessel out to sea.

***

Standing along the dock in the fading light of day, Conor was always amazed at the choreographed chaos of a vessel when it was being tied to the docks. As a young naval officer, he took every opportunity to watch his frigate being tied to the docks whenever possible. With a well-rehearsed crew, the longshoremen and the vessel's deckhands made the act of securing the warship look like child's play in most instances.

With the deckhands cinching the lines holding the *Standard-Apollo* fast to the docks, F/O Reid could be seen making her way from the bow to the aft working party, checking on the progress. "Is Captain McKenzie onboard?" Conor bellowed, coming upon the stern of the service vessel.

"Aye, who's asking?" the feisty woman from the highlands asked, coming closer to where Conor, and now Andrew, were standing on the dock.

Pulling out their credentials, they showed the first officer. "Scotland Yard," Conor exclaimed, taking a step onto the vessel's rail.

"Inform your cap'n that his vessel is being quarantined and that all hands will be made present and accounted for on the service deck immediately," the Scotland Yard inspector declared. Alison Reid looked up at the bridge wing just as Conor finished his demand, to see the figure of her captain silhouetted in the windows.

Dillan McKenzie looked down upon the aft deck of his ship from the bridge and saw his first officer in a verbal exchange with the inspectors at the same time he spied the gathering of uniformed constables converging on the ship under the growing illumination of the floodlights lining the dock perimeter.

No sooner had Conor stepped from the docks edge to the rail of the vessel making his declaration, he found himself face-to-face with Captain McKenzie.

"I'm Captain Dillan McKenzie. What is it that you want?" His weathered and tattooed arms pulled tightly across his chest.

"I'm CI McDermott of Scotland Yard. We've been made aware that there might be illegal drugs onboard, and you and your crew are under quarantine until a search is completed," he advised the captain of a bit of information he surely already knew.

"You've no authority on my vessel, Inspector," Dillan exclaimed, "and I'm not inclined to allow you free movement on it without permission."

Looking beyond the burly frame of the captain, Conor saw that the crew had assembled on the open deck, and they numbered nearly twenty, outnumbering the police contingent of constables by four. The gathered crew appeared restless but cooperative for the moment, and the correct number based on the harbormaster's records.

"The inspector has the permission and mandate to conduct the search, Captain McKenzie," the harbormaster said, conceding his position as the port authority to Scotland Yard.

Turning from the captain and his crew, Conor waved to Sergeant Giles and the assembled constables standing at the parked police cars along the quay. "Sergeant Giles, split your force up into teams of two," the chief inspector said. "Begin in the engine room and work your way topside, leaving two constables to mind the crew here on deck."

"Aye, Inspector; but who's going to authorize the night pay?" Sergeant Giles asked, knowing several of the officers would normally be let off their shift in a few hours.

"I'll see that things are taken care of with the chief."

Turning to Andrew, Conor said, "Go and call the Maritime office and have them provide a list of all calls between the *Apollo* and *Hercules* from the last forty-eight hours. We'll need the date and time of when they took place."

"And do we monitor calls from today on as well?" the young inspector asked, pointing out to his senior that he had the means to consider the potential for collaboration between the captains as well.

"Aye, good thinkin', lad," Conor said. "Make sure they track those calls as well."

"Captain McKenzie, if you'd be so kind as to provide a ship's roster," Conor said, requesting the vessel's master to submit his list of those assembled on the service deck.

As pairs of police officers left the service deck, one of the constables escorted Dillan back into the superstructure where the ship's roster was retrieved and presented to Conor.

With constables searching the interior spaces of the ship, Conor, with the help of Cadet Constable Howe, began the task of verifying the names of the crew members listed to work on this voyage. Walking along the ranks, he reviewed each seaman's credentials against the roster. One by one, names were verified and checked off, until he came across the second to last name and face.

"I've seen you before, haven't I? Umm…" He looked at the seaman's credentials. "Mister Campbell?" the inspector questioned the seaman who stood before him.

"I did *nae* believe I've had the pleasure making your acquaintance," the seaman replied, cocky and defiant.

"No, I'm sure I've seen you." He stepped closer to the seaman's face. "Because I've got several big eight by ten glossy photos of your stupid mug from several weeks back, hanging in my office," Conor declared, "and you're standing next to a rather mysterious fella from the Middle East."

Suddenly the color drained from the seaman's face, realizing that Conor was one of the two officers who interrupted the drug transaction between himself and Ewan Sutherland.

While Conor was singling out the deckhand, one of the constables emerged from below decks and stood beside the Scotland Yard inspector, whispering to him so that none of the others could hear the conversation. "We've got something suspicious in the machine shop, Inspector," the constable said.

Shortly after being told by the constable of the suspicious item, two other constables came through the hatch at the bottom of the superstructure, each one grappling with the end of a gas cylinder as they waddled across the deck under its weight.

"Seems that this cylinder needs serviced," the constable said, cracking the valve atop the green metallic container. What should have been a loud hiss of compressed gas being emitted from the brass opening turned out to be nothing at all. "We found it attached to a cutting rig ready for use," the constable said to Conor, "but there was no pressure registering on the gauge."

"That's rather careless of your machinist having an empty cylinder in his shop, isn't it, Cap'n?" Conor asked, walking up to Captain McKenzie.

"Officer Jefferies, get a spanner and open the cylinder," Conor directed the constable who had brought up the cylinder from the interior of the vessel.

"I happen to have one right here, Inspector," the constable said, pulling the tool from his back pocket. "Thought you might want to peek inside." Locking the spanner onto the valve, the constable pulled the tool towards him, loosening it to the point it turned easily on its threaded base.

Stepping to the side, Officer Jefferies handed the inspector a flashlight, allowing Conor to peer inside. What should have been a hollow metal container turned out to be a full bottle of a mysterious liquid.

"Inspector Fletcher, get the kit from the car like a good lad," Conor said, pleased in the notion that he was looking at hard evidence.

Doing as he was directed, Andrew happily leapt from the service vessel back onto the solid surface of the docks, heading for the parked police car. Even with the boat tied to the dock, the slight rocking motion was beginning to make him nauseous.

Opening the boot, Andrew reached in and pulled the heavy black drug kit onto the ground. Grabbing the handle, he tilted the box onto its side and wheeled it to the edge of the dock where Officer Jefferies gave him a hand, muscling it onto the deck.

As all this was taking place, Bernard King was watching from the bridge of the *Oceanic-Talisker*, relaying the events over the ship's phone to his captain, who was busy in the crew galley writing up his notes.

As Andrew opened the drug test kit, Captain McKenzie and First Officer Reid just stood in silence, an ashen-grey look on their faces, resigned in the knowledge that they knew the contents within the cylinder would test positive for hashish.

Pulling out a sample of the mixture, Andrew added the reagent chemical from the test kit to the specimen of thick brown liquid he'd placed into a glass vile. Giving the container a thorough shaking resulted in the substance to interact with the drug and turn a deep purple, like that of a thistle in full bloom. "It seems we have the potential presence of a cannabis-based narcotic, Chief Inspector McDermott," Andrew said, loud enough for the assembled crew to hear.

"Very well, Inspector Fletcher," Conor said, turning to look at Captain McKenzie. "Officer Jefferies, get Sergeant Giles and the rest of the constables, place the crew under arrest, and see that they're transported for processing."

As the constables gathered around the vessel's crew and began to place the restraints on their wrists, Conor took Dillan McKenzie by the arm and led him to the side and away from the rest of the crew.

"You know that as master of this vessel you'll endure the most responsibility for the drugs being onboard."

"You'll have a hard time keeping me locked up," Dillan McKenzie said.

"Is that so?" Conor asked. "And why is that, Captain?"

"I've said my peace till my barrister's present," Dillan announced.

"Andrew, see that the ship is secured per the harbormaster's direction after all the crewmen are situated in the transports, and, Sergeant Giles, see that a set of guards are posted on the dock to restrict access to the vessel."

With the crew and illegal cargo of the *Standard-Apollo* being handled by Andrew and the constables, Conor knew there was just one more thing to take care of. Making his way from the *Standard-Apollo*, he walked around to the opposite side of the docks to where the *Oceanic-Talisker* was moored.

Conor leapt onto the aft deck and started to make his way to the superstructure, where he knew Captain Kinkaid was waiting for him. Opening the outer hatch, he stepped over the threshold and down the narrow passageway to the crew's mess.

Seated at a table was Thomas Kinkaid, holding a spiral bound notebook, a cup of coffee in front of him. "Good evening, Inspector," he said, seeing Conor walk into the room. "I hear you've been busy."

"Aye, same to you too, Cap'n," Conor said, removing his coat and placing it on the back of the chair.

"I've got some interesting information for you," the ship's captain said, opening the notebook. "We were able to see what the *Standard-Apollo* and Captain McKenzie were engaged in for a wee bit yesterday evening."

"So, you saw them making a transfer from a freighter?" Conor asked. *This would make the case an open and shut event if he had information like that.* He took a cup of tea offered by one of the crew.

"Not exactly, but they're doing something out of the ordinary," the captain said. "Since they were at an abandoned derrick and we saw workers on the derrick when there shouldn't be anyone."

"What is the significance of that then?" Conor asked, unsure why this news was considered important.

"All vessels are advised to avoid the derricks that they are not assigned or commissioned to work on, partly because you're considered trespassing, and because many are now operated remotely from shore and have no safeguards for accidents," Captain Kinkaid explained. "In the case of the derrick we saw McKenzie and his vessel at, it's designated as 'abandoned' by British Petroleum, which makes one wonder why there were men working it at all."

"So, something 'illegal' could've been taking place after all then?" Conor asked, starting to piece together the puzzle as the captain explained the events to him.

"Yes. At the very least they could be cited for trespassing on private property, or scavenging without a permit, in simple terms," Captain Kinkaid said rather jokingly, "but only if we alerted BP and they wanted to investigate and press charges."

"That should do for the moment," the inspector said. *I know exactly how I plan to question Captain Dillan McKenzie and the crew of the Standard-Apollo about their most recent voyage to sea.* He drained the last of his tea from the cup. "Could you please have something 'official' prepared and sent to the district police headquarters, as well as the Maritime office regarding your sightings?" Conor asked. "And send the copy for the Maritime office attention to Miss O'Leary." He knew Ailene would let him know when it came in and to avoid the information being leaked.

"As you wish," the captain replied, a quizzical look on his face.

Getting up from his chair, Conor extended his hand to the captain. "Thank you for getting this information. I suspect you and I'll be heading to sea in the coming days."

"You'll be welcomed onboard, Inspector," the vessel's master answered, shaking the offered hand before him.

***

Returning to the office, Conor walked past the administration spaces and towards the office he and Andrew were now sharing. Sitting down at the desk, he grabbed the phone from its cradle and dialed the number for his superior, Chief Superintendent Collingsworth in London.

195

After the second ring, he heard the familiar voice of William on the other end of his call.

"Good evening, William," Conor spoke as his superior in London answered the phone.

"I'm hoping this call is to deliver some favorable news?" the senior officer asked, sitting back in his chair.

"Aye, we've come across the drugs just as the anonymous tip led us to."

"Then congratulations are in order," Collingsworth said.

"Aye, I'd like to think so," Conor said, rubbing a hand across his face. "But it seems too 'convenient' that we found the drugs on this boat, this time, and on this day." *What are we missing? My gut feeling is that there's more to this than just one boat.* "It makes me wonder if we weren't given this information on purpose to take us off the real activity." He sighed in despair.

Hearing this from his inspector, William Collingsworth could sense that Conor was not truly sure that they had achieved their goal of seizing the drug traffickers in tonight's action on the docks. "What do you propose our next step should be then, Conor?" William asked, leaning forward and resting his arms on the edge of his desk.

"We've made a pinch of one boat moving drugs, but we've still *nae* found out who's making the decisions. I still think we need to continue looking, William." Conor's voice showed the strain of the evening's activity.

Listening to the Scottish inspector, William knew all too well that Conor was right. Until they found out who was financing the drug shipments, they would still be fighting to stop the narcotics from entering through Aberdeen.

***

Having missed the opportunity to speak with her chief superintendent the other day, Sheila saw a chance noticing the senior officer enter the outer spaces of the Administrative department. Quickly walking back to her desk in the forensics lab, she took her keys and unlocked the center drawer and pulled the file with the notes from the Wallace investigation.

Walking briskly down the hall, she entered the admin offices where she caught Sergeant McKee talking with one of the cadet constables from the academy. "Excuse me, Sergeant, is the superintendent free?"

she queried the officer, trying to slow her labored breathing after the brisk sojourn from the forensics lab.

"He's in but give me a minute to see if he's free, though, Inspector," the sergeant answered, handing the cadet a folder from her desk. "See that this gets posted, Mister Collins." Walking a few paces behind her desk to the open door of the superintendent, the sergeant informed the senior officer that Inspector Gordon needed to see him.

"Show her in, Sergeant," Chief Superintendent MacCallum said, looking up from his papers spread about the desk.

Turning back to Sheila, Sergeant McKee motioned her to the door and stepped aside.

Entering the office, Sheila turned to the sergeant. "Thank you, Annie," she said, closing the door behind herself.

"What can I do for you, Inspector Gordon?" CS MacCallum asked, sitting at his desk, hands folded in front, giving the lab technician his full attention.

"Well, Chief Superintendent, I was reviewing the documents on the Wallace investigation when I noticed something peculiar," Sheila said, beginning to disclose her findings.

"And what might that be?" the senior officer asked. *How many times do I need to be reminded that a former constable under my watch has been an informant and leaked information to parties unknown?* He worked hard to control his expressions in front of the technician.

Looking down at her notes and trying very hard to fight back the tears welling up inside, Sheila disclosed what she feared most. "I believe one of my family members might be involved, sir," she said it quietly and with a tone of remorse in her voice.

This sudden news caught the chief superintendent by surprise, more so because he'd no indication that there were any other police members involved with the former sergeant's activities.

"How did you come about this information?" he asked Sheila, trying his best to remain calm seeing the emotions of the young woman beginning to take over.

"I was scanning the pages of numbers from the phone listing and came across one that was highlighted several times," she said, pointing to the paper laid out in front of the senior officer.

"And you recognized the number, did you?" he asked the obvious question.

"Yes, sir. It's my mum's," Sheila uttered, breaking down in tears.

# EPILOGUE

After maneuvering about the motorways of Edinburgh and Glasgow, the lorry with its cargo soon arrived at the Port Glasgow dock where 'Mr. Higgins' sat waiting in his rental vehicle. Tied to the dock was the support vessel *PSV Oceanic-Ranger*, captained by Clive Duncan's friend, Brodie Fraser.

As the lorry pulled up along the dock, Captain Fraser walked over to the crane operator and began to discuss the procedures for loading the container onto the deck. While the discussion between the operator and the captain took place, the first officer, Clancy Muir, gathered the deck crew on the aft of the vessel and prepared the chains and shackles for securing the container.

Exiting the lorry, Angus Dunbar walked up to Geoff, who was standing outside the rented Mercedes. "Good morning," he said, greeting the young Irishman, taking in the young man's posture, trying to sense anything amiss.

Opening the rear window of the German sedan, 'Mr. Higgins' motioned Angus to come back to the vehicle's side.

Careful not to place himself in danger, Angus walked back to the Ulsterman sitting in the backseat. "Good morning, sir," he announced.

"Good morning, Mister Dunbar," the Irishman said, much to Angus' surprise that he remembered what he looked like after so many years. "Please see that this is given to the driver." He held out a brown envelope. "And please accept this for your troubles as well." He handed out a second, smaller envelope to the syndicate member.

"Of course," Angus said, taking the first envelope. "And thank you," he said, acknowledging the second offering and sliding it into the inner pocket of his sport coat.

As the exchange of fees took place between 'Mr. Higgins' and Angus, the loaded container had been removed from the lorry and was being placed on the aft deck of the support vessel for its final voyage since leaving Marseille. With his first officer supervising the loading of the cargo, Captain Fraser was brought over to the waiting sedan by 'Mr. Higgins' driver.

"Captain Fraser, are you prepared to head for your destination?" the Irish businessman asked.

"Aye, I've *nae* worries with this load," Brodie declared, seeing that the container fit neatly in the thirteen by forty-two-meter footprint of the aft deck.

"Very well then. You're to proceed at normal sailing pace to Dublin and dock at Terminal Two. There you'll meet an individual in my employment, who will see that the container is removed, and your contract will be considered complete," 'Mr. Higgins' said. "Do you have any questions for me?"

"No," Brodie said, having been told by his friend Clive Duncan that he should be leery of asking too many questions.

"Very well. I wish you safe sailing then," 'Mr. Higgins' said, sliding the window closed and sitting back in the seat.

Taking his leave, Captain Fraser turned and began to walk back to his ship when Geoff walked up to him and handed him an envelope. Opening it slightly, Brodie saw the bundle of money, partial payment for making the voyage with the container, the remainder to be paid upon delivery in Dublin.

Seeing his captain safely over the rail and onboard, F/O Muir gave the command to let loose the mooring lines and proceeded to take the *Oceanic-Ranger* out into the River Clyde and the Irish Sea beyond.

As the service vessel moved slowly away from the dock, 'Mr. Higgins' pulled out his cell phone and dialed a number that would connect him with one of his staff in Dublin. After the second ring, a voice answered the call.

"Hello?" a man's voice asked.

"Liam, 'Mr. Higgins' here. The container is loaded and on its way. Please make the arrangements to transport it to the lab in Limerick."

"Certainly, sir." He knew what he must do since it had been in the plans for weeks.

"Geoff, time to head home," 'Mr. Higgins' declared, watching the service vessel sail westward. Sitting in the back, he smiled inwardly at the thought of his plan being executed without any mishaps.

Having the chemists at the pharmaceutical factory in Limerick replicate the French-Algerians narcotic cocktail of hashish and purified cannabis resin was moving forward, but so was the counterplan. Always thinking as a businessman, the counterplan that he proposed to his partner, Rupert Callaghan, was to have chemists create a drug to help rid the user of the addiction, thus creating the 'cure' to the cause he was perpetuating by selling a more potent narcotic to them. All the while he would be making money to help fund the creation of a private Irish militia.

Sitting in the back seat of the luxury car, he thought, *Business is looking up*, as his driver maneuvered the sedan along the highway that ran parallel to the River Clyde.

***The End***

Thank you for reading my book. If you enjoyed it, won't you please take a moment to leave me a review at your favorite retailer?
Thanks!
    Anthony

## Acknowledgements

First and most important, I'd like to thank my wife, Mary, for letting me scratch this itch called writing and for supporting me with her comments and encouragement, even after I locked myself away for hours at a time. Also, a big thank you to my daughter's Rebekah and Jennifer for letting 'Dad' to his thing without the need to keep asking "why'd you write that?"

Next, to my good friend and co-worker, Doretta Burgess, for providing the first level of sanity checks, grammar checks and being that punctuation pundit on all my many pages of random thoughts. Also, to the members of the Ventura Fiction Writer's Group for helping me understand the difference between 'showing' and 'telling' in my writing.

To my friend and fellow motorcyclist, Rob Gray for taking my ideas and descriptions for the cover and getting it right.

## About the Author

Anthony is a first generation American and native Californian, the son of Scottish immigrants, and who's fraternal grandparents hailed from Ireland. A product of a mixed education (part parochial and part public schools), he developed a thirst for reading early in his childhood and took to writing fiction as an escape from his work as an Instructional Systems Designer. When not working on improving his writing, Anthony can be found on the local golf course, honing his game created by his ancestors.

Anthony J. Harrison

## **<u>Discover other titles by Anthony J. Harrison:</u>**

Betrayed by A Scot – A Conor McDermott Novel

Suspicious by Design – A Geneviève Benoit Novel


## **<u>Provide your comments or feedback at;</u>**

mailto:fairwayscribe@gmail.com